Carter Avery's TRICKY Fourth-Grade Year

ALSO BY ROB BUYEA

The Daredevils
What Comes Next

THE MR. TERUPT SERIES

Because of Mr. Terupt
Mr. Terupt Falls Again
Saving Mr. Terupt
Goodbye, Mr. Terupt

THE PERFECT SCORE SERIES

The Perfect Score
The Perfect Secret
The Perfect Star

Carter Avery's TRICKY Fourth-Grade Year

ROB BUYEA

DELACORTE PRESS

Text copyright © 2024 by Rob Buyea
Jacket art, hand-lettering, and interior illustrations copyright © 2024 by Alexandra Bye
Owl ornaments and jelly roll art used under license from stock.adobe.com

All rights reserved. Published in the United States by Delacorte Press, an imprint of Random House Children's Books, a division of Penguin Random House LLC, New York.

Delacorte Press is a registered trademark and the colophon is a trademark of Penguin Random House LLC.

Visit us on the Web! rhcbooks.com

Educators and librarians, for a variety of teaching tools, visit us at RHTeachersLibrarians.com

Library of Congress Cataloging-in-Publication Data is available upon request.
ISBN 978-0-593-37618-8 (trade) — ISBN 978-0-593-37619-5 (lib. bdg.) — ISBN 978-0-593-37620-1 (ebook)

The text of this book is set in 12-point Adobe Garamond Pro.
Editor: Beverly Horowitz
Cover Designer: Jade Rector
Interior Designer: Cathy Bobak
Copy Editor: Colleen Fellingham
Managing Editor: Tamar Schwartz
Production Manager: Tracy Heydweiller

Printed in the United States of America
10 9 8 7 6 5 4 3 2 1
First Edition

FOR FRANÇOISE, BECAUSE ONLY MENTIONING YOU IN THE
ACKNOWLEDGMENTS IS NEVER ENOUGH

Prologue

THE TRUTH

When I first heard the rumor that Ms. Krane was pregnant, I immediately felt sorry for that baby. I was dreading being stuck with her as my fourth-grade teacher for one year; I couldn't imagine being stuck with her as my mother for the rest of eternity. That kid might as well not even be born, 'cause when it got here, its life was gonna be awful.

Part 1

END OF THIRD GRADE

1

MEET YOUR TEACHER DAY

We had this big thing at Bates Elementary called Meet Your Teacher Day. It happened at the end of the year, with everyone gathered outside on the blacktop behind the school. I had my fingers crossed, hoping not to see Ms. Krane, 'cause if she really was pregnant, then she wouldn't be teaching come September and I could stop worrying. I don't think a pregnant lady can teach fourth grade.

I should've crossed my toes too. She was there—and she sure didn't look like she had a baby on the way. Stupid rumor. I bet Missy Gerber started it. I kicked the ground. Then I quick double crossed all my fingers on both hands 'cause I needed all the luck I could get so that I didn't get stuck with Ms. Krane.

Every class from kindergarten all the way to fifth grade had a designated area where we sat and hung out while the teachers huddled in the middle—all except for Ms. Krane. She stood by herself, kinda like me whenever we had to choose partners for anything. Me and Ms. Krane weren't the same, though. No way.

Ms. Krane stood by herself 'cause she was mean. She was the meanest and nastiest teacher to ever step foot in a classroom. She was pretty old, I think like thirty-five or forty. She taught somewhere else before coming to Bates last month. Everyone said she got fired from her old school for being so mean.

She'd been hiding in the library ever since getting here, working as Ms. Beecher's assistant. Ms. Krane was rarely spotted, but now she was coming out of hiding 'cause next year she was getting her own classroom—and I wanted no part of it. No one did, 'cause not only was she mean, she was scary-looking. And that was the truth.

Ms. Krane had this giant reddish-purple mark that covered the left side of her face, all the way from her chin up past her eye. She reminded me of a raccoon, except her first name was Olivia and all the kids called her Owl-ivia—or the Owl, for short—'cause she could twist her head all the way around like an owl, which meant you could never do anything sneaky behind her back and get away with it. If you tried, she'd see you and then you were a goner.

I was sitting by myself at my lunch table when I overheard Kyle Pattie telling his buddies what happened after he tried shoving a book back on the shelf in the library where it didn't belong—which was Ms. Beecher's big no-no, but everyone did it.

" 'That's not how we do things here,' a voice behind me whispered all creepy. I could feel her hot breath on the back of my neck!" Kyle exclaimed. "I spun around and there she was, looming over me. I swear, she came out of nowhere, and when I looked up at her face, she made her purple eye narrow. Then she pulled my book out of the wrong spot and said, 'I'll take care of it this time—but not the next.' And she made that sound like a warning," Kyle finished.

His wasn't the only story I heard. There were others. If Ms. Krane could make the library scary, her classroom was gonna be the worst. I crossed my fingers super tight.

Here's how this meet-your-teacher thing worked: Starting with first grade, each teacher stepped forward and read off the student names on their new roster. When your name was called, you got up and went and stood in line with your new teacher. Then you walked to your next year's classroom with your next year's class and spent the last half hour of the day meeting your new teacher and classmates. The kindergarten teachers stayed behind with the fifth graders on the blacktop 'cause the preschoolers weren't here yet and the fifth graders were moving on to the middle school. So fourth grade was second to last—and that stunk 'cause I wasn't very good at waiting.

When it was finally our turn, Ms. Krane was the first

teacher to step forward, and all of third grade got real quiet. I held my breath and crossed my arms and legs and eyes. I had to do everything I could for extra good luck.

I wasn't supposed to have to wait long to find out if I was doomed or not, but then the Owl started with the end of the alphabet first. By the time she got to the As, my face had gone from red to blue. But breathing too early would've been bad luck, like breathing when you drive by a graveyard. You should never do that.

Little twinkly stars began popping up in front of me. I got wobbly—but I didn't breathe. And then Ms. Krane read the final name on her list.

"Carter Avery," she hooted.

The kids in Ms. Krane's line groaned and the ones still sitting near me on the blacktop sighed.

Normally I moved real fast. I was real good at running everywhere. The harder thing was sitting still. But I felt light-headed and dizzy.

"Carter Avery," the Owl hooted again.

It wasn't odd for teachers to call my name more than once, but I'd heard her the first time. I just needed a second to get air.

"Get in line, Carter," Missy Gerber whined from her spot behind Ms. Krane.

With the Owl *and* Missy Gerber, I was getting a double dose of awful for fourth grade. "I'm coming!" I yelled. "And you're not my boss."

Controlling my outbursts was one of the things I was supposed to be working on. That and sitting still. I had a lot of improving left to do on both.

"Missy, would you please come to the front of the line," Ms. Krane said.

I grinned. Now, that was unusual. Normally I was the one teachers called to the front. Missy glared at me and I stuck my tongue way out at her. That's what she got for being a bossy pants.

I grabbed my bag and got in line. The kids ahead of me grumbled and complained, but I was used to hearing that stuff whenever I got stuck in a group.

So anyway, there we were, the teacher no kid wanted and the kid no teacher wanted. What a start.

2

SCARFACE

Ms. Krane puffed her chest and stood perfectly straight. Then she turned and marched us to her room. We walked single file and didn't make a peep 'cause like I said, an owl can twist its head all the way around.

The fourth-grade classrooms were upstairs. They were the only ones there. You heard about them sometimes, but you never got to see them until you made it. Kinda like the Owl. I'd heard about her, but I'd never really seen her up close.

All that changed when she stopped outside our new room and spun around to stare at us. Ms. Krane was a taller, skinnier version of an owl with long hair. She wore these black pointy glasses that didn't hide her purple scar, but they did give her scary triangle eyes, just like the great horned owl. She sized us up and got ready to give us our orders, but my words jumped out first.

"What happened to your face?" I blurted. Told you self-control was one of the things I was supposed to be working on. I was trying. Really. But I just couldn't hold that in any longer.

Kids snickered. Missy Gerber gasped. "Carter!" she shrieked. "Ms. Krane, Carter doesn't have a filter on his mouth. He's sorry."

"I appreciate your concern, Missy, but Carter can ask if he wants. I imagine he isn't the only one wondering. He just happens to be the brave soul to speak it out loud."

Ms. Krane zeroed her eyes back on me. "My face is covered by a birthmark called a port-wine stain," she explained.

"I thought it was a scar," I said, all confused. "That's what I heard."

"In many ways it is," she replied.

That made my forehead wrinkle. "What do you mean?"

"My mark has made life challenging for me, Carter."

"But what made it happen to you?"

"No rhyme, no reason. No one's fault. I was just born with it."

After she said that, I got quiet. I didn't always understand everything teachers said, but I understood being born a certain way. Grams says I came out fidgety and full of life from the get-go. Only my mother could get me to settle down when I got upset. Grams says my mom had a way with me. But she's gone now.

My parents died in a car crash when I was just a baby.

Sometimes you're born a certain way—and sometimes things just happen for no rhyme and no reason. I understood that too.

Since I finally stopped with my questions, Ms. Krane went ahead and gave us our orders. "When you enter, I'd like you to drop your bags by the door and take a seat. You may sit in any open chair."

Teachers say I don't do a good job of following directions, but if they did a better job of giving directions, then maybe I'd be better at doing exactly what they meant. I dropped my bag and raced to the chair I wanted.

"Carter, you can't sit there!" Missy Gerber shouted.

I was ready to tell her to put a sock in it, 'cause I was still working on self-control, but the Owl beat me to it.

"Missy, I will be the teacher. You worry about you," Ms. Krane scolded. "Mr. Avery has followed my directions to a T. He dropped his bag by the door and found an open seat. Perhaps you're upset because he got that chair and not you?"

Boy, did that make me grin. But then Ms. Krane turned her pointy glasses on me and I shrank in her teacher chair. "It's yours as long as you can handle sitting in it properly," she said.

"Yes, ma'am," I hollered, and saluted, sitting up tall again.

"I'm your teacher, not your drill sergeant, so please don't salute me. And I'm much too young to be called *ma'am*, so please don't do that again either."

"But you're old," I countered, unable to stop myself.

"Old enough to know better, but definitely not old," she said.

That made my forehead wrinkle again and Missy Gerber snickered. I wanted to tell Missy to shut up, but I did a smart thing and slapped my hand over my mouth before those words jumped out. If Ms. Krane was getting mad at me for saluting her and calling her ma'am, we were in for a long year together.

3

TWO TRUTHS AND ONE LIE

The Owl began swooping around the classroom, passing out paper and pencils. I stuck both hands in my pockets and played with my marbles. What I really wanted to do was spin in Ms. Krane's chair but then I'd probly lose my seat. Fidgeting with things sometimes helped me sit still—sorta. Sitting still was really hard for me. Even harder than keeping quiet. Maybe.

"What're we supposed to do with this?" I blurted after Ms. Krane dropped a piece of blank computer paper in front of me. My hands were too busy with my marbles to cover my mouth and stop those words.

"For starters, I'd like you to print your name at the top," Ms. Krane answered. "And please make it legible."

"What's that mean?" I bellowed, letting more words jump free. At least I wasn't spinning.

"*Legible* means make it neat so that we can read it," Ms. Krane explained.

"Nothing about Carter is neat," Missy Gerber groaned.

You know something, that girl hadn't been in my class since first grade and I didn't miss her. Even if she wasn't trying to be funny, she got laughs.

"Missy, if you don't have something kind to say, then please keep your comments to yourself," Ms. Krane scolded.

Boy, that made me sit still—and I didn't even need my marbles. I'd never had a teacher stick up for me—and Ms. Krane had done it twice already. Yup, she was mean. Real mean. But since she was being mean to Missy Gerber, I liked it.

"Now for the fun part," Ms. Krane continued, confusing me again. There wasn't supposed to be any fun in her room. "I'd like each of you to write down three things about yourself. But . . . listen carefully. Two of your statements must be true, and one must be a lie. You can list them in any order you'd like, the lie first, second, or third, but you must have two truths and one lie. Once you've finished, we'll begin sharing and try to guess which are the truths and which is the lie about our classmates."

Yes, I blurted out stuff I probly shouldn't say sometimes, but it was always the truth. I never lied. Never. But Ms. Krane was giving us permission to lie now. She was asking us to do it. This *was* gonna be fun. I had my three things right away, but getting them written down was gonna take me a while 'cause I wasn't very good at writing. It was hard for me to make the letters. And doing it that legerble way that the Owl wanted made it even harder.

"Do I have any volunteers to share first?" Ms. Krane asked.

"Me!" I shouted, remembering to raise my hand. I waved my arm in the air, but Ms. Krane said I needed to have my statements written down before I could go. Told you she was mean. So annoying Missy Gerber went instead 'cause she was a fast writer *and* a know-it-all.

This is what she said:

1. *I've had perfect attendance my whole life.* (I knew that was true 'cause she bragged about it every chance she got.)

2. *I've never received a grade below an A.* (I also knew that was true 'cause she bragged about it every time we got report cards.)

3. *I've read the Mr. Terupt series six times.*

"No, you haven't!" I yelled. "That's a lie."

"You're right," Missy giggled. "I've only read it five times. But I'm on number six now."

If I had to write my truth about that girl, I woulda said Missy Gerber is annoying—with all capital letters.

Kyle Pattie was the next to go. We guessed his lie too. He loved sports and tried saying he'd met Tom Brady. He only wished that was true. Mary Fergus went after that and we guessed that she hadn't been to all fifty states, but she had been to thirty-one. And Vanessa Tucker didn't own a horse.

One of the coolest parts of Ms. Krane's game was how I learned something new about my classmates—even from their lies. I learned Kyle's favorite football player was Tom Brady, and Mary liked traveling, and Vanessa, besides wanting a horse, loved animals, same as me. And Missy Gerber was super annoying—but I already knew that.

"Carter, would you like to share yours next?" Ms. Krane asked.

I sighed. "I can't. I still don't have mine written down."

"Let me help you." Ms. Krane came over and had me whisper my three things in her ear. She gave a little laugh when she heard them and then she wrote my two truths and one lie down real quick. That was the opposite of mean. That was nice of her.

"Okay," she said. "Now you can share."

4

MY THREE THINGS

I hopped out of Ms. Krane's chair and held my paper in front of me with both hands. These were my three things. But I'm not going to tell you which was my lie.

1. One time I ate a worm.

2. One time I ate a worm with ketchup.

3. I have a sister.

"Ew!" Missy Gerber whined. "You ate a worm? Disgusting!"

"Ew!" the rest of the class joined in.

"Nuh-uh!" I exclaimed. "I ate a worm with ketchup!"

Missy and everyone else stuck their tongues out and gagged, but Ms. Krane was smiling. I was the only one to fool the class with my lie.

I laughed and jumped back in my chair. I was so excited

I accidentally spun around a few times, but Ms. Krane didn't yell.

"Would you like to hear my list next?" she asked us.

"Yeah!" everyone cheered.

I stopped spinning. I didn't know she'd made a list too. Teachers usually want to make sure you're doing your work, not do it with you.

Here's what Ms. Krane said:

1. *I love books.*

2. *I'm pregnant.*

"You're not pregnant!" I yelled. I didn't even let her finish.

"Really? How can you be so sure?"

"'Cause you don't look fat!"

There was lots of giggling after I said that—but it was the truth.

"Suppose I'm just early in my pregnancy," Ms. Krane wondered aloud. "A pregnant woman isn't big and round from the very beginning. It takes time to grow a belly like that, you know."

My forehead wrinkled. She had a good point, but I still didn't think she was pregnant. "Yeah, but if you were pregnant, you wouldn't be our teacher next year."

"Carter, a pregnant woman can work," Missy Gerber groaned.

Ms. Krane nodded.

Missy Gerber was such a know-it-all.

"You can't be pregnant," I argued. "You don't even like kids." That was something else I'd heard.

The room fell silent.

"Funny you should say that," Ms. Krane replied, "because the last statement on my list says, *I don't like kids.*"

"Told you," I bragged.

"Yes, but if you're convinced I love books, then that means only one of my last two statements can be true," Ms. Krane said, reminding me how the game worked.

She had to love books. You couldn't be a teacher if you didn't love books. That's a rule. But could you be a teacher if you didn't like kids? My head was starting to hurt.

"Does that mean you're having a baby?" I shouted. I wanted to know and I didn't want Missy Gerber to be right.

"When you see me after summer, you'll know for sure."

I didn't have enough patience for that. "Why can't you just tell us now?"

The PA system crackled from above and Ms. Krane pointed at the ceiling. "Because we're out of time."

Principal Ryan's voice came over the loudspeaker. Normally, I liked it when that happened 'cause it meant I was done with sitting still for the day, but I was mad this time 'cause I wanted Ms. Krane to tell us the answer, so I spun in her chair.

Principal Ryan did her job and wished us all a safe and happy summer with lots of reading. All the stuff a principal was supposed to say. And then she started calling buses. Mine was number nine. Mr. Wilson was my driver. He was always the last to arrive 'cause his first run with the middle schoolers took him the longest.

Ms. Krane walked around collecting our papers and saying goodbye to everyone as they left. I wheeled her chair over to the window so that I could watch for Mr. Wilson and the big yellow taxi. That was what he called our bus. When he pulled into the pickup circle, I jumped out of Ms. Krane's chair and made a beeline for the door, but the Owl was ready and stopped me before I got there.

"We do not run in our classroom," she said. Then she wrapped her wing around my shoulder and walked with me the rest of the way. "Have a good summer, Carter Avery," she added, releasing me.

"You too," I yelled back, and 'cause her rule was only about the classroom, I was already running down the hall.

5

MR. WILSON

I burst outside and bounded up the bus steps and slid into my seat behind Mr. Wilson. He had me sit in the front 'cause that way I steered clear of any trouble, and also 'cause we liked to talk on our rides. He said I kept him young even though I didn't know how.

"Mr. Wilson, have you ever heard stories about someone and then after you meet them you find out the stories maybe were wrong?"

He glanced at me in his rearview mirror and smirked. "Yeah, now that you mention it, I can think of a time that's happened before."

Hmm. So it was possible.

"Mr. Wilson, are owls sneaky tricksters?"

"I don't know about tricksters, but folks say they're full of wisdom. And they can be good at hiding too."

Hmm. So maybe Ms. Krane was hiding her pregnant belly.

And maybe she was trying to trick us into thinking she could be nice.

"Mr. Wilson, do teachers have to like kids?"

"You're sure doing a lot of thinking for a boy that just finished his last day of school. But your mind is always busy, isn't it?"

"Grams says I never slow down."

Mr. Wilson laughed. "She's right about that."

"But do you know if teachers need to like kids? Is that a rule?"

"I suppose they don't have to like all the kids all the time, but they always love them."

Mr. Wilson was being tricky now 'cause that was really confusing. I'd have to ask Grams about owls. She'd know because old people had lots of wisdom too. Plus, we were at my stop, so I couldn't ask Mr. Wilson any more questions. He opened the bus door and I hopped up from my seat.

"Have a great summer, young man. I'll be eager to hear what you find out about owls."

"See you later," I yelled as I jumped over the last step and hit the ground running.

"Thanks for the warning!" Mr. Wilson hollered, which was his favorite joke.

Grams called it sarcasm. I called it funny—and special, 'cause he only used it with me. I liked Mr. Wilson a lot.

6

BRYNN AND TORRIE

I ran into the house and kicked my sneakers off and threw my bag in the corner. Something smelled really good.

"Yum!" I yelled, sliding across the kitchen floor in my socks. "Cookies!"

"There he is," Grams cheered. "Happy summer."

I spun past Grams and twirled around my sister before grabbing a warm snickerdoodle from the plate on the counter. I bent down and shared a piece with Shelby, our basset hound. She usually greeted me at the door when I got home even though she was getting old and moving from one room to the next took lots of energy, but snickerdoodles were her favorite too. She had a belly that hung close to the floor to prove it.

"Grams, are owls tricksters?" I asked after swallowing my half and standing back up.

"Oh boy. You got Ms. Krane for your teacher, didn't you?" Brynn said, pulling a fresh batch of cookies out of the oven.

I'd made the mistake of telling my sister about Ms. Krane's nickname.

Brynn was going into eleventh grade. Shelby was her dog first. Brynn was a good sister but she always thought she knew everything and had to know everything, which could get annoying, but she was nowhere near as annoying as Missy Gerber.

"I wasn't talking to you," I groaned.

"I wasn't talking to you," she mimicked.

"Brynn, that's enough," Grams scolded.

Grams could see I was getting upset and didn't want us arguing, but it's really hard for me to stop once Brynn starts in. "You don't know everything," I shot back at my sister. "You've never even seen my teacher."

Brynn shrugged. "So. I've heard all about her."

"Yeah, did you know she's got a giant mark on her face?"

"*Pfft.* Everyone knows that," she scoffed.

"It's not a scar," I said, which was probly what she'd heard. "It's a part-jelly stain."

"What?!" Grams and Brynn both howled.

"A part-jelly stain," I said again. "She was born with it."

They laughed. "A port-wine stain," Grams said, correcting me. "That's a birthmark."

Brynn laughed more, so I stuck my tongue out at her and grabbed another one of her cookies.

"Are owls tricksters?" I asked again, going back to my first question.

"I don't know," Grams said. "And why the sudden interest in owls?"

"'Cause Ms. Krane is the Owl," I explained, which made Brynn smirk 'cause she thought she was so smart. "Her real name is Olivia," I continued, "but all the kids call her Owl-ivia 'cause she can twist her head all the way around."

Grams made a face. "Sounds like we better make a trip to the library. I'm no expert on owls, but if you've got one for your teacher, then we should probably read up on them."

"Okay," I agreed.

Going to the library would make Principal Ryan happy, plus I liked it there. Grams had been taking me and Brynn to the library since we were little. They had this really cool jungle gym area for a reading nook. You could crawl inside a tunnel or sit in a wagon or climb into a tree fort to look at your books. Reading was one of the few things that could get me to sit still—not for super long, and only if I was interested, but it was way better than dumb writing or boring math—especially if there was something I needed to research.

Brynn didn't go with us to the library much anymore 'cause she and her bestie, Torrie, had jobs and were on the swim team and were real busy with high school. Torrie was Brynn's best friend since forever. They were always together. So much so that sometimes it felt like I had two sisters.

"Hi!" a voice called from the front door. "Something sure smells good."

Speak of the devil. It was Torrie. She came inside and joined us in the kitchen, snatching one of my cookies. She was here so often that she didn't even need to knock or ring the doorbell anymore. She just let herself in.

"Guess what?" Brynn said. "CJ's got Ms. Krane for his teacher next year."

"Huh," Torrie gasped. "The Owl," she teased.

"CJ was just telling us about the giant birthmark Ms. Krane has on her face," Brynn said.

"You don't say," Torrie replied.

"Yup. And Ms. Krane is either pregnant or she doesn't like kids, but I don't know which yet," I added.

Brynn and Torrie shared a look, then glanced at Grams.

"That does sound tricky," Grams said.

Brynn pulled out the last batch of snickerdoodles and turned the oven off. She slid the cookies onto the cooling rack and then she and Torrie went to get ready for work.

I should've been wondering about that look Brynn and Torrie shared, and the way they quick glanced at Grams like there was some big secret I didn't know about—'cause there was. But me and Shelby were too busy licking our chops. Brynn's cookies were the best.

Part II

SUMMER

7

SUMMER READING

So my summer vacation started with me and Grams making a trip to the library, but even I knew not to go telling everybody that 'cause it wasn't gonna sound real cool compared to Mary Fergus going to Disney or wherever. I liked visiting the library, but that was something I only told Grams—and Brynn when she tagged along.

When we got there, Mr. Todd helped me and Grams track down books about owls. Mr. Todd was the youth librarian. I'd known him for a bunch of years now. He was really nice and smart—but even he couldn't tell me if owls were tricksters.

"Maybe you'll find the answer to your question here," he said, pointing to the shelf with owl books.

"Thanks, Mr. Todd."

"Sure thing, Carter. You let me know if I can be of more assistance. I look forward to hearing what you learn."

Mr. Todd went back to his desk, and me and Grams got

busy thumbing through those pages. There were way more kinds of owls than I'd realized. More than two hundred species. I had a lot of research to do.

After skimming through my choices, I picked four different books that I wanted to check out. We put the other ones back where they belonged and then walked to the front.

Me and Grams were the only ones in the children's area when we got to the library, but by the time we were ready to leave, there was a swarm of little kids coming in with their moms and dads.

"What's going on?" I asked Mr. Todd.

"There's a special program happening today to kick off summer reading. Would you like to join?"

"What kind of program?"

Mr. Todd pointed.

I looked and saw a man wearing a fancy hat and sunglasses getting settled near the jungle gym area—and he had his dog with him.

"That's Mason. And his dog, Susie," Mr. Todd said.

"Can I meet Susie?" I asked. I didn't have Ms. Krane write it on my list of three things, but I loved dogs.

"That's the idea behind the program, Carter. If you document your independent reading at least five times a week, the name of the book and amount of time you read for, and your grams signs off on it, then you can come and spend time reading to Susie and some of the other dogs when they visit us.

You'll get to meet the owners and learn more about their special companions."

"What makes Susie special?"

"She's Mason's eyes."

I glanced back at them. Mason still had his sunglasses on. "You mean he's blind."

"Yes," Mr. Todd said. "Susie is an amazing dog. Mason will be giving us a short demonstration to show off some of her smarts. One of the other dogs joining us later is a retired Frisbee champion."

I'd heard enough. "Can we stay, Grams? Can we? Please?"

"Okay," she agreed. "We can stay for a little while, but then we've got to get home because Brynn needs the car this afternoon."

"Yay!" I cheered. I ran over to join the others. And that was how I got signed up for summer reading and met Mason and Susie. They got to hear me talk all about owls.

8

FARMER DON'S

I got myself a bowl of Fruity Pebbles and sat down at the breakfast table with Grams and her coffee. It was just the two of us 'cause Brynn made sleeping her job.

"You know something, Grams? I think Brynn's a nocturnal creature like the owls I've been reading about. She's up all night and sleeps all day."

"That's a teenager for ya," Grams explained.

"That's dumb for ya," I replied.

"Leave your sister alone. Between swim and dive, her job, and school, she burns the candle at both ends all year long, so it's okay if she sleeps in during the summer."

That was true but I wasn't gonna say so. I shrugged and shoveled a scoop of Fruity Pebbles into my mouth.

Me and Grams had gone to the North Pole two nights ago and it was super busy. Not the real North Pole, but the ice cream shop where my sister and Torrie worked. They didn't even have time to say hi to me and Grams 'cause the lines were so long. And it was like that every night 'cause the North Pole had the best homemade ice cream in the whole state. And that was the truth 'cause they had a sign from the state fair that said so: VOTED BEST HOMEMADE ICE CREAM. I always got the soft serve twist 'cause it was really creamy and you could get rainbow or chocolate sprinkles on top. And if Brynn or Torrie made my cone, I got extra.

"Well, we're not sleeping our days away," I told Grams after a few more mouthfuls. "So what're we gonna do?"

"I was thinking we better go get some milk and eggs from Farmer Don. Brynn used the last of the eggs for those brownies she made and you're drowning that cereal in milk."

Slurp. "Okay!" I cheered. I'd finished with my owl books, so I didn't have more research to do until we got back to the library. And I liked going to Farmer Don's. He was real friendly and he had lots of animals.

So after cleaning up and brushing my teeth—'cause Grams always made me do that—we left Brynn sleeping 'cause waking her up would mean a heavy dose of attitude, and we hopped in Leopold. That was the name Grams gave her old clunker 'cause that at least made the car sound fancy. It wasn't fancy. But like Grams always said, it got us where we were going— most of the time. It only broke down on us once last year.

"Farmer Don!" I yelled, waving to him when we got there.

"Hi, Carter!" he called, waving back from his garden.

"We're here to get milk and eggs!" I hollered.

Farmer Don took off his hat and wiped his forehead, and then he walked over to properly greet us. He was a big guy that Grams called a gentle giant 'cause he was easygoing and soft-spoken. He had his usual plaid shirt tucked inside his overalls, with thick boots on his feet and a green John Deere cap on his head. He handed Grams a couple of tomatoes.

"Oh, Don. You don't need to give me these."

"I got more than I know what to do with, so you take them."

"Thank you," Grams said. "Guess we'll be having tomato sandwiches for lunch," she told me.

"That sounds good," Farmer Don agreed.

"Enough of the small talk," I groaned. "Can we collect eggs now?"

Farmer Don laughed. "Let's go see what we can find."

Me and Grams grabbed our empty egg cartons from inside Leopold and walked with Farmer Don around the side of the barn and out to his chicken coop. The coop was the house where the hens laid their prizes. It wasn't real big or real small, but it was nice. Farmer Don kept it clean 'cause coops can get super stinky. Lucky for him, the chicks spent most of their time strutting around inside the fenced-in area he'd built surrounding the coop, which he said was the idea, so that helped. The birds looked too much alike and moved too fast for me to give them individual names, so I just called them all Chicken.

The only one I named was the pain-in-the-butt who followed me everywhere, pecking at my feet and being super annoying. I called that one Missy.

Normally, Farmer Don stayed and helped us, but he left me and Grams to collect our eggs after we got inside the coop 'cause we heard another car pulling into his gravel driveway and he went to see who it was.

"Bawk! Bawk! Bawk!" I chattered with the hens as I filled my carton with their hard work.

Bawk! Bawk! Bawk! they replied.

Grams didn't join in the conversation, but she laughed. "What in the heavens are you even saying to each other?"

"I'm complimenting them on their fine eggs and they're telling me they'd be happy to lay more."

"Oh my goodness," Grams said, shaking her head.

We got our cartons filled and stepped out of the coop, and you're not going to believe this next part, 'cause I couldn't believe it, either. Guess who came walking over with Farmer Don? The Owl!

9

COLLECTING EGGS WITH MY TEACHER

School and summer vacation weren't supposed to mix. That was a rule. And the one person you absolutely weren't supposed to see over summer was your teacher! But Ms. Krane sure didn't look like a teacher. She wasn't wearing any nice school clothes or special shoes. She was dressed in baggy overalls and barn boots, so maybe that made it okay.

"Ms. Krane, what're you doing here?!" I squawked with the hens when she entered their yard alongside Farmer Don.

"By the looks of it, I'd say I'm doing the same thing as you."

"You're getting eggs?"

"I am."

"CJ, is this your teacher?" Grams asked.

I nodded. "This is my grams," I told Ms. Krane.

"Nice to meet you," Ms. Krane said, tipping her head toward Grams.

"Likewise," Grams replied.

"Ms. Krane, do you need help?" I asked. "These chickens can be a handful."

"I'm sure after dealing with you turkeys in her classroom, she can manage chickens," Farmer Don said.

Ms. Krane and Grams laughed at Farmer Don's joke, but then Ms. Krane said, "I'd love some help, Carter. Thank you."

I stuck my tongue out at Farmer Don, same as I do for Brynn and Missy Gerber, and he chuckled.

Ms. Krane took her time getting inside the coop. I was thinking Grams walked faster than she did, but I didn't say anything. Somehow I kept those words inside my head. Maybe I was getting better.

"There's lots of different kinds of chickens," I told Ms. Krane. "Farmer Don has leghorns. Like that cartoon character, Foghorn Leghorn, that real old people grew up watching. Do you know that one?"

"Yes, I'm familiar with Foghorn Leghorn, but that most certainly doesn't make me real old," she made clear.

"Just old enough to know better," I said, repeating her line from the last day of school.

Ms. Krane grinned. "That's right. And one might also say it serves as evidence of me being well-read."

"Well-read?" I repeated, scowling. "What's that mean?"

"That's something you might say about somebody who knows quite a lot about many things or about a particular subject. You, for instance, seem to know your fair share about chickens."

"Yup. I'm read-well all right. Me and Grams read all about chickens in the library last summer. This summer we're reading about owls."

I slapped my hand over my mouth as soon as I said it.

"I love owls," Ms. Krane said, and smirked, which made her part-jelly stain wrinkle. "They're both beautiful and fierce."

"Do you know if they're tricky?"

Ms. Krane looked at me and tilted her head to one side, which owls weren't supposed to be able to do. "Carter, I believe you could say owls are tough, loyal, reliable, or honest, but tricky isn't one of the adjectives I'd use to describe them, though someone else might."

I nodded, even though I wasn't sure if Ms. Krane was describing herself or a real owl. We weren't even in school and she had me doing all kinds of thinking, which had to be against all summer rules. But I couldn't help it. Like Mr. Wilson said, my mind was always busy.

After we got her carton filled up, we left the coop to join Grams and Farmer Don. On the way, we crossed paths with Farmer Don's barn cat.

"Careful," I warned Ms. Krane. "I love animals, but Hector can be nasty."

Ms. Krane nodded, but you know what happened next? Hector strolled over and rubbed against her leg, and Ms. Krane reached down and petted his side and scratched his butt. All's I could figure was owls and cats must be friends.

"So tell me, Carter. What does the J in CJ stand for?" Ms. Krane asked after we started walking again. "I heard your grams call you that."

"Joseph," I said. "That was my dad's name. But CJ is only something my grams and Brynn and her bestie, Torrie, ever call me."

"Brynn's your sister?" Ms. Krane asked.

"My older sister. Brynn's middle name is Meghan. That was my mom's name. But we don't call Brynn BM."

Ms. Krane chuckled. "I like the connections with your middle names," she said, smiling at me. "It's nice. And I'm sorry your parents aren't alive anymore. I read that in your school file."

I nodded. I liked the connection too.

"Looks like you got your eggs," Farmer Don said when he saw us approaching.

"Yes, and Carter was a big help," Ms. Krane replied.

Farmer Don gave me a quick wink, just between him and me, which felt good and made me stand up taller.

"Well, we better get going," Grams said.

"Did you get the milk?" I asked her.

"Yup, already in the car."

"You all have a good day," Farmer Don replied. "I'll see you later."

"And I'll be seeing you soon," Ms. Krane told me. "September will be here before we know it."

I wasn't sure how I felt about that, but I nodded, and then me and Grams hopped in Leopold and gave a wave as we drove off.

10

BRYNN'S UP EARLY

"Your teacher seems like a very nice woman," Grams said after she had Leopold on the road.

That was the confusing part, 'cause she wasn't supposed to be. "Can someone be nice in one place but not in another?" I asked her.

"You mean, like nice at the farm but not in school?"

"Yeah!" I exclaimed.

"That would be tricky," Grams replied, smirking.

"You're not helping," I groaned.

Grams snorted. But then she got serious when she saw I wasn't laughing. "CJ, rumors are often one-sided and stories often exaggerated. You've got a brain and a heart. You're gonna have to use them."

That was Grams dishing out some of her old-school tough love, which she claimed was a whole lot better than that everything's-gotta-be-fair stuff they handed out in school these days. Grams didn't say anything more and I knew that was 'cause she wanted me to think about what she'd just said. That, and it was also a good opportunity for me to practice being quiet. I did both—though the quiet stopped when we got home.

Me and Grams walked into the house with our fresh eggs and milk and found Brynn sitting at the kitchen table with a glass of OJ. She wasn't being a sleepyhead teenager.

"You're up early," Grams said.

"Not really," I corrected. "It's almost lunchtime."

Brynn didn't stick her tongue out at me like she was supposed to. She sneezed instead. I shrugged and bent down so Shelby could give our eggs a thorough sniffing. Maybe she was getting old, but she still had a good nose.

"So what's the occasion?" Grams asked after pouring herself some lemonade and joining my sister at the table.

"Torrie wants to go to the mall," Brynn groaned, then sneezed again.

"Sounds like you'd be better off going back to bed," Grams said.

"No. I can't. I promised Torrie I'd go with her."

A few sniffles couldn't stop my sister. She and Torrie never got tired of shopping.

"Torrie will understand," Grams said. "If you're coming down with something, you need to rest."

"I'm fine," Brynn insisted. "Torrie's meeting a boy she met at work last night. She wants me to check him out."

I rolled my eyes. I'd heard enough. I got the eggs put away and went into the living room. I flipped on the TV and plopped down on the couch to watch some cartoons. But our TV was having a rough morning too. The picture kept glitching. It'd been acting up more and more lately. It was one of those real old fat-back models. Grams wouldn't let us turn the volume up past twenty anymore 'cause she worried that it would fry the tube.

"Grrr!" I growled. "It's time to put this blasted TV to pasture and get a new one!" I yelled, repeating one of Grams's favorite lines.

I tossed the remote on the coffee table and marched back into the kitchen. "Did you hear me? Dumb TV is acting up again."

"I heard you," Grams said.

"I'm going outside," I huffed. "But first I'm getting myself a popsicle."

I rummaged through the box until I found a blue one and then I slammed the freezer shut. The bang made Brynn slop her orange juice and cover her ears. But that was okay 'cause Shelby waddled over and got busy licking the mess up off the floor.

"Smooth move, slick," I teased like we always did after one of us did something clumsy.

Nothing. Not a sneer or stuck-out tongue or any kind of comeback. My sister definitely wasn't feeling like herself. But Grams would take care of her.

11

LIBRARY TRIP

Mr. Todd's summer reading program was supposed to be about reading—and I did that at home—but not so much when I was at the library. I talked more about my owl research (I still didn't know if they were tricky or not) when it was my turn with the dogs so that I could spend more time visiting with them.

Murphy was the retired Frisbee champion Mr. Todd had mentioned. He was an Australian shepherd, which I learned was also excellent at herding sheep or cows or just about anything with legs—kids included. If one of the younger readers got bored and started wandering around, Murphy went to work, steering that kid back to their reading spot. So visiting with Murphy was entertaining, but we were always getting interrupted. He had a harder time sitting still than me—and that's saying something. And Bowie and Buster, the other dogs who showed up, liked being around the little kids.

Mason and his dog, Susie, were different. Susie was a golden retriever who never left Mason's side, and she liked me 'cause I didn't put sticky fingers in her fur, so I got to spend lots of time with them. They were both real friendly and Mason didn't mind my talking. He told me all about Susie and the three dogs he had before her and I got to tell him all about owls and Ms. Krane and Missy Gerber and Brynn and Grams too. Mason and Susie had lots of patience, and I told them that.

"Being blind teaches one a fair amount of patience," Mason replied. "And being a seeing-eye dog requires it."

"I guess I wouldn't be very good at either one of those things, then."

Mason laughed and Susie picked her head up and looked at me.

"Do you like ice cream?" I asked Mason.

"I do. A good old-fashion twist is still my favorite during the summer."

"Me too!" I exclaimed. "Have you ever been to the North Pole? They got voted best ice cream in the whole state and they've got the sign to prove it. My sister works there with her bestie, Torrie. They do everything together. Work, swim team, homework, clothes shopping, you name it. Torrie spends a lot of time at our place 'cause her brother and sister are away at college, so she says her house is boring."

"Oh, I see," Mason said, even though he couldn't see

anything. "And, no, I haven't been to the North Pole, but I'm looking forward to it."

"Looking forward to it when? Maybe me and Grams can go with you."

"We'll all be going," Mason said. "Mr. Todd arranged an end-of-summer outing for everyone involved in the reading program to go to the North Pole to celebrate our successes."

"Really?! Hooray!"

"You can thank Mr. Todd. He's the mastermind."

"Mr. Todd's really smart," I said, "but even he couldn't tell me if owls are tricky."

"You still haven't found an answer to that one, huh?"

"No."

"Well, as much as I love books, I've got to say, I don't think you're going to find your answer there. And unfortunately, I don't have the answer for you, either, but the good news is school will be starting soon, and something tells me you'll find out then."

I didn't know if school starting soon really was good news, but I was beginning to think Mason was right. I'd have to wait a little bit longer to get my answer about owls.

12

SWIM LESSONS

Swim lessons weren't as exciting as Farmer Don's or my library trips. Maybe if we'd had Susie and Murphy doing dog paddles in the pool with us it would've been better. Or Shelby teaching us how to float, 'cause she wasn't built for slicing through the water with those short legs and low belly. But instead of dogs, I got stuck with Missy Gerber and Samantha Yelber. It was a good thing Samantha wasn't with us in Ms. Krane's class 'cause I couldn't take her *and* Missy every day for a whole year. All they did was cry about how cold the water was. It was the same thing every Friday morning—and it was really annoying.

"Mr. Justin, did you turn the temperature up?" they'd whine.

Mr. Justin was our instructor. He was one grade ahead of Brynn and Torrie but all three of them were on the same club swim team, so I knew him. Justin was my favorite swimmer 'cause he was super-fast.

"Yup. I've got it nice and warm for you today," he'd reply.

Then they'd jump in and let out high-pitched squeals and shout, "No, you didn't!"

Grams said Justin had about as much control over the pool temperature as I did over the weather and that the girls knew it but kept up their game 'cause it was their way of flirting with a cute older boy. When I heard that, I realized those girls were even dumber than I'd thought. So I decided it was time to teach them a lesson.

I hurried and got out to the pool first so I was ready when they showed up. I rushed for no reason, 'cause those girls took forever, but Justin was already there.

"How's your sister?" he asked while we were waiting. "I don't get to see her as much during the summer."

"Okay," I said, and shrugged. "She's busy working at the North Pole with Torrie."

"I forgot she works there. Maybe I'll swing by and say hi. They've got great ice cream."

"You should," I told him. "Their twist is my favorite. And if you're nice, Brynn will give you extra sprinkles."

Justin laughed. "I'll be nice," he promised.

Missy and Samantha finally came strolling out of the locker room after that, so we were able to get started. But first things first. As soon as they dropped their towels on the bench and stepped toward the edge to do their flirting, I ran past them and let my killer cannonball fly. I tilted my butt in their direction on impact and my monster splash soaked them from head to foot.

Boy, did they ever scream—and it sounded way better than their stupid high-pitched squeals.

"It's warm today!" I yelled up to them.

"You're insufferable," Missy Gerber spat, trying to confuse me with her big words.

"You're in—whatever you said. And annoying too," I shot back.

"I can't wait for my mom to get me switched into Samantha's class so I won't have to put up with you."

Samantha nodded along in agreement.

"You can't get switched. That's the rule," I told Missy, even though I liked the idea of being done with her.

"My mom is meeting with Principal Ryan. I'm getting switched."

"Why?"

"Because she doesn't want me dealing with any disruptions."

I thought she was talking about me when she said disruptions—but she wasn't. Not just me, anyway.

Justin blew his whistle and the girls jumped in and did their annoying high-pitched squeals, then swam to the far side to give him their googly eyes. And it didn't bother me one bit, 'cause I just got great news. Missy Gerber wasn't gonna be in my class!

13

END OF SUMMER READING CELEBRATION

Asking me to be patient and wait for the End of Summer Reading Celebration at the North Pole was like asking ice cream not to melt on a hot day—impossible. I must've asked Grams a hundred times if we could go already.

"Carter Avery, if you ask me that one more time—"

"Then let's go so I don't have to."

Grams huffed. "The event doesn't even start until seven o'clock, so we're gonna be early, but I suppose that's better than you driving me nuts."

"Exactly," I agreed.

"Let me use the bathroom and get my things. You should do the same."

It was my turn to huff now. "Why do I always have to use the bathroom before I can go anywhere? And when will you stop making me?"

"Because I said so and when you're old enough to know better."

"Old enough to know better is how old Ms. Krane is."

"Then I guess you'd better get used to me telling you to use the bathroom before going anywhere and doing so without complaining about it," Grams said.

I didn't find her joke funny and Grams said that was 'cause she wasn't joking. That wasn't funny either.

I let her use the bathroom first 'cause I wanted her to know I was annoyed and also 'cause it wasn't gonna take me as long. I tried moving slow, but I was still stuck standing next to Leopold and waiting for her. And I even washed my hands when I got done.

"Oh, calm your horses," Grams said when she came out of the house and saw me tapping my foot in the dirt. She unlocked the doors and tossed her purse in the back. Then we got ourselves situated and buckled, and finally we got going—and it's a good thing we did.

"Wow. Look at how many people are already here," I said when we arrived. "Betcha you're glad we came early now, huh? Any later and we wouldn't have found a place to park."

"Betcha you're glad we came early now," Grams mimicked.

I grinned but didn't say anything more.

Grams squeezed Leopold into a parking spot and I jumped out and ran to the event area that was behind the building 'cause that was where Mr. Todd said we'd all meet. He'd arranged for a magician to come and perform for us, and then we were all getting coupons for a free cone.

The event area was just a big field where people could

spread out on blankets or plop down in lawn chairs if you brought them, and in the middle was a small stage. As Grams liked to say, it wasn't much but it got the job done.

I was happy when I found Mason and Susie already sitting back there. I ran right over to join them. Susie's tail started wagging the second she saw me.

"Hi, Carter," Mason said.

"How did you know it was me?"

"Susie's tail always thumps that way for you. And your feet always make the same rhythmic running sound."

I knew Mason couldn't see it, but my eyebrows went up real high after he said that. I was impressed.

I sat down with them. "You wanted to get here early too, huh?"

"Yes," Mason said. "There are fewer tripping hazards if I arrive before the crowds."

I nodded real big. That made sense. But then I thought of something. "How'd you get here? If you can't see, you can't drive, right?" I was pretty sure about that but asked 'cause Mason had a way of surprising me.

"No, I can't drive," he laughed, "though I might argue I could do as good a job as some drivers based on the number of horns honking and people yelling at each other that I hear. But the law says I can't, so I make arrangements to have a driver."

"Do you live far from here?"

"Not too far. Just a few towns away. Are you excited for the magician's show?"

"Yeah," I said. "I hope they cut somebody in half."

"Oooh. That would be good," Mason agreed.

I wanted to ask him how he was gonna enjoy the show if he couldn't see but before I got to, Grams joined us.

"Hello, Mrs. Sims," Mason said.

"Good evening," Grams replied. "And a good evening to you too," she told Susie.

Grams got her lawn chair set up, and lots of other families and dogs and owners from the reading program started filling in the space around us. Murphy was already busy herding a few runaway kids. Mason and Grams chatted and I spent the time petting Susie and watching Mr. Todd get the equipment ready on the stage. He put out two big speakers and wrestled with a wad of black electrical cords until he had things plugged in. Then he opened some sort of stand thingy and stuck a sign on it that said, NOW YOU SEE IT, NOW YOU DON'T.

When Mr. Todd finished, he took the microphone and got our event underway. "Good evening and welcome to our End of Summer Reading Celebration," he announced. "How about a big hand for our thirty-seven amazing readers?"

The lawn area got loud with grown-ups clapping.

"In total, our readers have read over fifty thousand minutes this summer," Mr. Todd continued. "And our special visitors have been there for much of it. How about a round of applause for our furry friends and their handlers."

This time I clapped too, 'cause it was for Mason and Susie and Murphy and the other dogs and their owners.

"You should all be proud of your accomplishments," Mr. Todd said. "I know I am. And that's why we're here to celebrate your success. So without further delay, let's welcome Abracadabra Adam. I hope you all enjoy tonight's show."

Mr. Todd left the stage and our special magician stepped up. He was dressed in black and wore a top hat like he was supposed to, so that was a good start.

14

NOW YOU SEE IT, NOW YOU DON'T

Abracadabra Adam didn't say anything. He motioned with his hand to call one of the younger kids sitting near the front onto the stage with him. He had the girl face the audience. Then he wiggled his fingers and waved them around her ear and pulled out a coin.

I'd seen that one before. Who hadn't? So I wasn't real impressed.

Adam looked over the crowd and shrugged. He waved his hand around the girl's ear again and the coin disappeared and was replaced by a feather.

I perked up, 'cause that was better.

But Adam shrugged and waved his hand again—and this time the feather disappeared and was replaced by a real live bird.

The crowd gasped and clapped. I wanted to know how he did that. *How did he do that?*

Abracadabra Adam gave his young helper a slight bow and then had her sit back down. A different older girl entered from the side of the stage then and wheeled out a small cage. She had to be his assistant 'cause she was dressed in black too.

Adam placed his bird inside the cage. Then he draped the cage in a blanket, spun it around several times, and fast yanked the blanket away. And the bird was gone!

Abracadabra Adam pointed to his sign.

"Now you see it, now you don't!" the crowd cheered.

He didn't saw anybody in half, but Abracadabra Adam put on a great show that night. He was real good. So good I forgot about getting my free ice cream cone until he was done. But when he was, I jumped to my feet.

I wanted to run to the first open window, but I didn't 'cause me and Grams walked with Mason and Susie. I wanted Brynn and Torrie to meet them.

"Hi, Brynn. These are my friends Mason and Susie," I said, making introductions when it was finally our turn at her window.

Brynn quick grabbed Torrie from the next window over so she could say hi too.

"Carter has told me all about this dynamic duo," Mason said. "It's nice to meet the amazing baker and her bestie."

Brynn and Torrie laughed. "It's nice to meet you too," they replied.

"Carter tells me you can't beat the twist here, so I'll take that," Mason said, giving his order.

"Would you like the classic chocolate and vanilla or we have a Creamsicle twist tonight?" Brynn asked.

"*Hmm.* I'll try the Creamsicle," Mason decided.

"Coming right up," Brynn responded, and hurried off.

Torrie waved and went back to her window. My sister returned a minute later carrying Mason's cone and a short vanilla one for Susie, which she handed to me. I grinned.

"Susie says thank you," Mason said.

Brynn seemed stunned that Mason knew. "Susie's enthusiastic butt shake tells me she got a treat," Mason said, explaining himself to Brynn.

Brynn smiled. "I hope you both enjoy them," she said.

"Susie did," I answered. She was a patient dog, but not when it came to ice cream. She wolfed it down faster than me.

Mason laughed, then went with Susie to find a place to sit while me and Grams waited for our orders. Brynn got me mine first 'cause she knew I was anxious to be with my friends. And even though she was my sister, I told her thanks 'cause Grams would've made me anyway, but I meant it this time, and then I dashed off. Grams could join us after she had her yucky maple walnut.

I rounded the corner of the building and spotted Mason stopped halfway to the nearest picnic table. His ice cream was on the ground—and Susie wasn't licking it up. Her hair was raised and her eyes were narrowed and focused on two older guys sitting on a bench off to the side.

"Now you see it, now you don't," one sang.

"Ha ha ha," they laughed together.

"Wait, you never saw it," the first one joked.

"Ha ha ha!" More laughing.

Those jerks were bigger and older than me, but I didn't care. I wanted to march over and tell them to leave my friend alone—or else. But wanting and doing are two different things. I stayed rooted where I was. Too scared to move.

"C'mon, bro, let's get outta here," the second jerk urged, tugging on his buddy's elbow. "We'll come back later."

"Now you see it, now you don't," the bro sang again as he waltzed off all cocky.

Once they were out of sight, Susie took care of cleaning up the mess on the ground and I got busy licking my own cone 'cause it was already dripping all down my hand and wrist. "I'll have Brynn make you another one," I told Mason.

"No, that's okay. I'm happy to share mine with Susie today. Let's find a place to sit."

I spotted an open picnic table and led us over to it. At the same time we took our seats, a rusty brown pickup burped and roared in the distance, peeling rubber as it tore out of the parking lot. I felt like Mason right then, 'cause I didn't need to see to know who was behind that wheel.

"How come you're not upset?" I asked him. "If that happened to my ice cream, I'd be madder than the devil."

"And once upon a time, I probably would've been too. But not anymore."

"Why?"

Mason took a deep breath. "Carter, I haven't always been

blind. I lost my sight when I was a teenager, and while that was happening, I was angry. Angry at the world. It wasn't fair. But here's the thing. There's a lot about life that isn't fair. So you either spend your days being angry and crying about it, or you play the hand you're dealt the best you can."

"My grams says that too."

"Yes, she told me life hasn't always been fair for you, either, has it?"

I shook my head. And even though Mason couldn't see that, he knew my answer. "Brynn remembers more than me," I said, "so it's harder for her."

"You're lucky to have each other, and your grams too."

"My grandpa died before I was born, and my other grand-parents were older and died even before Brynn came along, so it's just been my sister and Grams and me for as long as I can remember."

"And you're a great family."

I nodded.

"The funny thing is, Carter, it took me losing my vision before I was able to really see the world."

That was Mason being tricky now. His watch buzzed and he tapped it. "My ride's here," he said. "Looks like it's time for me to head home."

"Will I see you and Susie again?" I asked, suddenly ner-vous that I might not since our reading program was over and school would be starting.

"I hope so. I need you to tell me what you learn about owls firsthand."

I smiled. Susie gave my fingers a quick kiss and then she helped Mason to their ride.

Now I see them, now I don't. But you want to know who I did see? Justin. He was standing in Brynn's line.

Part III

FALL: THE START OF FOURTH GRADE

15

THE BULLETIN BOARD WARNING

Some kids get excited for the first day of school 'cause they can't wait to wear their new clothes, but not me. I hated clothes shopping and trying on all that stiff, itchy stuff. I was happy to stick with my old shorts and T-shirt. I liked how they felt and I could move in them. But Missy Gerber was a different story.

"Carter Avery, what're you wearing?" she shrieked when she saw me buzzing down the sidewalk. Missy was on the student council, and one of their jobs on the first day was to hold the main doors open and welcome students back to a new year. She skipped over the welcoming part and went straight to being annoying.

"What? These are my regular shorts and T-shirt," I said. "I even slept in them last night so they're compterfied."

"Compterfied?" she repeated. "That's not even a word."

"Is too. It means making something comfortable."

"Sleeping in your clothes overnight doesn't make them

comfortable," Missy argued. "It makes them dirty. That's the word you should be using—and that's disgusting."

"Yeah, but you can't run in that stuff," I said, pointing at her fancy skirt and shoes.

"I don't need to run. In case you forgot, there's no running in school."

She was right, but I wasn't about to tell her that. I left her and her dumb new clothes in the dust and skipped into the building and up the stairs 'cause that wasn't the same as running. When I reached the top, I got mad at myself 'cause I forgot to ask Missy if her mom got her switched to a different class, but I wasn't going back. I darted out of the stairwell and around the corner and hurried down the hallway, searching for my locker. We'd never had lockers before. Fourth grade was our first time getting them.

I found mine all the way at the end, closest to the classroom door—which was right next to the bulletin board. I froze, staring at the display. There was a full moon at the top, with our room number written on it, and below that Ms. Krane had twenty-two mice scurrying across a meadow, one for each student. I scanned the names, looking for mine. I was in the middle but facing the opposite direction. I smiled. How did Ms. Krane know I liked running backward?

My smile faded when I spotted Missy's mouse with pigtails running above mine. And I gulped when I noticed what loomed overhead. Perched in the tree that stretched out from the side of the bulletin board was a great horned owl. Its fierce yellow eyes, pointed ears, and razor-sharp talons zeroed in on the mice. Stamped across the owl's chest was my teacher's name—Ms. Krane.

As soon as I saw that, I knew Ms. Krane had tricked us. She only did something fun on Meet Your Teacher Day to fool us into thinking she was maybe a little bit nice. But we were getting the real Ms. Krane now. I didn't need to do any more research. The real Ms. Krane sat on that branch. She was the Owl—and she was ready to gobble us up!

16

THE REAL MS. KRANE

"You going to stare at that all day or are you coming?" Kyle asked on his way past me and the bulletin board.

I shook my head and blinked a bunch of times. I was the last one in the hall. "I'm coming!" I shouted.

I quick shoved my bag inside my locker and slammed it shut. Then I stole one last glance at the owl and my mouse before scurrying into my new classroom.

When I spotted Ms. Krane, it looked like she'd already swallowed a few students. I hoped she'd started with Missy Gerber.

"Ms. Krane!" I exclaimed. "What happened to you?"

She smiled. "Welcome to fourth grade, Mr. Avery. You'll find your seat over there." She pointed.

My desk was pushed up against the counter that ran along the windows. And sitting on the table in front of me was a fish tank. Except it wasn't a fish tank. It was a jungle tank.

"What's in there?" I asked, rushing over to inspect it.

Ms. Krane came and stood next to me as I peered inside.

"That would be a bog, which is sort of like a miniature rainforest habitat, and there's a tree frog in there. I thought we should have a class pet."

Did you catch that? She said *we*.

"Really? Where is he? What's his name?"

"Actually, he could be a she, and the frog doesn't have a name yet. Maybe you can give it one for us?"

Did you catch that? She said *us*.

"Me?" I squeaked, looking at Ms. Krane with wide eyes. That seemed like a pretty important job, not one any of my other teachers would've given me before.

"Sure," she answered. "I know you'll think of a good one."

I gulped. Then I searched inside the tank again. "I'll need to get to know him a little bit first."

"That sounds like a good plan," Ms. Krane agreed.

She walked away and started chatting with some of my classmates, and I went back to staring in the tank. I forgot all about asking her how she got so fat 'cause I was distracted with trying to find our frog.

I had to slow my eyes down and look real careful before I finally spotted him resting near the top. He was hiding on a leaf. He blended in with the colors so it was really hard to see him. I thought about naming him Hider or Camo, which would be short for camouflage 'cause that's what he was doing, but I wanted to give it more time before deciding, in case other ideas came to me.

Speaking of names, Ms. Krane got started calling ours for morning attendance. She never even told me to get to my seat. She let me keep standing at the tank, which was way better than trying to sit still behind my desk, but guess who couldn't handle that.

"Carter, you need to sit in your seat now," Missy Gerber said, already bossing me around.

I ignored her. Ignoring was one of the strategies Grams was always telling me to try—and Principal Ryan, too, when I got sent to her office.

"Carter!" she cried again, her voice sounding irritated like my old teachers.

Me and Camo were doing good ignoring. (That was me trying out his name. He was definitely a boy frog. I'd had enough of girls already—thanks to Missy.)

"Ms. Krane, Carter won't sit down," Missy whined.

Now you know why Missy Gerber was a double dose of annoying. She was bossy *and* a tattletale.

"Missy, I'd like you to worry about you," Ms. Krane said. "Carter isn't bothering anyone."

Boy, did I grin when I heard that. "Yeah, worry about yourself, bossy pants."

Kids laughed even though I wasn't trying to be funny. I quick slapped my hand over my mouth, but it was too late.

Those words had skipped ahead of my brain again. The idea that it was okay to think certain things but not say them was something I was still working on.

Ms. Krane lasered her triangle pointy eyes at me, giving me her death stare. The Owl was so scary and mean she didn't even have to say anything—and I didn't need to keep my hand over my mouth, 'cause I knew if I let one more word slip, I'd be a dead mouse.

Missy Gerber didn't say anything, either. Instead, she hid her face in her hands. Missy wasn't double trouble. She was a triple threat: bossy, tattletale, and crybaby.

Ms. Krane finished taking attendance and began passing out those black-and-white notebooks that reminded me of a cow. She put mine on my desk even though I still wasn't sitting there. I grabbed it and sat on the counter between my seat and Hider's tank. (That was me testing out his other name.)

"These will be your personal journals for the year," Ms. Krane explained as she walked around. "Personal means it's yours and you may use it for anything you want. There will also be times when I ask you to work in them. If you want me to look in yours or read something in it, I will. But only if you want."

"Is that for real or a trick?" I asked.

The Owl twisted her head around and lasered her triangle pointy eyes on me again. "I don't play tricks, Carter."

I gulped a second time.

Ms. Krane took her position at the front of the room and continued giving us directions. "Please put your names on the front covers. You may work in your journals now or choose silent reading."

I didn't like writing very much 'cause it was hard for me, but I took my pencil and printed my name on the cover like she'd asked. I got done and then the great horned owl swooped over and landed next to me when I wasn't looking. One thing me and Grams read this summer was that owls can make silent flight, which is something that makes them scary hunters. That was pretty cool, unless your teacher was an owl.

"Carter, I'd like to speak to you in the hallway."

17

A HIGH-FIVE KICK

This was it. My mouth blurted stuff it wasn't supposed to and now the Owl was taking me outside to bite my head off. I'd made this trip with my teachers lots of times before. This was when they told me how bad I was and left me out there to think about my behavior. I never did much thinking 'cause they were the bad ones. Instead, I practiced holding my breath for as long as possible. I played with the stuff I had in my pockets and picked at the carpet or counted the dots on the ceiling. I tried to see how many times I could spin around in place before I got super dizzy. I kept busy.

Ms. Krane pulled the door closed after we stepped into the hallway—but not all the way closed 'cause she still wanted to hear what was going on inside the classroom. Since it was reading or personal journal time, it had better be silent or she'd be biting off more heads when she got done with me.

"Carter, I'm sorry Missy was telling you what to do. I will speak to her later. Regardless, I cannot have you calling her names or using hurtful words in our classroom."

Did you catch that? She said *our* classroom, not *my*. With my old teachers, it was always, *"I will not let you disrupt MY classroom."*

"Did it make you feel better to see her get upset?" Ms. Krane asked.

"Yes!" I exclaimed.

"Really?"

My shoulders sagged. "It felt good to say it."

"But not the rest?" Ms. Krane asked.

"No," I admitted. "But she deserved it."

"Maybe so, but making someone else feel bad is never a good way to make yourself feel better. On the contrary, helping others can be very rewarding. Our big rule this year is that we have to bring positive attitudes to our classroom, which is why I know you're going to do great. You're full of positive energy. Too much sometimes, but we'll work on that."

Did you catch it that time? She said *our* again—a couple times. And she said I was gonna do great.

"Huh," Ms. Krane suddenly gasped.

My eyes popped. "What's wrong?" Was she going to eat me now?

She put her hands on her belly. "Carter," she said in a tiny voice.

"What?"

Ms. Krane kept looking down at her tummy. She moved her hands around slowly, then stopped and held them in one spot. Suddenly, she glanced up at me, her face turning from serious to bright and happy.

"What? Can I touch?"

Ms. Krane took my hand and placed it on her stomach. "Feel it?" she whispered.

"Feel what?" I whispered back, 'cause that's what we were doing. But she didn't have to answer. All of a sudden, something inside her belly hit my hand.

"Did you feel it?!"

I nodded fast, my eyes real big now.

"That's my baby."

"You mean you really are pregnant? You didn't just get fat?"

Ms. Krane laughed. "Yes, I'm really pregnant."

I didn't know owls could smile. I'd heard Ms. Krane had never been seen smiling, but I'd witnessed it a few times already. And she had a big smile on her face now. Me too.

We held our breaths, waiting to see if it happened again. And then it did! Her baby kicked my hand. It was like giving me a high five or fist bump. I squealed and so did Ms. Krane.

"Wow!" I said. It was the most amazing thing I'd ever felt. I didn't know a baby was moving and doing stuff inside its mom before coming out.

"Can your baby hear us?" I asked.

"I believe so, which is another reason why we've got to try hard to be positive and use nice words."

I nodded fast 'cause I understood that. Then I leaned closer to my teacher's belly. "Hi, baby," I said.

Ms. Krane felt it move again. "I think my baby likes you, Carter."

I grinned.

"C'mon," she said, wrapping her wing around my shoulder. "We should get back inside."

I glanced at my mouse on the bulletin board. He was still there. And you know what? I didn't see it earlier, but he looked happy.

"Sorry, Missy," I hollered when I reentered our classroom. I was using nice words for the baby.

I walked to my side of the room but I didn't sit in my seat. Apologizing to Missy didn't mean I had to do what she said. I grabbed my pencil and personal cow journal and opened it to the first page. And then I drew a picture of Ms. Krane's baby giving me a high-five kick.

When I finished, I leaned closer to the tank and held up my artwork for Camo to see. (I decided that was his name.) He didn't do anything, but that didn't matter 'cause I was proud. And then I thought of something else—Ms. Krane's three things, her two truths and a lie. Since she was for real pregnant, that meant her last statement was false.

She really did like kids—maybe even me.

18

THE SECRET

I bounded up the bus steps and slid into my seat behind Mr. Wilson, but I didn't sit down.

"Guess what? My teacher's pregnant," I exclaimed.

"Well, that's exciting."

"Yup. I got to feel her baby move today."

Mr. Wilson's eyebrows went up. "Really?"

"Yup. We were having a private chat out in the hall when it happened."

"A private chat, huh? That sounds familiar."

"Yeah, but it was different with Ms. Krane. She's nice."

Mr. Wilson's eyebrows shot up again. "Not sure I've ever heard you say that about a teacher before."

I shrugged. "It's true. And it's not a trick 'cause she really does like kids."

"Huh," Mr. Wilson said, and smirked. "That's great to hear, Carter, but I need you to pop a squat now. It's time for me to put this big yellow taxi in drive."

I plopped my butt on the seat and stared out the window. Mason never said I'd have to do hands-on research, but that was what I'd done—and I'd learned a lot! He was gonna flip if I ever got to tell him.

Grams was waiting for me when we got to my stop. I jumped to my feet. "See you tomorrow," I cheered.

"Thanks for the warning," Mr. Wilson replied.

I stuck my tongue out at him and hopped down the bus steps. Me and Grams waved as he drove away and then we turned toward the house.

"Your sister and Torrie are inside," Grams said.

"No swim today?"

"Practice is later. They're getting an after-school snack ready before tackling their homework."

"Yay!"

"Maybe you can tell us about your day while we eat?"

"I've got lots to tell," I teased.

"Really?" Grams sounded shocked 'cause I wasn't usually thrilled to talk about school.

"Yup," I teased more. Then I ran ahead 'cause Grams walked too slow for me and 'cause I was hoping Brynn had fresh snickerdoodles waiting. Plus, I didn't want to tell Grams the news until everyone was together. I hurried inside and booked it to the bathroom 'cause I had to go bad.

"Did you wash your hands?" Torrie asked when I slid into the kitchen. Told you she was like another sister.

"Yes," I groaned. If she didn't ask, then Grams or Brynn would. Someone always checked on that 'cause I didn't always remember, especially when I was in a hurry.

Brynn handed me a plate and ruffled my hair.

"So what's your exciting news?" Grams asked.

I loaded up on Brynn and Torrie's warm mini-muffins, which weren't snickerdoodles but were still really yummy, and sat down. "Ms. Krane is pregnant and I got to feel her baby move today. Just me," I blurted.

Brynn and Torrie looked at each other and then at Grams, but no one said anything. "Did you hear me?" I shouted.

"Yes. Yes," Grams replied. "That certainly is exciting. Sounds like you learned something big about your teacher on the first day."

"Yup, I sure did. I learned she's pregnant and she really does like kids."

Grams chuckled. "Well, that's a relief."

"Did you learn anything else about Ms. Krane?" Brynn wondered, glancing at Torrie again.

"Like what?" I asked.

"Brynn," Grams cautioned.

"What? He might as well know. He's gonna hear about it."

"Know what?" I asked.

"Never mind," Grams said. "Why were you the only one who got to feel the baby move?"

"Know what?" I repeated.

"CJ, you're on the need-to-know list, and right now you don't need to know, so drop it," Brynn said.

"That's right," Grams snapped. "I said never mind. Now, why were you the only one who got to feel the baby move?"

I wanted to know their secret, but I knew better than to argue with Grams. Besides, I was still excited to tell them about the baby moving. I also told them about Camo and a little bit about annoying Missy Gerber 'cause she didn't get switched into a different class.

"CJ, it's gonna be real important for you to try hard for Ms. Krane. You don't want her to get upset or stressed out, because that won't be good for her baby," Grams explained.

"Don't worry. Our classroom rule is that we have to be positive and use nice words."

Grams smiled. "That's good to hear," she said.

When I got done eating my snack and telling my story, I let Shelby lick my plate clean, and then I put it in the sink and ran outside to play. I'd forgotten all about Brynn and Torrie and Grams's secret—but Brynn was right. I was gonna hear about it sooner or later.

19

MY SEAT GETS EVEN BETTER

I already loved where my desk was in our classroom 'cause I was near Camo and had the windows and big counter space next to me. When I got tired of my chair, I sat on the counter. And when I got tired of sitting still, I spun in circles on it. And Ms. Krane never stopped me or yelled at me.

Missy Gerber wanted to, but Ms. Krane did something real clever that made my seat even better. She switched Missy's desk with Vanessa Tucker's, so now Missy was on the other side of the room, as far away from me as possible, so she wasn't bossing me around all the time—even though she still wanted to. Asking Missy to stop telling me what to do was like asking me to sit still. Moving her desk was the smartest thing Ms. Krane ever did.

The only stinky part was putting Missy on the other side of the room still didn't stop her from bugging me at recess. "Carter Avery, you can't go on these monkey bars," she whined.

"Yes, I can. You're not my boss."

"I'm not bossing you. I'm telling you the rules. These are the bars for the girls. Boys are on those." She pointed to the other set.

I stuck my tongue out at her. "You don't make the rules."

"I didn't make those rules. That's how it's always been. Everyone knows that."

"Yeah, well, I know something you don't know."

"I doubt that," she scoffed.

"Ms. Krane is pregnant and I felt her baby move."

"Carter, the whole school knows she's pregnant. Are you really that dumb?"

"No, they don't."

"Yes, they do. Parents have been talking about it all summer because Ms. Krane did it artificial."

I scowled. "What's that?"

"I don't know, and you better not ask her because she might get upset," Missy sneered, then swung down the bars and ran off to catch up with Samantha Yelber.

I'd never heard Missy say she didn't know something before. Any other time and that woulda put a big smile on my face 'cause she was such a know-it-all, but now I was just left with the word *artificial* stuck in my head and it was taking up my whole brain.

Was Ms. Krane having an alien baby?

20

"ARTIFICIAL" RESEARCH

I really, really wanted to ask Ms. Krane what her being artificial meant, but I was worried Missy Gerber was right and that I could upset Ms. Krane, and Grams had told me it was real important for her baby that Ms. Krane not get upset. So I kept my question inside for the rest of the school day, even though I thought I might explode. To get it out just a little before I popped, I tried writing the word in my personal cow journal—and I didn't like writing! That's how bad it was!

I thought about asking Vanessa Tucker what she knew about Ms. Krane being artificial, but I didn't know if she would tell me 'cause she hardly ever said anything to me, so I stuck with whispering my question to Camo instead. I could trust him to stay quiet and telling someone helped me get through the rest of the day without bursting.

But as soon as I got on the big yellow taxi and slid into my seat behind Mr. Wilson, I asked him if he knew what artificial meant.

"Artificial?" he repeated, eyeing me with one of those curious looks in his mirror.

"Yeah."

"Well, I guess artificial means not natural, like those fake sweeteners," he answered, putting the bus in gear. "You know, the stuff that's not real sugar. You've probably seen them before. Those blue or pink packets."

I did know. I remembered a time when I was at the diner with Grams and I tried giving her the colored packets to put in her coffee.

"Not those!" she hollered. "That artificial stuff is terrible. I want the white packets."

Did that mean my teacher was terrible, too?

"Artificial can also refer to something being man-made," Mr. Wilson said, adding to his answer a little while later, after we'd dropped off a few kids. "I guess that's another way of thinking about it."

I scowled. "Can it be girl-made?" I asked, 'cause Ms. Krane was a girl.

Mr. Wilson laughed. "Yes. 'Man-made' is just an expression, but that doesn't mean girls can't do it."

"The expression should be person-made, then."

Mr. Wilson snorted. "I suppose you're right."

But how could Ms. Krane's baby be not natural if it was

person-made? That didn't make sense. "Mr. Wilson, can something natural be person-made?"

"*Oof.* That's a tough one. Hard to say. Probably. But you better ask your grams that question."

That was just what I was thinking. We slowed at my stop and I hopped up from my seat.

"Well, here you are, young man," Mr. Wilson said, opening the door. "Home sweet home. Good luck with that question of yours."

"Thanks," I said. "I'll see you tomorrow."

"Not if I see you first," he teased, reciting another one of his favorite jokes.

I grinned. I didn't get that one the first time he said it, but Grams explained it to me. She said Mr. Wilson was a man of one-liners. Brynn liked to add "cheesy" to that description.

Speaking of Grams and Brynn, since neither one was waiting for me, I knew they had to be busy with something. I jumped down the bus steps and hit the ground running. Mr. Wilson honked the horn and drove away.

I was right. I burst into the house and found Grams having fits with our TV again.

"Hi, Grams," I said, poking my head into the living room.

"Shhh!" she spit. "I'm trying to fix this blasted thing so I can watch my show later."

"Where's Brynn?"

"Swim practice. There's a snack in the kitchen. Now stop asking me questions. I need to concentrate."

"You can fix that thing by putting it out to pasture," I reminded her. "You've said so yourself."

"I'm about ready to," she groaned.

I left her alone and scooted into the kitchen. Shelby came with me 'cause the kitchen was definitely more exciting than a broken TV—not much, though. Snack was one of the healthy options—ants on a log. The name made it sound fun, but it was just celery with peanut butter and raisins. Or you can do cream cheese instead of peanut butter, but me and Shelby both preferred the peanut butter—and no raisins on Shelby's, 'cause raisins are poisonous for dogs.

I ate mine and Shelby took care of hers, and we washed it down with some nice cold milk. And then I got Grams's big fat dictionary that was almost as old as her. Back when I was too short to see over the counter, the book was my stepping block, and after that it got put under Shelby's bowls so she didn't have to bend down as far to reach her food and water. But today it was gonna help me by being itself, 'cause without Brynn to ask and Grams up to her neck with the TV, that big fat dictionary was the only thing I could think of that might be able to answer my question.

I plopped it open on my bedroom floor. It took me a bit to find the word 'cause *artificial* wasn't an easy one to spell, but I did my best sounding it out and finally found it. I knew I had the right word 'cause one of the definitions said what Mr. Wilson had mentioned.

artificial: (adj)—that meant adjective—*made by human skill; produced by humans (opposed to natural)*

I didn't get it. If babies were made by humans, how could they be not natural? That didn't make sense, so I decided Missy Gerber didn't know what she was talking about this time. And I left it at that—until the next thing happened.

21

BIG CHICKENS

"I thought we'd start today with a fun book," Ms. Krane announced.

I stopped spinning on my counter space. Everybody stopped what they were doing, 'cause if there was one thing we all agreed on at this point, it was that Ms. Krane was the greatest at reading aloud.

"Ms. Krane, no offense, but that's a picture book. Aren't we getting too old for those?" Missy Gerber complained the first time Ms. Krane tried reading to us.

"I like picture books," I argued. And that wasn't me trying to be the teacher's pet.

"Me too," Ms. Krane agreed. "We'll read lots of them this year. And, actually, I prefer to call them 'everybody books.' I happen to be of the opinion that a person never outgrows them."

And she wasn't lying. We'd read a bunch already—and Missy Gerber wasn't complaining anymore, 'cause like I said, Ms. Krane was the greatest at reading aloud.

"What everybody book do you have today?" Kyle asked.

"*Big Chickens,* written by Leslie Helakoski and illustrated by Henry Cole," Ms. Krane replied, holding the cover up for us to see.

I glanced at Camo and shrugged. I'd never heard this one before, but I grabbed my personal cow journal and got ready. Ms. Krane wanted us to have our journals nearby whenever she read to us in case we got the urge to write something—I never did; I only added a sketch once in a while.

Ms. Krane lowered the book and began to read. And, boy, did she get into it. Ms. Krane gave those big chickens super-funny personalities. She had our whole class laughing and snorting at those ridiculous birds—even Missy Gerber.

"Ms. Krane, you make the best voices!" I shouted when she finished.

I'd already told her that many times, but I couldn't hold it in. And even though it'd happened before, there was still a chorus of enthusiastic "yeahs."

"How'd you do that? How'd you make all those chickens sound different?" Kyle asked.

"By having fun with the story," she answered. "Simple as that. I want you all to see how much fun reading can be."

"Except when it comes to those boring workbook passages and dumb questions," Kyle groaned.

There were more "yeahs" 'cause everyone agreed with Kyle. Even Ms. Krane nodded. "A fair point," she said. "But just because you dislike one passage, doesn't mean you have to dislike reading altogether. You need to give it a chance, same as you do other things in life."

Don't ask me why, but me and Missy Gerber looked at each other at the exact same time after Ms. Krane said that.

"Now, I must confess," Ms. Krane continued. "Other than having fun, there is another reason why I chose today's book."

"What?" we wondered.

"Well, we'll be taking our very first field trip at the end of this week."

"Where?" I squawked, sounding like those chickens, but I couldn't help myself. Field trips were exciting.

"We'll be visiting a local farm where they have chickens, among other things. The gentleman there will give us a tour and tell us about his job and all of his animals."

"Are we going to Farmer Don's?" I squawked louder, bouncing on the counter.

"Yes," Ms. Krane replied. "And easy on the bouncing."

"Are we going to see elephants and giraffes?" Vanessa asked, perking up 'cause she loved animals.

"It's a farm, not the zoo," Missy Gerber groaned. "Why couldn't it be a trip to a museum or the theater?"

"No way! Farmer Don's is awesome!" I cheered. "You'll see."

Vanessa looked at me and gave a tiny smile.

I wasn't kidding, Farmer Don's *was* awesome. But even though I'd been there a bunch of times, I had no clue what was in store for us.

22

IF I WAS IN CHARGE

Me and Grams had this game we played called If I Was in Charge. Grams might say something like, "If I was in charge, a person's knees wouldn't get creaky and achy as they get older."

And then I might say, "If I was in charge, Missy Gerber would slip and fall in a cow patty when we visit Farmer Don's. And she'd get poop in her eye and in her mouth!"

And then Grams would squawk, "Carter!" 'cause we weren't supposed to wish harmful things. So then I'd change my answer to something silly. I never said what I really wanted—to be brave or to have friends or to have my mom and dad alive, 'cause I didn't want to get Grams upset. The game was supposed to be fun, not serious. But I was eating alone in the cafeteria again, and if I were playing the game right now, I knew what I'd say.

"If I was in charge, I'd make a rule that you could go to recess as soon as you finished your lunch," 'cause sitting by yourself was something that could make you feel bad. And no one even had to say anything mean to you. I'd been eating alone for a long time, so I knew what I was talking about.

Our cafeteria had square tables spread out across the floor. There were four chairs at every table, one on each side—except for mine. There was only one. Kids took the other three and added them to their tables so they could sit with five or six friends. As long as they didn't make messes and put the chairs back at the end, the cafeteria aides never stopped them.

Grams didn't like that I always sat alone, but I told her that was better than making kids sit with me. Some of the grown-ups in the cafeteria had tried that once and the kids stuck at my table just sat there and whispered about me. That was worse, so Grams didn't push it. Besides, every once in a while I got invited to a lunch bunch with our school guidance counselor, Ms. Garcia. It was called a lunch bunch 'cause you could bring a bunch of friends with you if you wanted, but I never brought anyone. There was no one I wanted to invite. I was happy just to eat with Ms. Garcia.

The other thing I never did was buy school lunch 'cause what Grams packed me was way better. She made my peanut butter and jelly with the kind of peanut butter that I liked 'cause not all peanut butter tastes the same, and she put just the right amount of jelly on my sandwich. Enough that it fought against the peanut butter, but not so much that it got my bread soggy. If you can see a dark spot through the top of the bread, there's too much jelly. Usually I could count on a bag of Goldfish, but if Brynn had done any baking, then I'd get a few snickerdoodles or muffies, and Grams also liked to put something like applesauce or yogurt in there 'cause there was supposed to be a healthy item. If I was real hungry, I'd eat that stuff—but not always.

There were two other things I found in my lunch box every day. One was a prize. Something that I'd be able to play with—Legos or a couple Matchbox cars—after I got done eating, 'cause I ate fast and always had to spend time sitting and waiting before we could leave the cafeteria. The second thing was a note. Sometimes Grams would write a word on my napkin, like *SMILE*. It wasn't much, but it always made me feel better—even when I was sitting by myself. And other times she'd jot down my horoscope on a scrap of paper 'cause Grams read hers and mine and Brynn's every morning.

"Hey, Carter," a voice said, startling me. I looked up from my lunch box and found Vanessa standing there. "What kind of animals will we see at Farmer Don's?"

I shifted in my seat. "He has a horse, and cows, chickens, a moody barn cat, and a few pigs," I told her.

"Wow, that's a lot."

"Yeah," I agreed.

"I can't wait to go."

I grinned. "Me either."

"Thanks," she said before walking back to her table.

I watched her leave, then glanced down at the note Grams had given me. *Expect the unexpected because things are looking up.*

23

FIELD TRIP

Ms. Krane let me be our line leader when it finally came time for our field trip 'cause she knew it was gonna be hard to slow me down. I knew it was gonna be a great day when I saw Mr. Wilson was our bus driver.

I bounded up the steps and jumped into my seat behind him.

"Fancy seeing you again so soon," he said.

"Must be your lucky day," I replied.

Mr. Wilson snorted. Thanks to him, I was getting better at my one-liners.

Ms. Krane climbed aboard last and took attendance one more time. When she got done calling our names, she sat in the seat across from me and introduced herself to Mr. Wilson.

"I'm Olivia," Ms. Krane said.

"Henry," Mr. Wilson replied, putting the bus in motion. (It sounded funny hearing them say their first names.) "It's nice to meet the teacher Carter has told me so much about."

The Owl lasered her triangle eyes on me and I shrank against the window. "Good things, I hope," she said.

"Oh, yes," Mr. Wilson assured her. "And if you didn't know, Carter only tells the truth. He might stretch it a bit from time to time, but he's a straight shooter."

Ms. Krane's eyes softened. She grinned and I smiled back.

After a few minutes of traveling, Ms. Krane did that teacher thing where she stood up and checked to make sure everyone was behaving. I stared out the window 'cause I knew where we were going and I was anxious to get there. I breathed on the glass and drew a chicken picture to help pass the time. And then I got to thinking about Ms. Krane and my game with Grams.

"Ms. Krane, if I was in charge, I'd pay my old teachers less and you more," I suddenly announced. "And I'd also change the rules so school was four days a week and the weekend was three days."

Mr. Wilson laughed, but I wasn't joking.

"If we're lucky, maybe you'll be in charge and can make the rules one day," Ms. Krane said.

"If we're lucky, I'll be in charge so Missy isn't," I said.

I quick covered my mouth. That was definitely one of those things I was okay to think but not say out loud.

Ms. Krane smirked.

Just then, Mr. Wilson turned off the main road and started down the dusty and bumpy gravel drive that led to Farmer

Don's. We were getting close, which Mr. Wilson must've decided called for celebration, 'cause he burst into song, singing one of his favorite melodies for everyone to hear. I hadn't heard it in a while, but I remembered it, so I joined him. The occasion called for it.

Birdie, Birdie in the sky
Dropped a little whitewash in my eye
I'm no sailor; I won't cry
I'm sure glad that cows don't fly

We sang it through a second time, and after that the whole class jumped in and belted it with us. Ms. Krane laughed and shook her head. We musta been the loudest bunch on wheels to ever pull into Farmer Don's driveway, which wasn't really a driveway but more like a parking lot in front of his barn. Mr. Wilson stopped and threw the side door open.

When the dust settled, I saw Farmer Don standing outside, waiting for us. Hector was also nearby, sprawled out in the sun.

I hopped up from my seat.

"Have fun," Mr. Wilson said.

"I will."

24

COWS AND HEIFERS

I was the first one to jump off the bus. Hector streaked away, which was probly for the better before somebody tried to pet him and got clawed. Ms. Krane was the only person I knew who could get away with that.

"Hi, Farmer Don."

"Hi there, Carter. That was some mighty fine singing."

"Thanks, but it wasn't just me. It was my whole class. And Mr. Wilson."

Farmer Don chuckled. "So, you ready to show this place off to your friends?"

I grinned. "Yeah!"

"Hi, Don," Ms. Krane said, greeting Farmer Don when she stepped off the bus. "We're all here now."

Farmer Don nodded. "Welcome," he hollered to everyone. "Follow me," he instructed, waving his arm. We took a few steps but then he stopped and turned back around. "I almost forgot. Better watch where you're walking today. Cow patties can make a mess."

There were "ewws!" mixed with laughs after he said that—but it was true. You needed to pay attention around the farm.

Farmer Don had us enter the barn for our first stop. "How about some ice cream to start?" he said, pointing at a table where there were small cups set out for us. We each got one and a spoon. It was really good. There was plain vanilla or vanilla with Oreo pieces inside. I noticed Missy Gerber didn't wrinkle her nose at that.

"Thank you," many of us remembered to say, but I had my mouth full so I didn't get to say it.

"Don't thank me," Famer Don said. "Thank Ellie." He pointed to the brown cow standing in one of the stalls farther down. "She's the one who gave us the milk to make your treat."

Farmer Don brought us over so we could say hi to Ellie and even touch her if we wanted. I didn't know her as well as the chickens, but I'd met her before. I gave her head a big scratch and made sure to thank her. Vanessa stood on Ellie's other side and rubbed her neck.

"She's not an elephant," I whispered, "but she's still pretty terrific."

"She's sweet," Vanessa whispered back.

A lot of other kids got in line to pet Ellie after us—even Missy Gerber. But when Missy took her turn, her fancy bracelet got Ellie's attention and the cow gave her arm a big lick with her long sandpaper tongue. Missy let out one of those hurt-your-ears screams and everyone laughed—including Farmer Don and Ms. Krane. I gave Ellie an extra scratch for that one.

Farmer Don told us Ellie was a Jersey breed, and no, she didn't make chocolate milk just 'cause she was a brown cow. He showed us the milking equipment and gave us a quick demonstration without actually doing it 'cause Ellie had already given her milk for the morning. And then Farmer Don explained the difference between a heifer and a cow. A heifer hasn't had a baby yet. She needs to have a calf in order to start making milk.

"Do you have heifers?" Kyle asked.

"Come with me," Farmer Don said.

We followed him to the back of the barn where there was a gate on one side. "I've got two heifers in this pen," he said. "Looks like they're outside at the moment so we can head out and try to catch a glimpse of them. Both are pregnant. One of them is due to deliver any day now."

There was lots of whispering and excitement after Farmer Don told us that—and even more when we got outside, 'cause we saw which heifer he was talking about right away. Her baby was starting to come out! And if we didn't see it, we heard it, 'cause the mom bellowed.

"Will you look at that!" Farmer Don exclaimed. "It's time."

We stood along the fence with eyes bigger than the cow's.

And we watched the whole thing. The baby calf's head poked out, then slid back inside a little, then poked out more. It went on like that for a couple of minutes, with the mom hollering every so often. I'd never seen anything so gross and so exciting all at once.

"This is like Animal Planet in person!" Kyle cried.

I glanced at Ms. Krane and saw her smiling and holding her belly. Vanessa Tucker leaned on the fence, glued to the action. Missy Gerber and Mary Fergus had their hands over their faces, but they were peeking through their fingers.

I turned back just in time to see the calf fall from its momma onto the ground. The mom cow turned around and started kissing and licking her newborn right away. There were a bunch of "ewws!" when we saw that 'cause the baby was all slimy and wet.

"It's not every day that you get to witness the miracle of life right before your eyes," Farmer Don said. "You kids sure are lucky."

I didn't know if Missy or Mary would say lucky, but I knew that was something none of us would ever forget. Vanessa hadn't taken her eyes off the mom and baby yet. I definitely didn't think there was gonna be anything more amazing than that on our field trip—but Farmer Don and Ms. Krane still had something big waiting for us.

25

SCRAMBLED EGGS AND BABY CHICKS

"Last stop, the chicken coop," Farmer Don announced when we reached the birds. The hens strutted around their fenced-in yard, pecking at the ground.

"Those are some big chickens!" Kyle bawked, trying to sound like Ms. Krane did during our read-aloud, which was pretty funny.

"These birds are called leghorns," Farmer Don explained. "I could've had scrambled eggs waiting for you when you got here, but I figured you'd like Ellie's ice cream more."

"You eat their eggs?" Missy asked, pointing at the chickens.

"You betcha," Farmer Don replied. "Nothing like fresh eggs."

"They're really good," I said. "Me and my grams get them here all the time."

Missy's nose wrinkled.

"Farmer Don and I have a surprise for you today," Ms. Krane announced.

"Another one?!" I yelped.

"We get eggs?" Kyle asked.

"Yes," Farmer Don answered, "but not to eat. To hatch."

"To hatch!" I flipped. "You mean we're gonna grow baby chicks?"

"We're going to try," Ms. Krane replied. "I thought it would be neat for us to watch something grow and develop at the same time it's happening with me."

The girls squealed 'cause that's what girls do when it comes to cute. First it was Lifeguard Justin; now it was baby chicks.

"So if we don't eat the eggs, they'll become babies?" Missy asked.

"Is that what happens with the eggs in your refrigerator?" Farmer Don responded. "The ones you don't eat become chicks?"

"No," Missy mumbled, turning red and hiding her face.

"Don't be embarrassed," I said. "A lot of people get confused about that."

Those words skipped ahead of my brain and came out before I realized it was Missy Gerber I was trying to make feel better. Maybe it happened 'cause I remembered that was the same thing Farmer Don had said to me when I asked him that question last summer. Or maybe it happened 'cause I knew the answer and was eager to explain.

"Carter's right," Farmer Don said. "I get asked that question all the time. I didn't mean to make you feel bad. I'm sorry."

Missy wiped her eyes and nodded.

"The way it works," I began, "is that you need a rooster with the hens to make fertilizer eggs. Those are the ones that become baby chicks. No rooster, then you get the eggs we buy in the grocery store."

"Fertilized, not fertilizer," Missy corrected me. She was back to being annoying again.

"So how are we getting baby chicks?" Kyle asked. "I don't see a rooster."

"Just because the rooster isn't with them now doesn't mean he wasn't with them before you got here," Farmer Don said. "Ms. Krane will be picking up your eggs this weekend. There's no real way to tell if they'll be fertilized or not, but some should be. You'll just have to take care of them and wait and see."

"Is that why we didn't see any boy cows?" Vanessa asked. "They were here before us?"

"Well, actually, the heifers never saw a bull, which is what we call a boy cow. That is one option, but these cows were done artificial by the vet."

My head jerked around. Did he say *artificial*?

"What do you mean?" Kyle asked.

"Well," Farmer Don said, pausing and rubbing his chin. "It's like this. The vet was able to take the seeds from the boy and plant them inside the girl where they can grow," he explained.

"Oh," Kyle said. "Makes sense."

That answer seemed to satisfy him and Vanessa, even

Missy Gerber and everyone else in my class—but not me. I was stuck wondering if that was what Ms. Krane had done. Did the vet give her the seeds? Is that how she got pregnant the artificial way?

I could wonder all I wanted, but I wasn't gonna say anything 'cause I didn't want to upset Ms. Krane. Too bad I couldn't keep others from getting her upset—and me too. Turns out my old teachers didn't like Ms. Krane any more than they did me.

26

THE RED CHAIR

When we got back to school, the only thing we had left in our day was music. I liked music—even though I spent last week's class spinning circles in the hallway. But that wasn't my fault.

Fourth grade was the year when we got to play recorders. I was super psyched to get my first instrument. The problem was that music was our last activity and by then I had to pee real bad 'cause I always drank extra at the fountain when we came in from recess. I was trying to break my record of twelve swallows in thirty seconds. Kyle and Austin kept time for me to make it official, and also 'cause they thought it was funny and they both loved sports, but I came up short, so I'd have to try again.

Anyways, I was in the bathroom when Ms. Crawford passed out our brand-new instruments. And I missed her giving directions. When I got back to class, I saw a shiny black recorder waiting on my desk. It was too hard to resist.

I grabbed it and stuck it in my mouth and blew as hard as I could. The screech that came out would've made Shelby cover her ears—but Missy Gerber's shriek and Ms. Crawford's holler would've made Shelby run and hide. That was way worse.

"What did I say?" Ms. Crawford roared.

I shrugged. "I don't know. I was in the bathroom."

"What's the rule?"

"I don't know. I was in the bathroom," I repeated. (Ms. Crawford needed to work on her listening skills.)

"Do NOT play your recorder until I tell you to," she thundered.

"Oh."

"What's the rule?" she asked again.

"Do NOT play your recorder until I tell you to," I repeated, emphasizing the "not" part like she had.

"Until *I* tell you to," she groaned in disgust.

"Oh."

I didn't like getting scolded, but I was relieved Ms. Crawford didn't take my recorder. I only wish she'd thought of repeating her other directions—like the one about how to clean our recorder—'cause I'd missed that too. Then she wouldn't have had to kick me out. Ms. Crawford was bad at listening and she was bad at giving directions.

So here's what happened. After ten minutes of blowing on my recorder—after Ms. Crawford said we could—the neck got clogged with my spit. It was making my recorder gurgle and sound funny. So I held it away from me and shook it as hard as I could. And that did the trick—except Missy's first shriek was nothing compared to the one she let out after getting splattered by my spit.

"Give me that recorder and get in the hall!" Ms. Crawford yelled.

And that was that. I spent my last music class spinning circles in the hallway. Told you it wasn't my fault.

Now that I knew the directions, I was ready to do much better—except I didn't get the chance. Instead, I was stuck sitting in the main office, wiggling in the red chair by the door.

Ms. Garcia wanted to have a meeting just to check in and see how things were going 'cause we hadn't done a lunch bunch and she hadn't seen me yet this year. I saw her a lot during first grade and second grade and third grade 'cause my teachers didn't like me very much. What they did like was sending me to the office whenever they got tired of me not sitting still or not raising my hand or not doing my work. Sometimes I had to talk to Principal Ryan about my behavior and sometimes it was Ms. Garcia. Either way, I always had to wait for them to be ready to see me, which was why I was familiar with the red chair.

Even the teachers who weren't my teachers knew who I was by now 'cause their mailboxes were on the wall opposite my waiting spot. And Mrs. Rosa, our administrative assistant, also knew me well 'cause her desk was near the door too. (I made the mistake of calling Mrs. Rosa our secretary once and Brynn gave me a lecture about why she wasn't a secretary and made me swear I'd only refer to her as the administrative assistant forever more.)

The teachers and Mrs. Rosa got so used to me being there that they went about their business like I was invisible. The teachers chatted away in the workroom that was just around the corner, forgetting that just 'cause I couldn't see them and they couldn't see me, that didn't mean I couldn't hear them. But they were teachers, and old, so I never listened for long 'cause it was always dumb boring stuff that they talked about, like shopping sales or new recipes and ridiculous husbands—until today.

I recognized their voices right away 'cause I'd heard them yell at me so many times. There was my old third-grade teacher, Ms. Hornet, and my horrible teacher from second grade, Mrs. Stinger.

"Ms. Krane, how're things with Carter?" Stinger asked in a singsong voice. "Can't say I miss having that boy in my class."

I slumped in my chair and stared at the floor.

"Worst student I ever had," Hornet added.

I slumped farther.

"The worst," Stinger agreed. "I feel like all I did was put out fires with that boy."

Farther.

"Couldn't sit still. Never followed directions. A nightmare," Hornet said.

"I like the boy," Ms. Krane replied. "In fact, I like him a lot."

The workroom fell silent. I sat up and waited for what they'd say next.

"Well, you're just a rebel in more ways than one, aren't you?" Stinger responded.

"What's that supposed to mean?" Ms. Krane challenged. There was an edge to her voice. Owls don't back down—that was something else I'd learned in my research.

"You know exactly what it means," Stinger pushed back. "We'll see if you still like the boy after a few more weeks with him, or if he's too much for even your liberal ways."

I turned my body and hid my face when Stinger and Hornet came buzzing by my chair on their way out of the office. I didn't want them to see me and suddenly feel bad. Having them lie and try making excuses for what they'd said would've been worse than the truth. Even though I was the worst student in the whole wide world, I understood feelings.

I fooled them, but there was no hiding from Ms. Krane when she came out of the workroom 'cause an owl has really good eyesight. She spotted me right away.

"Carter, how long have you been sitting here?"

I shrugged.

"Long enough, huh?"

I wiped my eyes and nodded.

Ms. Krane sat in the chair next to me. "The only thing you

need to remember is what you heard me say. The rest you can forget. You understand?"

I nodded.

"You understand?" she repeated, wanting my answer. This was tough love, same as Grams dished out.

I nodded again.

"Good. You're a special kid, Carter Avery. And don't ever let anyone tell you different." She wrapped her wing around me and gave me a firm hug, then let go and flew away.

27

WORD BOY

My meeting with Ms. Garcia was short. I told her fourth grade was good and that we could do a lunch bunch if she wanted but I was okay. I didn't complain about Missy Gerber, even though I could've, and I didn't ask her anything about *artificial* or *rebel* or *liberal* 'cause I didn't want Ms. Garcia asking me why I was asking. She was on my need-to-know list, and right now she didn't need to know.

I did make sure to tell Ms. Garcia that Ms. Krane was the best teacher I'd ever had, though. I'd already seen enough and heard enough with the Owl to know that was the truth.

Ms. Garcia smiled. "That's great to hear, Carter. It's time for you to have a good year."

So basically, our meeting told Ms. Garcia she could relax when it came to me, but it did nothing for me. When I hopped on the bus after school, I was still wondering and worrying about Ms. Krane's baby being artificial, but I'd already asked Mr. Wilson what he knew about that, so I didn't mention it.

But once we got going, I did ask him about the other words Stinger had hurled at Ms. Krane, 'cause Mr. Wilson was my preferred guidance counselor.

"Mr. Wilson, what's a rebel?"

"That's the question you have for me after visiting the farm?"

"No. It came up after we got back to school."

"Oh," he said, glancing at me with a raised eyebrow. "Well, I'm no wordsmith, but when I hear *rebel*, I think of someone who kinda goes against the ordinary. Maybe goes against the rules. A rebel tends to have new or different ideas."

"Is that good or bad?"

Mr. Wilson stopped and opened the door to let a few kids off.

"Is that good or bad?" I repeated.

"That depends, I suppose," he answered after we were rolling again. "But I can tell you this. Going against the ordinary isn't easy. People don't often like change, so they resist. But if we never have new ideas or challenge things, then how're we ever supposed to grow?"

"Mr. Wilson, are you a rebel?"

"Me?! No. I'm not brave enough for that. I could see you being a rebel, though."

"Me?!" I exclaimed.

"Sure. You know, in all that time we've talked about your teacher, you never once mentioned her birthmark."

I shrugged. "It's a part-jelly stain on her face," I said, explaining the truth to Mr. Wilson.

"Well, that's the first thing most people would've brought up when talking about her. But not you."

I shrugged again, which made Mr. Wilson shake his head and laugh to himself. "You're a good egg, Carter Avery. They don't make enough like you."

Mr. Wilson stopped and opened the side door to let another group of kids off and I sat there wondering how he and Ms. Krane could say almost the same thing on the same day. And if they both said it, did that mean it was for real and not just a nice thing to say that wasn't true?

"I've got another word for you," I said after he started driving again.

"Another one?" Mr. Wilson exclaimed. "What happened in school this afternoon that's got you wondering about these things?"

I shrugged. "Nothing."

That wasn't true, but that wasn't me lying either. "Nothing" was an answer you could give that meant you didn't want to say. Mr. Wilson understood, which was something that made him a good guidance counselor even though he was a bus driver.

"What's the other word?" he asked.

"Liberal."

"*Hmm.* That makes sense. Liberal and rebel sorta go together. Someone who's liberal tends to like change and new ideas, but that word is usually reserved for politics or religion."

"*Hmm,*" I replied. This was getting more and more confusing, but I couldn't ask any other questions 'cause we'd reached my stop.

Mr. Wilson pulled the side door open. "Okay, Word Boy, I'll see you tomorrow," he teased.

"Thanks for the warning," I replied.

We both grinned and then I jumped down the steps and ran toward the house. I had *rebel* and *liberal* mixed in with *artificial,* all jumbled in my head. I'd researched and asked about those words, but now came the big question: How did the jumble go together with Ms. Krane?

It was time for Grams and Brynn to start giving me some answers.

28

I NEED ANSWERS

I dumped my bag by the door and gave Shelby a good butt scratch; then we made our way into the kitchen 'cause it was snack time. I found a small plate of cheese and crackers waiting for us, but no Grams and no Brynn.

My sister coulda been at swim practice or work or staying late at school for a review session or who knows where. If I had her schedule, I'd need it written down on a big chart 'cause I'd definitely forget where I was supposed to be and when. But Grams had to be around somewhere.

I snatched a chunk of cheese and handed it to Shelby. Even though I was hungry, I wasn't interested in eating. Not yet. First, I wanted answers. So I left the plate on the counter and went searching.

Just as I suspected, Grams didn't meet me by the road or in the kitchen 'cause she was busy all right. Busy catching flies! I found her zonked out in the recliner with her feet kicked up, head tipped back, and mouth wide open.

"Grams!" I yelped.

She jump-kicked awake, then brought her feet down and quick wiped her mouth and fixed her glasses. "You're home," she said. "I was just resting my eyes for a second."

I walked across the room and plopped on the couch. "Well, wake up. I need answers."

"I am awake," she insisted.

"Did Ms. Krane have the vet plant seeds in her belly?"

"What in the world?!" Grams exclaimed, sitting forward. Now she was for-real awake.

"Did she?" I pressed.

"No, the vet didn't plant seeds in her belly! What kind of question is that?"

"Then why did Missy Gerber say Ms. Krane's baby is artificial?"

Before Grams could answer, the front door banged open. "I'm home," Brynn called.

"Me too," Torrie announced.

"Why?" I pressed Grams. I wasn't letting her off the hook.

"I've got no clue," she huffed.

"Yes, you do. Tell me!" I yelled.

That was one thing I never did. I never yelled at Grams. I'd yelled at Brynn before 'cause she was my sister, but not Grams, 'cause she was my grams—but I was upset. Real upset. So upset that tears started running down my cheeks and I couldn't stop them. So upset that Shelby put her head on my knee.

"What's going on?" Brynn shouted, running into the living room after hearing my outburst, Torrie right behind her.

The instant they saw I was crying, they rushed over. Brynn sat on one side of me and Torrie on the other. They both hugged me tight, but that just made my crying turn into sobbing. "Shhh," they whispered. "It's all right."

I got myself to slow down and breathe, and then Grams wanted to know what had got me so worked up, and it all came spilling out. I told them about everything that had happened in the school office. What Ms. Hornet and Mrs. Stinger had said about me. And, most important, how Ms. Krane didn't let them get away with it.

I wiped my face and nose and sat up, remembering my questions. "So, is Missy Gerber right or not? Is Ms. Krane's baby artificial?"

Brynn glanced at Grams. "I told you he'd hear about it."

"Tell me," I demanded. Shelby put her head on my other knee, reminding me she was there. I rubbed her ears.

Grams sighed, then nodded. Whether that was her granting permission or giving in, I didn't know or care, 'cause it was good enough for me. I turned toward Brynn and waited for her to start explaining.

29

THE ARTIFICIAL TRUTH

"Here's what we know," my sister began.

"And that's not everything, just remember," Grams interrupted.

"That's true," Brynn admitted. "These are only the bits and pieces Torrie's mother told us about after seeing them posted on Village Moms."

"Which means it could all be nonsense," Grams interrupted again.

"What's Village Moms?" I asked.

"It's an online group that moms in our community can join and post messages to," Torrie explained. "The idea is that it takes a village to raise a child, so in theory it's a place where people are supposed to look out for one another."

"In theory," Brynn scoffed. "Lately, it's more for slinging mud. The whole concept is dumb. Even calling it Village Moms is wrong. Why can't dads join?"

"Settle down, Brynn," Grams said. "You getting upset isn't going to help anything right now."

Brynn huffed.

"My mother joined the group and started following it when my older brother was going through school," Torrie continued. "She's never posted anything and only continues to follow it because she likes keeping up with the gossip."

"Yet another great example of how we'd be better off if we didn't have cell phones and all this blasted technology and social media nonsense," Grams griped.

"Not now," Brynn groaned. "Getting on your soapbox isn't going to help anything."

"Well, it's true," Grams shot back. "Those highfalutin women wouldn't be able to gossip so freely without their darn phones and computers."

"They'd still talk," Torrie said. "If not online, then in the grocery store, in the pickup line at school, or at church."

"They best be going to church," Grams added. "Their high-'n'-mighty souls all need help."

Between the three of them, they had my head twisting back and forth faster than an owl's—and I still didn't know what was going on. "What's artificial?" I asked louder 'cause I was running out of patience—and I didn't have any to begin with.

"Go ahead," Grams said. "Tell him."

My sister took a breath and began explaining. "CJ, Ms.

Krane doesn't have a husband or fiancé or any partner. But that hasn't stopped her from wanting to be a mother. So she went to a doctor who was able to take seeds that had been donated, and put them inside her so that she can have a baby."

"Is she alone 'cause of her part-jelly stain?"

Grams sighed. "We don't know. . . . Maybe."

That was sad. And if it was true, then how else was Ms. Krane supposed to have a baby? "Why is artificial bad?" I asked.

"It's not," Brynn was quick to say. "Lots of women choose that kind of pregnancy, whether they're single or not. But we live in a small town where we're sheltered from big-city life, so this sort of thing hasn't happened here before. At least not that we know of."

"People here are just stuck in their ways and scared of anything even remotely different," Torrie added.

"CJ, Ms. Krane didn't get fired from her last school for being mean or whatever other silly rumors you may have heard," Grams said. "She had to leave because it was a religious school and they couldn't support her personal decision to have a baby on her own. Mrs. Stinger's sister works at that other school, which is why Mrs. Stinger knows too much and can't seem to keep her trap shut. Pardon my French."

It wasn't often that I was quiet, but after hearing that, I didn't know what to say. And Grams wasn't done telling me everything yet.

"Unfortunately, Mrs. Stinger's not alone," Grams continued. "Ms. Krane's situation is a first for traditional folks around here, so Mrs. Stinger's got others on her side who disapprove. They think having babies should be left in the hands of God, not doctors and scientists."

I knew I didn't like Mrs. Stinger; that was nothing new. But I did have a different question now. "If Ms. Krane got her seeds from a doctor, who's the dad?"

"We don't know. The seeds come from an anonymous donor," Brynn explained, "which means Ms. Krane and her baby may never find out, and that's something else people are gossiping about."

"It takes all kinds to make the world go 'round, CJ. You've heard me say that before," Grams reminded me. "People don't always agree on matters like this. These days, especially. Let's just hope it doesn't become anything more than a few voices on Village Moms."

"What do you mean become more?"

Grams grumbled under her breath, but then let it out. "We kept this a secret because you have a hard time not saying stuff, and the fewer kids talking about it the better for Ms. Krane. If your classmates start going home and asking questions and getting the adults riled up, that could spell trouble. This isn't anything Ms. Krane can be fired for at your school, but if people want to, they can make her life unpleasant enough that she doesn't feel welcome and chooses to leave on her own. That's a dirty trick to play to get rid of someone."

"The grown-ups here need a lesson in kindness," Brynn said.

"That's true in a lot of places today," Torrie muttered.

"That's it!" I erupted. If Ms. Krane was willing to stick up for me, I was ready to do the same for her. "I'm gonna make Ms. Krane's life at school extra special."

"How?" all three of them wondered, looking at me with wide eyes.

"I'm gonna prove she belongs here by being her best student and doing all of my work."

I jumped up from the couch and ran to get my backpack. I'd just given myself a secret mission—secret 'cause I wasn't gonna say anything to anyone about Ms. Krane, but the mission part meant I needed to get started on my math problems.

30

THE PROOF IS IN THE PUDDING

"The proof is in the pudding" was another one of those funny sayings from when Grams was a young girl that she still used sometimes. Like when she had me picking blackberries with her so she could make a pie and my hands turned all purple. When we got home, Grams made me scrub with stinky vinegar 'cause she said that was the surefire way to get those stains to come off.

"Is this really gonna work?" I groaned. "This stuff smells terrible!"

"The proof is in the pudding," she answered, nodding at my hands, "so keep scrubbing and stop whining."

I looked down but I couldn't see anything 'cause that stinky vinegar had my eyes watering so bad. Grams didn't care. She made me keep scrubbing and when I finally got done, my hands were only a little purple.

Maybe the vinegar helped, but I still thought her proof-in-the-pudding mumbo jumbo was dumb—until I made it my secret mission to help Ms. Krane by proving she was the best teacher. 'Cause to do that, I had to be her proof in the pudding.

Here's what I can say about all that. Funny old-timer talk is called sayings instead of doings 'cause it's a lot easier to say something than it is to actually do it—like wanting to be brave is easier than being brave. I could say I was gonna be Ms. Krane's proof in her pudding and I was gonna be her best student and do my work all I wanted, but actually doing it was a whole other can of worms—especially since I had a hard time sitting still and an even harder time finishing my work. But Ms. Krane made all that easier 'cause she had great ideas, starting with us hatching baby chicks. I couldn't wait to get going on that project.

When we got back to school after the weekend, Ms. Krane had our eggs keeping nice and warm inside a fancy-schmancy incubator. She told us she bought it online, which would've made Grams bawk, but our eggs needed it.

And the incubator was only the start. There was lots to be done over the next twenty-one days. Hens work hard to hatch their babies, so we had to too.

"We'll care for our eggs as best we can," Ms. Krane told us, "but even so, there are no guarantees any of them will hatch. And sometimes a chick doesn't make it."

"Why?" Vanessa asked.

Ms. Krane shrugged. "Sometimes there's a medical explanation, and sometimes there's no explanation at all. It just happens and it's no one's fault."

"That's sad," Missy said.

"Yes, it is," Ms. Krane agreed, "which is why we want to try our hardest to have healthy chicks. If all goes well, Farmer Don will be picking up his new flock just in time for Thanksgiving."

"You mean we don't get to keep them?" I blurted.

"No, Carter, I'm afraid not. Baby chicks are cute and cuddly, but they grow fast and turn into chickens, and we can't have chickens running around our classroom."

"'Cause you've already got your hands full with us turkeys?" I said.

My classmates burst into laughter. They thought that was a good one. Ms. Krane eyed me and smirked 'cause we both knew I got that joke from Farmer Don—but she didn't tell.

"Ms. Krane, you keep saying we're going to do our best, but if the eggs are already inside the incubator, what's there left for us to do?" Kyle wondered.

"I'm glad you asked, because the answer is plenty."

And she wasn't lying. Ms. Krane explained everything we'd be responsible for, and after that we got busy doing. First, we had to mark each egg with a rhombus on one side and a trapezoid on the other. Ms. Krane chose those shapes 'cause they weren't the easy ones and this was gonna help us learn their names and remember them. She was real smart like that. The reason the eggs needed to be marked was 'cause we had to turn them three times a day and the shapes helped us keep track of which side was supposed to be up and down.

After gently tattooing our eggs, we made a big calendar on chart paper and listed who was in charge of turning them each day, and when you got your turn, you also had to record the temperature and humidity inside the incubator 'cause if things got out of whack, our eggs almost definitely wouldn't hatch. Keeping the right temperature and humidity was real important.

It was amazing to think hens did all this stuff with just their beaks and butts—which was why I didn't understand the importance of washing our hands before doing any of the touching 'cause the hens sure weren't washing their rear ends. Now I had to worry about washing my hands after going to the bathroom *and* before touching our eggs. But I didn't complain 'cause I was trying to be Ms. Krane's proof, remember.

That still wasn't everything we had to do. You need to be prepared for the baby chicks before they arrive.

"Just like I need to make sure I have a crib before my baby comes home, and a car seat and stroller and diapers and bottles and all sorts of things, we need to have a play yard for our chicks, and food and a heat lamp," Ms. Krane explained.

"Do you already have all those things you just mentioned for your baby?" Mary asked.

"Some," Ms. Krane answered, and smiled. "Getting ready

for a baby's arrival is exciting and requires a lot of planning. And so, too, will getting prepped for our chicks."

She wasn't kidding. When I found out we had to build play yards for our chicks, I was pumped. This was gonna be the coolest project I'd ever done in school. What was really great was Ms. Krane wanted us to break into small groups and work on our own. Of course, no one picked Missy Gerber to be in their group 'cause she was too bossy, and no one picked me 'cause they didn't know about my secret mission. That meant me and Missy ended up together—"by default" was what Ms. Krane said.

I wasn't happy about it and neither was Missy, but Ms. Krane told us we'd better figure out how to make the two of us work 'cause our baby chicks were depending on it. That was some good old-fashioned tough love. And you know what? It worked, 'cause me and Missy didn't want chicks dying on our watch. And then I remembered my secret mission and realized something. What better way was there for me to be the proof in the pudding than by working with annoying Missy Gerber?

31

MAKING OUR PLAY YARD

To help get us started, Ms. Krane shared different examples and ideas for play yards. Basically, we had to build a structure with walls to keep the chicks inside, and we needed to be able to hook up a heat lamp and have a food and water station and soft bedding. That didn't sound too hard, but remember, saying and doing are two different things. And double remember, I was working with Missy Gerber.

After showing us the different examples, Ms. Krane turned us loose. It was time to get started brainstorming with our partners. The only directions she gave us was what the maximum and minimum area were, and also the minimum height for the sides. That might not seem like much information, but it meant we had to do lots of measuring and estimating, which was Ms. Krane being real smart again 'cause those were things we were working on in math. That and problem solving, and there was lots of that with this project—like how to work with Missy Gerber.

"We have all kinds of stuff in my basement that we could use," I told Missy after we found a spot on the rug and started talking about ideas and materials.

"What kind of stuff?"

"Everything," I said, spinning a quick circle. "Cardboard, newspaper, old dishes, paint sticks, rusty old screws. You name it and we've probably got it. My grams has a real hard time throwing anything away." I whipped another spin.

Missy's nose wrinkled. "Why does she keep all that stuff?"

"*'Cause you never know when you might need it,*" I said, mimicking Grams's voice. "That's the answer I get whenever I ask her the same question. So then I tell her, *probly never,* 'cause when're we ever gonna want a rusty old screw?"

Missy giggled at my story and I grinned.

"Do you have stuff at your house that we can use?" I asked her before spinning again.

"I doubt it. My mother is a perfectionist. Between her and the cleaning service that comes, we don't have anything nifty like that lying around."

"Well, that's okay. I've got enough sturdy cardboard for us to build a spaceship."

"Using cardboard is practical, but it's going to be all brown," Missy said, wrinkling her nose again.

"What's practical? And who cares?" I said, coming to a stop before I got too dizzy.

"Practical means it's a wise decision because it makes sense," she explained. "But brown is boring."

"The baby chicks won't mind."

"You don't know that. And besides, it bothers me. I don't want an ugly play yard."

"Well, we're gonna have to use duct tape to hold the walls together, so that'll give it some gray color," I said, trying to make her feel better.

"Oh, wait! I forgot. I have all kinds of colored duct tape in my crafting bin at home. Carter, that's perfect!" Missy exclaimed.

That made my eyes pop and look all around. Never in a million years did I think Missy Gerber would say something I suggested was perfect, but she did. I caught the Owl looking at us with a big smirk on her face—like she knew something all along.

Ms. Krane gave our groups time to work on our play yards every afternoon for the next couple of weeks, 'cause we had to be ready when the babies hatched. Mine and Missy's structure was extra sturdy—thanks to my strong cardboard. And it was extra colorful (and sturdy)—thanks to all the duct tape Missy added. We had a great play yard—and that wasn't just me talking.

"Wow, yours is awesome," Kyle said when he saw it.

"Yup," I agreed.

"Actually, it's bedazzled," Missy corrected, sticking her nose in the air.

In addition to her colorful duct tape, Missy had also glued sparkly gems and sprinkled glitter along the tops of the walls. But only the tops, 'cause I told her we didn't want the chicks trying to eat that stuff—and she didn't argue.

My favorite part was the feeding and drinking carousel we'd built in the middle. Kyle said it was legit.

Our play yard project took a lot of time and was loads of fun, but that didn't mean everything else in our classroom stopped. Ms. Krane kept reading to us all along. She read another silly chicken book, but she also read some nonfiction stuff that showed us pictures and diagrams of what was happening inside the eggs, so we could see how our baby chicks were growing and changing.

"Is the same growing and changing happening with your baby?" Mary asked.

The growing was! Ms. Krane's belly was getting bigger by the day. It looked like she had a basketball in there now, but I slapped my hand over my mouth before those words jumped out.

"Yes," Ms. Krane answered.

Kyle freaked. "The same growing and changing?!"

"Well, not exactly the same. I'm having a baby, not a chicken."

Everyone laughed, which was something I never remembered happening in my other classes.

Besides building our play yards and reading and talking

about our chicks, we also had to keep up with our daily calendar and make sure we were turning our eggs inside the incubator. When it was Missy's turn to rotate the eggs, she asked me to do it for her 'cause she was afraid. She didn't want to hurt them. I almost forgot to wash my hands until Missy reminded me, but that didn't annoy me 'cause she wasn't being bossy about it. I didn't know how it happened, but we were being a good team.

A good team at chicken time, but Missy still wouldn't let me anywhere near the girl monkey bars. Except she wasn't mean about it anymore. We even spent a few of our recess periods working on our play yards. It really was the coolest school project I'd ever done. The only bad thing was waiting for Day 21 when the eggs were supposed to hatch.

Luckily, Ms. Krane found a way to make the waiting easier.

32

DRAGON SLAYER

Ms. Krane had more tricks up her sleeve than Abracadabra Adam. You're gonna think I lost my head, but she even managed to get me excited about writing.

She started out by reading us the everybody book *Brave Irene.* I'd heard that one before, but not like Ms. Krane read it. When she finished, she told us she was going to read it again, which made some kids groan a little, but not me 'cause I was being her pudding. I mean, her proof. Ms. Krane said she wanted us to pay close attention to the strong verbs the author used throughout the story. She listed a bunch of those words on chart paper—*whirled, ripped, flung, swept,* and others—so that we could see them while she read, and then she talked to us about how strong verbs make strong writing. She wanted us to take one of the small moment ideas that we'd brainstormed earlier in the year and start writing about it, but we were supposed to focus on using strong verbs.

Ms. Krane shared her own example to help us better understand what she was looking for. Her small moment was from when we watched the calf being born at Farmer Don's.

"'My fingers *gripped* the fence when the mama cow *bellowed*,'" Ms. Krane read. "'The more she *hollered*, the more my fingers dug into the wood railing and the harder my heart *railed* against my chest. And then, after one final push, the newborn calf fell from its mother and landed in the dirt. Tears *streamed* down my cheeks as the two bonded.'"

Ms. Krane only shared a few sentences, but, boy, was it good—and she used a bunch of strong verbs.

We got to work.

I didn't have any brainstorming list to look at 'cause we did that before I was the proof in the pudding, but I had my idea. I was gonna write about trick-or-treating 'cause Halloween was only a few days away and I couldn't wait. Brynn and Torrie were gonna go with me, dressed as queens, and I was gonna be their fearless knight.

Coming up with ideas wasn't my problem. And I was good at coming up with verbs too. Everything I did was a strong verb: run, blurt, shout, interrupt. *I* was a strong verb.

It was the actual writing and doing it the legerble way that slowed me down 'cause it took me forever to make all the letters with my pencil. And I was even slower on the computer. But I was gonna try my best today 'cause you know why.

I was hunkered over my paper, showing Camo that I could

do it, when the Owl silently glided over and landed next to me on the counter. "Carter, I'm proud to see how hard you're working on your writing."

"I'm trying."

Ms. Krane leaned closer. "It's called the Dragon," she whispered.

"What is?" I whispered back, 'cause this felt like a secret.

Still whispering, Ms. Krane told me all about the Dragon, which was a special computer program. The way it worked was I wore this fancy headset with a microphone attached that I talked into. All I had to do was tell the Dragon my story and then the computer typed out all my words for me. Ms. Krane said doctors and reporters and lots of smart people used the Dragon for their jobs, so she knew I could too. And the school had it.

"Just think, Carter, now when it comes time to write, you'll get to be a dragon slayer."

I looked at Camo and smiled. What kid doesn't want to be a dragon slayer?! I couldn't wait to try it out.

Ms. Krane was nice—but she was still a teacher, so there were a few catches with her plan. For starters, the Dragon was on a computer in the workroom next to Principal Ryan's office. Ms. Krane worried that me telling my stories out loud to our classroom computer could be distracting to my classmates, and since I could get energetic when telling my stories, I saw her point. Also, Principal Ryan was interested in trying the Dragon for her job, so she was curious to see how it worked. She was the one who helped me get my computer up and running the first time I went down. She gave me a quick lesson on what to push and how to use my program and then told me I was ready for battle—which got me excited again.

Ms. Krane's other catch was this. After I told my story and got it typed and printed, I had to read it over real careful and do the edit and revise stuff. I never did that 'cause I never had writing to reread, but Ms. Krane said that was about to change. And after doing my edit and revise stuff, I was supposed to retell the Dragon my story, but better, and if I couldn't do that part, then Ms. Krane said I wasn't ready to be a dragon slayer. And when a grown-up says something like that, it just makes you want to try even harder to prove them wrong. All of a sudden, I had lots of proving to do.

It took some getting used to, but I got the hang of it. The best part about my Dragon was it did whatever I told it to do. Whatever I said, it typed. So I tried out a few zingers.

"Missy Gerber has a butt for a face," I said. That was mean, but I wasn't the one who came up with it. Brynn called me a butt face once when we were arguing. I wasn't sure I liked saying that about Missy anymore, though, so I deleted it and tried something different.

"Mrs. Stinger farts out her mouth!" I exclaimed. That was much better.

After fooling around, I got serious and told the Dragon my Halloween story three times, not just two—and with lots of strong verbs. I needed those 'cause no matter how animated I got when I shouted different parts of my story, the sentences still sounded boring without them. I had to get better at the fixing stuff 'cause I'd only used a couple of periods, which meant I had those run-on sentences everywhere, but so what. For the first time ever, I had my complete story written on paper. I did more writing on that assignment than I'd done in all my school days before that. You wanna know why? 'Cause I was a dragon slayer!

33

THINKERS, NOT SIMON SAYSERS

Ms. Krane began our day with another book. She was big on books. And bigger on us being thinkers.

"I want you to pay careful attention to this story because I'll be interested in hearing what you think when we finish. Think," she stressed again. "In case you haven't figured it out yet, I want our classroom to be full of thinkers. A bunch of Simon Saysers would be boring."

"I'm not very good at that game, so don't worry, Ms. Krane, I'm not one of them," I blurted.

She chuckled, then held up her book. "Today's title is *Last Stop on Market Street*. This book won a Caldecott Medal as well as the Newbery Medal, putting it in rare company."

That was as far as Ms. Krane got before I interrupted her 'cause I was already doing some thinking.

"Ms. Krane, your baby is gonna be real smart from listening to all these stories before even being born."

"I'm just hoping for happy and healthy," she replied.

"Nah, you want smart too. It's no fun not being smart."

"Having a hard time with self-control doesn't equal not smart," Missy Gerber said.

"Truer words were never spoken," Ms. Krane agreed, looking very proud and pleased with Missy.

I didn't know if Missy meant to let those words out, or if her mouth got ahead of her brain like mine does sometimes. Was she being for-real nice on purpose?

It was hard for me to stop thinking about what she'd said and start thinking about that book, but Ms. Krane's reading voice lured me in—and when I found out the boy in the story was also named CJ, I got to paying careful attention like Ms. Krane wanted and like I needed to if I was gonna be her pudding. I mean, proof.

I kept spinning on my counter seat, but I didn't write anything in my cow journal like I saw Vanessa doing. I listened real good, though, and was quiet so Ms. Krane's baby could hear too. And when Ms. Krane finished and closed the book, I couldn't hold it in any longer 'cause there was a lot that story made me think about.

"Ms. Krane, I met a blind man with a dog this summer," I said before raising my hand and before she called on anyone else. That was something that happened with the boy named CJ in the book. My old mean teachers would've yelled at me for blurting out, but Ms. Krane let me keep going. "His name is Mason and his dog is Susie. They're my friends. And just like the blind man in the book, Mason can see things with his ears."

"I'm glad you were able to make that connection to the story, Carter. I can tell that helps you visualize and also better understand CJ's feelings."

I didn't know what she meant by that, but I smiled 'cause she was happy with what I'd said.

"Let's give your classmates a chance to share now," she reminded me. "Listening to their connections should help us think even deeper."

I nodded. Giving others a turn was something me and Ms. Krane had chatted about and that I was working on.

"Yes, Kyle," Ms. Krane said, calling on him next.

"I know what it's like to have to go places when you don't want to," he explained, which was something else that happened with the CJ in the book. "Sometimes my mom makes me go with her when she visits her aunt Marge. It's a long drive and Aunt Marge's house is old like her, and it's always hot and stinky 'cause she smokes cigarettes, and I never want to go. But once I get there, it usually isn't that bad, just like it turns out for that boy in the book. Aunt Marge lives by a lake, so sometimes I get to go fishing and that's cool."

"That's a really good connection," I told Kyle.

"Yes, it is," Ms. Krane agreed. "And I like how you're being positive and complimenting your classmate, Carter."

That just made me smile more. I was on a roll.

Ms. Krane called on Vanessa next. "Sometimes my dad and I volunteer at an animal shelter," Vanessa said, "so I know what volunteering feels like. And sometimes we foster puppies until they get permanent homes," she added.

"Another excellent connection," Ms. Krane replied. "I've also spent time volunteering, but my experiences have been at a food pantry similar to the one in our story. I've met some wonderful people there."

"That's a lot of connections," Mary said. "I didn't think of all that stuff."

"Me neither," Missy admitted, sounding disappointed.

"And that's okay," Ms. Krane replied. "Sometimes we connect with texts in many ways and other times not as much. But what I want you all to see is that when we do connect, it helps us understand the characters' feelings and picture things even better, and oftentimes leads to us enjoying our reading that much more."

"That's why I like sports books," Kyle said. "Tim Green is my favorite author."

Ms. Krane nodded. "Exactly."

Then she turned back to me. "Carter, I like how you're raising your hand. Did you have another connection you wanted to share?"

"No, I've got an idea," I announced.

"I'm listening."

"We should get Mason to come visit us so that everyone can meet him and read to Susie. She's a super-friendly and super-smart dog—and she loves books."

"That would be so cool," Kyle said. "She could be like our mascot."

"Can we, Ms. Krane?" Vanessa asked, 'cause she loved animals and liked my idea too.

"I'm making no promises, but I will speak to Principal Ryan about the possibility," Ms. Krane said. She left it at that, but that was enough to get the rest of my classmates buzzing.

When I peeked at Missy Gerber, she gave me a small smile. And when I glanced back at the Owl, she gave me a quick wink with her triangle pointy eye. I was doing a good job with my secret mission.

34

FLY HIGH!

I sat at my spot and opened my lunch box. While kids dragged the other chairs away from my table, I rummaged through the contents, searching for whatever prize Grams had for me today. I hoped it was good. I lifted my grapes out of the way and found a small glider airplane with the note *Fly High!* I grinned. This was gonna be great at recess.

Grams says my dad loved airplanes. When he was a kid, he wanted to be a pilot. I might do that when I grow up. Or I could be a vet like my mom was. I wondered if Vanessa Tucker wanted to be a vet. Speak of the devil.

"Hey, Carter. What kind of dog is Susie?" Vanessa asked, stopping by my table. "You never said."

"She's a golden retriever," I answered, looking up from my plane.

Vanessa beamed. "They're one of my favorites."

"Did you ever foster a golden retriever?" I asked, remembering her connection.

"Just once. Do you really think your friend will bring her to school?"

"Mason? He'll definitely bring Susie if Principal Ryan says they can come. He'll want to know what I've learned about owls since summer."

"About owls?" she repeated.

"Yup. What does *foster* mean?" I asked.

Vanessa giggled. Then she pulled out the last chair still left at my table and sat down across from me with her tray before one of the lunch aides barked at her for loitering. *No loitering* was their favorite thing to yell. That meant no standing around. You had to be in your seat unless you were throwing your garbage out.

I glanced around the cafeteria to see if anyone was watching what just happened.

"Fostering means we keep the puppy until it gets a permanent home," Vanessa explained. "That's usually four to eight weeks."

She dipped her chicken nugget in ketchup and bit into it. Since she was eating, I took out my sandwich.

"And then you give the puppy away? Isn't that hard?" I asked before taking a bite, 'cause Brynn woulda yelled at me if I tried talking with my mouth full.

"It's a lot of work training them," Vanessa said, "but it's fun too. And saying goodbye is sad, but the puppies get to go to good homes, so I try to be happy for them."

"Well, Susie's not a puppy, but you'll love her," I promised. "She's the smartest dog I've ever known."

I poked around in my lunch box to see what yummy treat Grams had packed for me and found a small bag of iced animal cookies. I saw Vanessa eyeing them.

"Want one?" I whispered, 'cause you weren't supposed to share food, but Vanessa loved animals and it was either my cookies or yucky school green beans.

"Sure," she said.

And real quick I handed her an elephant, 'cause I remembered she liked those. I snuck her a giraffe too.

"Thanks, Carter."

"You're welcome."

When Vanessa finished eating, she got up and tossed out her trash, then went to sit at her usual spot with her friends. But . . . for a few minutes, I didn't sit alone that day. And it felt good.

Grams's note said *Fly High!*—and I was soaring.

35

TRICK-OR-TREATING

A lot of kids hit the party stores for their Halloween costumes, but me and Brynn and Torrie hit the basement. You'd be amazed what you can do with some cardboard, tinfoil, a little creativity—and a teenage sister and her bestie.

Going around and collecting candy was great, and eating it was yummy, but getting ready for the big night was still my favorite part. Technically, Brynn and Torrie were too old for trick-or-treating, but as long as they were with me, they got away with it. And Grams didn't have a cow about it 'cause she liked knowing I was with them and safe.

"If you're going to be my knight in shining armor, you need a big sword," Torrie said, drawing the outline for my blade in black Sharpie on a large piece of cardboard.

"I thought Jay was your knight in shining armor," Brynn teased.

I scowled. "Who's Jay?" I asked.

"The guy Torrie met at the North Pole," my sister said, batting her eyelashes and making her voice sound all lovey-dovey.

"And I thought Justin was yours," Torrie jabbed back, making a face at Brynn.

"Lifeguard Justin?!" I exclaimed.

They giggled but never bothered answering me. I swear, teenage girls were impossible. But I didn't care. They could be dumb all they wanted as long as I got my costume.

Once Torrie had my weapon outlined, she took a pair of scissors and cut it out. Then we wrapped the blade in shiny tinfoil so it looked like the real deal. Brynn helped me wind black string around and around the handle to fatten it up and give me something good to grip. Then we glued a row of gems where the blade and handle came together to make it fancy. Brynn and Torrie were both real good at arts and crafts.

My sword was cool, but that was only the beginning of my costume. I also got a shield and special armor. I had a front and back plate that was more cardboard tied together over my shoulders and around my waist—which was plain and boring until Brynn and Torrie got to work and decorated it in red and blue and gold tinfoil that Grams had stashed in the basement. After that, I looked awesome! The final touch was my hat, which was a medieval hood that resembled real chain mail. Grams got it for me 'cause it was supposed to be cold on Halloween night and she wanted something covering my ears. I didn't argue 'cause it was perfect.

Brynn and Torrie didn't work as hard on their own costumes. They did makeup and wore long black dresses and added capes made out of some sparkly material that they'd found in Grams's stuff—the capes were kinda cool—and they had tiaras, but not much more than that. They didn't need to bother 'cause everyone was gonna be looking at me anyways.

When the big night finally arrived, I was amped. Words and phrases like *walk* and *slow down* and *take your time* weren't in my regular vocabulary—forget about Halloween. But that was just what my sister tried to make me do.

Shelby was my buddy, but I didn't want to bring her trick-or-treating. I promised her I'd share my haul when I got home. There was no way her short legs could keep up—but Brynn insisted.

"Adding Shelby makes you look like Dorothy from the *Wizard of Oz* instead of my queen," I grumbled.

"I don't care," Brynn snapped. "Shelby likes seeing all the other dogs and kids. You know that. She shouldn't have to miss out."

"You can run ahead of them," Grams said. "Just make sure Brynn and Torrie know where you are. They'll keep Shelby."

"Fine," I huffed. "Can we just get going?" I stomped out the door and to the car.

"Have fun!" Grams hollered as we were leaving. Grams stayed back to pass out candy to any trick-or-treaters who happened to swing by our house, which was never many.

Brynn parked Leopold at the town common and then I got to go wild running from house to house while my two queens lollygagged behind with their ferocious guard dog. I had to keep going back and checking in with my sister and Torrie, like Grams said, but that was okay 'cause I had lots of energy—and I hadn't even eaten any of my candy yet.

Turns out bringing Shelby didn't ruin anything. I even agreed to keep her for a minute after Brynn and Torrie saw some boys they wanted to go and say hi to. Me and Shelby were having a good time—until we ran into a witch and a black cat. Shelby growled when they came near—and she only growled for the specialist occasions. I knew exactly how she felt 'cause Missy Gerber was the witch and Samantha Yelber was the cat.

Even though she had a green face and black hat, Missy tried acting like a good witch, 'cause first thing she did was bend down and hand Shelby some Goldfish from her bag. Fastest way to get Shelby to like you was to give her a treat. A witch can be tricky like that. I didn't have a chance to warn Shelby not to fall for it.

"Hi, Carter," Missy said after standing back up.

"Carter isn't here," I replied. "I'm Sir Lancelot, protector of two queens."

Missy giggled.

"Ha. More like Sir Wimpsalot," Samantha said, 'cause she wasn't ever nice.

Shelby growled again.

"Your dog doesn't like cats," Missy said.

"Or mean people," I added, glaring at Samantha.

Samantha hissed at me and Shelby and I thought about slicing her with my sword.

"Melissa," a woman called from farther up the sidewalk, interrupting my thoughts. I recognized Missy's mother. "We're leaving," she yelled. "Let's go."

"Leaving?" Samantha whispered. "Why? What happened?"

"I don't know," Missy said. "But I better not keep my mom waiting."

"Where's *my* mother?" Samantha wondered.

Missy shrugged. "I think she's over there," she said, pointing to a small group ringing a doorbell at the end of the block. "I better go."

She was right 'cause Ms. Gerber did not sound happy.

"Bye," I told Missy, feeling sorta sorry that her Halloween was ending early.

"Bye, Carter. I mean, Sir Lancelot."

Missy flew off on her broomstick, which left me and Shelby with Samantha Yelber. And once again, I missed my chance to slice Samantha with my sword, 'cause the black cat hissed a second time, then turned and dashed across the road and ran off into the darkness to catch up to her mom.

I held my breath when she did that 'cause a black cat crossing your path is bad luck—especially on Halloween. Must be I wasn't fast enough or didn't stop breathing long enough 'cause bad luck found me soon after.

"Hey, CJ," Brynn said, rejoining me.

"Where's Torrie?" I asked.

"She's getting a ride home with someone else."

"Someone else? Is it that Jay guy she met at the North Pole?"

"Yes," Brynn huffed. "I'm starting to think he's not so great."

"Why?"

"Let's just say it's all about him." She took Shelby from me and started walking.

My sister was upset, but this was no time to worry about that. There was still more candy to be had. I kicked it in gear and hurried past her.

36

MY WISH COMES TRUE

Ms. Krane did one of her mini-lessons, which was what she called it when she took time at the beginning of our writing period to talk to us about writing and writers. I never minded 'cause I liked talking about writing, just not doing it. But that was before I became a dragon slayer.

This time, Ms. Krane wanted us to work on taking a real moment, like when we watched the calf being born, which was the example she used again 'cause she said it was one we could all relate to, and have fun adding imagination to what was real to make it even better in our stories. In her example, Ms. Krane had twin calves born, and Farmer Don helped deliver the second one 'cause the mom was beginning to struggle. She made it real suspenseful.

Adding imagination sounded fun but it was gonna be hard for me 'cause I always told the truth. But Ms. Krane gave me permission to stretch the truth this time, 'cause she said it was okay to do that in our creative writing. And stretching the truth wasn't the same as lying.

So I hurried down to the Dragon and got situated. Principal Ryan had given me a special green swivel chair to sit in at my computer station 'cause Ms. Krane told her I did my best work when I was able to keep moving. It didn't matter if I was spinning while telling my story as long as the Dragon could still hear me. I just had to be careful I didn't move too far away from the computer 'cause the cord to my headset was only so long and could get yanked off my head. I learned that the hard way.

I was still thinking about Mason and Susie and hoping they could come to visit our class when I sat down to be a dragon slayer, so I decided to write about what happened at the North Pole over the summer when those boys were mean to Mason. I had the whole story in my head so I jumped into telling the Dragon all about it. I kept pretty close to the truth 'cause it was still hard for me to stretch things—until I got to the good part.

Once I started adding imagination to the bad guys, I got on a roll. In my story, they were even bigger and scarier. I gave them tattoos and rotten breath and bulging muscles. And my favorite part was that I didn't just want to be brave, I *was* brave. I marched over and warned those jerks to leave Mason alone—"Or else." The leader bad guy got in my face and growled, "Or else what?" So I showed him. I grabbed his hand

and twisted it, squeezing a secret pressure point. He dropped to his knees. "Uncle!" he cried, begging for mercy. "Uncle!"

I had a good time telling my story to the Dragon and changing it into what I wished had happened in real life. The next step was printing and doing the edit and revise stuff, 'cause that was my deal with Ms. Krane. So I took my headset off, 'cause the printer was on the other side of the room, and wheeled over to fetch my paper. That's when I got distracted. There were voices coming from Principal Ryan's office next door.

"I'm not here to argue about Ms. Krane's personal decisions," a woman said, "though there are some in our town ready to make a stink. Some who are uncomfortable with the idea of our children coming home with questions. Even some who say that her facial birthmark scares the kids."

"Careful. Now you're crossing the line," Principal Ryan warned.

"I'm only telling you what I've heard," the woman replied. "Perhaps you're not aware, but there's a group starting a petition to have Ms. Krane reassigned to a new job."

"What?!" Principal Ryan exclaimed, taking that exact word right out of my mouth.

"I ran into them on Halloween. While our kids were getting candy, this group was trying to gather signatures. Susan Yelber, Samantha's mother, and your teachers, Mrs. Stinger and Ms. Hornet, were among them. I was appalled."

"Unbelievable," Principal Ryan said. "Some people will stop at nothing. You can be assured I will be speaking to those teachers, but the fact of the matter is the children love Ms. Krane. They're not scared or confused or asking any of the questions these adults are so worried about. The children don't care. It's the adults who have the problem."

Principal Ryan was right about all that except for one part. I did care—a lot!

"I don't disagree," the woman said. "I'm not signing any petition. I'm not interested in making things difficult for Ms. Krane. As a divorced working mom, I have respect for any woman raising a child on her own, but a teacher leaving in the middle of the school year is disruptive. Add to that what could happen with this petition and you've got the potential for major disruption, and I won't stand for it. My daughter only gets the best. I want Missy moved to a different classroom."

I gasped. It was Missy's mom on the other side. She wasn't giving up. This was my wish come true—but suddenly, I didn't want it anymore.

"Ms. Gerber, I thought we'd been over—"

"You've ignored my requests," Ms. Gerber snapped, cutting off Principal Ryan. "Ms. Krane must be seven or eight months into her pregnancy and you haven't done anything to prepare for the situation. The school hasn't even hired for the position yet. That is unacceptable. I want Missy moved."

"Ms. Gerber, if I give in and grant your request, that is going to open the floodgates. I'll have parents knocking down my door, demanding the same for their child. If you're truly not interested in making things difficult for Ms. Krane, then you'll drop this."

"I want Missy moved." She wasn't dropping it.

Principal Ryan sighed. "Finding and hiring the right individual takes time. And moving a student this far into the school year would be disruptive for all the children," Principal Ryan replied, "so I strongly disagree with your request, but I will discuss the possibility with Dr. Morris—again."

Who was Dr. Morris?

"And when will that be?" Ms. Gerber demanded.

"I have a scheduled superintendent's meeting at the end of the week."

"Good. I'll be expecting an answer, and it better be what I want to hear," Ms. Gerber threatened. She stormed out the door and down the hallway. Even her heels sounded angry *tap-tap-tap*ping against the floor as she marched off.

I kicked both feet against the ground and fast wheeled over to the computer and put my headset back on. I didn't want Principal Ryan to know I'd been listening. When she peeked in on me, I showed her my printed page and told her I was done.

"Good job, Carter. Ms. Krane will be pleased."

She didn't ask to hear it like she did the last time, but I knew that was 'cause of Ms. Gerber. I quick gathered my things and hurried out of there before I burst and told Principal Ryan that I'd just overheard everything.

37

SOMETHING TO THINK ABOUT

I was so busy replaying Ms. Gerber's words in my head that I walked up the stairs instead of running. And I shuffled down the hall, past our bulletin board without so much as a glance, and into my classroom.

Leave it to Ms. Krane to find a way to break my trance. "Carter, you're just in time. How would you like to read your story today? We've just started sharing."

"What?" I asked in disbelief, my eyes growing bigger.

"Would you like to read your story to the class?" she repeated.

That was something I'd never done before. I'd never written a story that I could share. But now that I was a dragon slayer, my sentences were on paper and waiting for me to read out loud.

"Let's hear it," Mary encouraged.

"Yeah," Kyle agreed.

"But I didn't get to edit and revise," I told Ms. Krane.

"That's okay. You can work more on it later. Your classmates would like to hear what you've got."

I shrugged. "Okay."

I made my way to the front of the room and took my position. I stood there holding my paper, then cleared my throat and began, trying hard to add good expression and pacing like Ms. Krane does when she reads.

My classmates were silent when I finished. I thought that was 'cause no one liked my story, but it was 'cause none of them could believe I wrote it.

"That was so good," Vanessa said, making me smile. "I could picture it. I felt like I was there."

"Carter, did that really happen?" Missy asked.

"Yup. Well, sorta. I did see those bullies at the North Pole. But I had to add imagination 'cause that was what Ms. Krane said to do."

"Carter, you must've added lots of imagination because you couldn't beat up a flea," Kyle exclaimed.

My shoulders sagged.

"Kyle, I'd like to remind you that we're positive in our classroom," Ms. Krane said.

"Sorry," Kyle murmured.

"My friends, Carter has just given us an opportunity to do some serious thinking and reflecting," Ms. Krane continued. "We should be asking ourselves what kind of friend we are and want to be. Because doing something heroic doesn't require muscles. Being a hero takes courage and heart—and that's something each of you is capable of."

Told you the Owl was big on us being thinkers. But usually our thinking had to do with the books we were reading or projects we were doing, not 'cause of something I'd written. So I thought about my own words.

And you know what came to mind? Ms. Krane. She was sticking up for me—again. I was ready to do the same for her if she ever needed me to. And I'd stick up for Grams and Brynn and Torrie too.

But plot twist. (That was something Brynn liked to say when there was a surprise.) Turns out there was somebody else that I had to stick up for.

38

THE CROW

After I told Grams about Ms. Gerber and what I'd heard in the office, she blew out one of those heavy breaths that meant what she was hearing wasn't good.

"A petition?" she repeated. "Unbelievable."

"That's just what Principal Ryan said. What's a petition?"

"A piece of a paper that people can sign if they agree with what you want," Grams huffed. "If you gather enough signatures, a petition can be very convincing, so I'm glad Ms. Gerber declined, but there's no telling what she's gonna do next—or any of the rest of them. But we can't sit around worrying about it. You control what you can control, CJ. And in your case, that means continuing to work really hard in school. Understand?"

Control what you can control, I thought. Guess that made sense. I nodded.

"Good. The rest will take care of itself."

If by that Grams meant we'd get answers about what was gonna happen, then she was right, 'cause the part of "the rest" that involved Ms. Gerber took care of itself on Friday afternoon. We were busy packing up for the weekend when she stormed into our classroom. Ms. Gerber looked meaner than the great horned owl ever could. Scarier, too, like a crow with her long pointy nose. I shivered, 'cause the crow and owl are fierce enemies. But it wasn't the Owl that Ms. Gerber wanted.

"Melissa, gather all your things," her mother cawed.

Missy scrambled to cram her stuff inside her backpack while the Crow flew across our room and grabbed the stack of papers sitting inside her daughter's mail slot. Missy's spelling test was on the top.

"You couldn't spell *exuberant*?" her mother scolded, waving the paper in the air.

Missy shrugged and looked away. She'd gotten a hundred on the test. *Exuberant* was Ms. Krane's bonus word. It was the only one Missy had missed. None of us spelled it right. But we knew what it meant.

My mouth got started before my brain could catch up and slow it down. "Ms. Gerber, we have a rule in our classroom that you can only say positive things. We *exuberate* positive attitudes here," I explained.

The Crow didn't appreciate that 'cause her chest puffed and I thought for a minute she was gonna breathe fire like a real-live crow dragon. But the Owl stepped beside me before she could do that so the Crow quick turned and swept her daughter out of the classroom.

"I don't think I like Missy's mom," I confessed. Even if she wasn't signing the petition that Grams made me promise I wouldn't mention to Ms. Krane, she was still making things difficult by being mean.

"Maybe not, but let's remember, we don't really know her," Ms. Krane replied.

"I don't want to." And that was the truth.

I grabbed my backpack and went over to the window to wait for Mr. Wilson. During all the excitement, Principal Ryan had come over the loudspeaker and made a few announcements and already started calling buses. Mr. Wilson wasn't here yet, but I saw Missy leaving with her mom. Missy glanced up at our classroom and I gave her a small wave. The Crow must've sensed that 'cause she whipped around and glared at me, so then I waved real big. *Take that, Crow. I'm with the Owl!*

Ms. Gerber's eyes narrowed and then she took Missy's hand and pulled her along.

Ms. Krane squeezed my shoulder. She'd been behind me and I didn't know 'cause owls are masters of silent flight.

"Ms. Krane, I know you want me to be a thinker, but I can't right now 'cause I've got too many questions."

"Just because you have questions doesn't mean you aren't thinking, Carter. Quite the opposite. People who fail to ask questions are the ones not thinking."

That made me smile a little. "I'm good at asking questions," I said.

"Yes, you are. But now I need you to be a good friend too—to Missy."

I didn't say anything 'cause she was asking something that used to sound impossible—but was it still?

"I know you can do that. You've already proven it."

Mr. Wilson pulled in then and I looked into my teacher's eyes. "I'll try," I promised.

Ms. Krane smiled and her purple stain wrinkled. "Thank you, Carter."

"Bye, baby," I said to her belly. "Have a good night." I didn't want her baby feeling upset after what had happened. That wouldn't be good.

"Bye, Carter," Ms. Krane said. "We'll see you Monday morning."

I thought about thanking her for the warning, but then thought better of it. I stepped into the hall and turned on the burners. It was the weekend!

39

A GOOD FRIEND

"Well, what did you learn today, young man?" Mr. Wilson asked after I bounded up the steps and slid into my seat behind him.

"That I can be a good friend."

"I coulda told you that," Mr. Wilson exclaimed. "You've been my good friend for a long while now."

I grinned. "Yeah, but you don't count, Mr. Wilson. I need to be a friend to somebody in my class now. Somebody that I thought I could never be friends with."

"Well, how lucky for that kid that they have the chance to get to know you," he said, kicking our big yellow taxi into gear.

We pulled out of the parking lot, and as we rode along, I got to thinking about what Mr. Wilson had just said. About Missy getting to know me. That was one of those things Grams would call a two-way street, 'cause Missy getting to know me also meant I'd have to get to know her. I already knew some stuff, like she could be bossy and annoying and her mother was the Crow. But she was a good teammate too. We were on Day 18 with the eggs and couldn't wait for them to hatch so we could introduce the baby chicks to our play yard. And there was one other thing I knew about Missy. Me and Mr. Wilson drove by her house every morning and afternoon, but she never rode the big yellow taxi. Except I didn't know why.

"Carter, you've asked me about several different words so far this year, but I've got one for you now," Mr. Wilson said, interrupting my daydreaming.

"Really? What's the word?" I asked.

"I want you to tell me what that word *friend* means to you."

Guess I wasn't done thinking after all, 'cause I had to think about that for a minute. Mr. Wilson was my friend, and so was Mason, so what did that mean?

"It means I wouldn't do anything to hurt you," I said, "and I'd always try and help if you needed me to—even if it's scary."

"I like that," Mr. Wilson said, nodding. "So just remember, you've got a friend in me, and I'm here for you if you need me."

We came to a stop and he threw open the side door. My eyes bugged. We were already at my house. I'd been so lost in my thinking and daydreaming that I hadn't been paying attention to where we were. Grams stood in the driveway waiting for me.

I hopped up. "Thanks, Mr. Wilson."

"Hey?" he replied, stopping me 'cause I almost forgot.

"Oh yeah. See you later!" I yelled over my shoulder on my way down the steps.

"Thanks for the warning!" he shouted.

Grams shook her head. "You two are a pair of fools, you know that."

"Have a great weekend, Mrs. Sims!" Mr. Wilson hollered, honking the horn as he drove away.

Me and Grams laughed—'cause she liked Mr. Wilson too. He was a good friend.

40

SURPRISES

I like surprises. That's why birthdays and Christmas are so great. But those surprises are only the halfway kind, 'cause you've been asking for certain things.

My favorite surprise is the all-the-way kind. The one that comes out of nowhere, when you're not expecting it. Like one time, after Brynn got her driver's license, she told me to get ready and hop in Leopold 'cause we were going for milkshakes. And another time when she went shopping with Torrie, she came home with this awesome new toy for me—for no reason.

"I got something for you, CJ," she said.

"Really?! What is it?!" I clapped, and reached for the bag.

Brynn held it away. "It wasn't cheap, but when I saw it, I knew you'd love it, and I had to get it."

"What is it?!" I yelled again.

She finally handed over the bag and I tore it open. I couldn't believe my eyes. It was my very own bug-shooting salt gun! It came equipped with a laser beam pointer that you put on your target to help you aim. Now if there's a fly in the house, I kill it dead with one shot. No more stinky fly swatter. Grams is not a fan of guns, but she appreciates my sharp eye—even though she gets annoyed with the salt that's left lying all over the place.

"We've got more salt around here than Carter's got liver pills," she liked to complain, which was another one of her old-timer sayings that made no sense to anyone that wasn't halfway to ancient.

"But we don't got more flies than Carter's got liver pills," I always tell her. "You can't have it both ways, Grams. You win some, you lose some," I liked to remind her, which was another one of her sayings.

My bug-shooting salt gun was one of the awesomest surprises I ever got. Brynn really was the best sister sometimes.

So why all this stuff about surprises? 'Cause this was the week of surprises at school. The first one belonged to Missy Gerber. She pulled off her own Abracadabra Adam disappearing act. She didn't come to school on Monday. That made being her friend easy 'cause I didn't have to do anything.

I got at the end of the line on our way to art and waited for everyone to get ahead of me and then I jumped down the stairs 'cause Missy wasn't here to tell me I couldn't. And when I jumped to slap the wall above the double doors on our way down the hall, Missy wasn't here to tell me to stop. But when I spotted the sign for Ms. Krane's baby shower on the teachers' room door, Missy wasn't here for me to ask what a baby shower was, 'cause how could you give a baby a shower before it was born?

So I asked Kyle and he told me it was a party where people gave the pregnant lady presents like diapers and rattles and maybe a high chair and whatever other things a new mom might need for her baby. He knew 'cause he had to go shopping with his mom before she went to one of them for somebody she worked with. Kyle said he hated the shopping but I was happy for Ms. Krane. I just hoped Stinger and Hornet weren't invited. They could go to Ms. Gerber's for the mean-person party.

But Missing Missy and the baby shower were just two of the surprises that I was talking about. It was Ms. Krane who unveiled the biggest surprise of all.

41

WE HAVE VISITORS

I was at the end of the line heading back from art, but once I heard the gasps and squeals coming from inside our class-room, I broke the no-running rule and booked it to see what was happening.

"Mason!" I exclaimed when I rounded the corner and saw him.

Susie greeted me with a bark—and she never barked. She trotted over and rubbed against my legs, so I had her yellow hair all over my sweatpants, but I didn't care. I bent down and hugged her and got her yellow hair all over my shirt too. I was just as excited to see her.

"Mason, what're you doing here?" I asked after standing up.

"Ms. Krane got in touch and asked if Susie and I would like to pay a visit. Maybe let some of you do a little reading with her. It seems somebody thought that might be a good idea."

I glanced at Ms. Krane. She gave me the same one-eyebrow-raised look that Mr. Wilson was good at. Maybe owls could be tricky?

"Thank you, Ms. Krane," I said, and grinned.

She nodded.

"This is Mason and Susie, everybody," I said, introducing my friends to the class.

"This is everybody, except Missy Gerber," I said to Mason, introducing him to my class.

"Ms. Krane, I know the idea is for us to read to Susie, but maybe you can do the reading today so everyone can spend time with her," Vanessa Tucker suggested, 'cause one of her three things that wasn't a lie was that she loved animals.

"Yeah," Kyle agreed. "Plus, it's snack time, and you always read to us during snack."

"Yeah, and Susie and Mason deserve to hear your great reading voice," I added.

Ms. Krane smiled. "Okay. We'll try it for today and see how it goes," she said.

"Yay!" everyone cheered.

We hurried and got our snacks and personal cow journals and pushed a few desks aside so there was room to gather on the floor. Then we sat in a circle with Susie in the middle while Mason stayed in his chair nearby and Ms. Krane sat on the table in the front of the room. Susie was already scooting around the circle 'cause she was a fan of snack time. She really liked Mary's Cheetos.

"Susie, don't think I can't see what you're doing," Mason said.

Kyle's face scrunched, and so did a bunch of others around the circle. They were confused, 'cause how could the blind guy see anything? I smirked.

"Told you Mason could see things with his ears," I bragged.

"No begging," Mason told Susie. "It's reading time, but you can still visit."

Susie stopped her sniffing and settled in front of Mary and Vanessa so Ms. Krane could get started. Susie was the best-listening dog I'd ever met.

Ms. Krane opened our newest read-aloud, called *Summer of the Gypsy Moths,* and picked up where we last left off. There were two girls in the story and they didn't like each other. They were sorta like me and Missy Gerber, which made me wonder if maybe they would start to get along 'cause things weren't as bad with Missy anymore—but she wasn't here.

The more Ms. Krane read, the more we were all sucked into the story. Those two girls were in a big pickle that I won't tell you about 'cause I don't want to ruin the book, but they were starting to work together 'cause they had no choice— kinda like how it was for me and Missy with our play yard.

Susie scooted to a different spot every few minutes so we all got turns petting her. I wished I could listen and follow directions as good as her—but I was getting better. When I glanced at Mason, he had his head tipped back with a smile on his face. Yup, Ms. Krane's reading voice could do that to you.

"Mason, what were you smiling about?" Mary Fergus asked after Ms. Krane finished the chapter and closed the book. I wasn't the only one who'd noticed.

"The ocean," he replied. "Your story takes place on Cape Cod, so I was remembering the ocean. The breeze on my face. The smell. The sound. The sheer power of it. Everything. When you breathe it all in—"

"It fills you with a calming happiness," Ms. Krane finished.

"Yes," Mason agreed.

"My friends, that is exactly what I mean when I talk to you about visualizing as a reader," Ms. Krane said, never missing a teaching opportunity. "Mason sees it better than any of us. And his sharing helps the rest of us get there, even if we've never experienced it ourselves."

"I haven't been to the ocean," I blurted.

"Put it on your bucket list, then," Mason advised. "It's something not to be missed."

"Absolutely," Ms. Krane said. "And the Cape is one of my favorite spots too," she added, smiling.

"Our family goes there every summer," Mary said. "It's always a blast." No wonder she loved traveling.

"But what's a bucket list?" I asked.

"A list of things a person hasn't done before but wants to accomplish before their final day on Earth," Ms. Krane explained.

"Before kicking the bucket, which means dying," Kyle added.

I nodded. I'd mention it to Brynn and Grams, but the ocean was probably too far away for Leopold to get us there, so unless we got a new car, I didn't know when I'd ever make the trip. But it was still going to be number one on my bucket list. I opened my cow journal and drew a bucket at the top of the page and underlined it 'cause it was my title, and then I drew waves next to my number one 'cause that was faster than trying to write the word *ocean*.

Suddenly, Susie sprang up and hurried over and sat in front of Mason. She stared past us to the corner of the room, her tail swishing back and forth across the ground. Her ears twitched and perked.

"She hears something," Mason said. "Listen."

We got quiet and listened real careful, holding our breaths—and then we heard it. A tiny peep.

"Baby chicks!" we shouted. "They're hatching!"

42

PIPPING

"The pipping has started," Ms. Krane announced, sliding off the table. "No running," she reminded us. Then she motioned to join her at the incubator.

Susie danced in circles 'cause she was excited, too, but she was a good girl and waited for Mason. So did I—and I ran to everything.

"Carter, you know Susie will help me. You don't have to stay behind," Mason said.

"That's okay, I'm not in a hurry."

"I've never known you not to be in a hurry. What's wrong?"

I shrugged. "Nothing."

"That's a nothing that means something. Same goes for the shrug."

Told you Mason sees everything. "I've been waiting and waiting for the eggs to hatch," I said, "but Missy is supposed to be here for it. She helped me build our play yard and she talked and talked about when we'd get to put baby chicks inside it. Now she's missing it. It's not fair."

"The fact that you're upset for Missy tells me your feelings about her have changed. Perhaps she's even your friend now?" Mason wondered.

I shrugged again. "Maybe."

Mason flashed a smile mixed with a told-you-so expression, but he didn't make a big deal of it. "Tell me, how many eggs do you have in that incubator?" he asked.

"Twelve."

"Well, then there's still a chance some will hold out longer and hatch tomorrow, and maybe Missy will be here to witness those."

"Yeah, maybe," I said, suddenly feeling better.

Mason grinned. "Good. Now let's check out this pipping event."

I gave Susie a pat on the head for being patient. "Make room," I hollered. "Mason and Susie want to see."

Kyle and Mary moved apart and made a spot for us and we slid up to the incubator. Ms. Krane looked at me from the other side and smiled.

We stood there, all of us crowded and smooshed together, rooting for the first baby chick as he pecked his way through the shell. It took him a long time and he was exhausted by the end, but he made it. He came out all wet and slimy with his feathers stuck down, but he sure was a cute little bugger.

"Peep," he said. "Peep."

"Why's he all wet?" Vanessa asked, scrunching her nose.

"From the environment inside the egg," Ms. Krane explained, "similar to how the baby calf we witnessed being born came out all wet. The difference is the heat lamp will help dry this little fella and not his mama."

By the time Mason and Susie had to leave, half of the chicks had hatched, and all were doing well. And by the end of the school day, eight of them had arrived, which meant Mason was right, there was still hope for Missy to see some pipping tomorrow.

But Missy didn't come to school again.

43

PIT STOP

Missy didn't come to school the next day or the next or the next. I asked Mary and Vanessa if Missy was sick, and they said Samantha Yelber told them Missy's mother wasn't letting her come to school. Thanks to the Crow, Missy's perfect attendance record was long gone, but I was glad she wasn't there when we found one of our chicks not breathing. But when she still wasn't back on Friday and missed our turn to put the chicks inside our play yard, I found Samantha Yelber at lunchtime and asked her how long Missy's mother planned on keeping Missy home. Samantha said the rest of the year 'cause Ms. Gerber was *aaangry* at the school. And then Samantha told me to get away from her.

I didn't care about Samantha Yelber. But I went from feeling bad to feeling mad for Missy. What her mom was doing wasn't fair—and I was gonna do something about it.

Now that it was November, it had turned chilly in the

mornings, so Grams started insisting I wear my zip-up hoodie. I put it on to make her happy, but as soon as I got to my locker, I took it off and stuffed it at the bottom of my backpack. The tag was itchy and I didn't like wearing it, but I sure was glad Grams didn't let me out of the house without it now—'cause a wadded-up hoodie at the bottom of a backpack made the perfect nesting spot for a baby chick. If the Crow wasn't gonna let Missy come to school and see the baby chicks, then I was bringing the baby chick to her.

I waited until the end of the day, when everyone was busy packing up and zigzagging around the classroom, to make my move. I had my unzipped bag nearby and as soon as Ms. Krane did the teacher thing and stepped into the hall to check the scene, I quick snatched a baby chick and dumped him inside my pack and zipped it shut. I was fast as lightning so no one saw me 'cause there woulda been squawking if I got caught. Now I just had to hope the little bugger didn't make a peep.

I said bye to Ms. Krane when Mr. Wilson pulled into the loop, then speed walked toward the door.

"Carter," Ms. Krane called out.

I stopped and glanced back. The Owl gave me one of those sideways looks that meant she was wondering something and trying to decide what to do about it. I gulped.

"Have a nice weekend," she said.

"You too!" I exclaimed. Then I turned and burned rubber before she could say anything else.

I bounded up the steps and took my seat behind Mr. Wilson and real careful slid my backpack off my shoulders and peeked inside. Baby chick was still there and he looked okay.

"What's the news today, young man?" Mr. Wilson asked.

"We need to make a pit stop on the way home," I informed him.

Mr. Wilson's head jerked around. "A pit stop? What kind of pit stop?"

"We need to stop at Missy Gerber's house."

"Gerber's house? What in the devil for?"

I stood up and leaned close and whispered the reason in Mr. Wilson's ear.

"You've got that thing with you now?" he yelped.

"*Shhh.* Yes, he's in my bag. And be quiet about it."

"It's okay in there?" he asked, keeping his voice low.

I nodded.

"You're sure?"

I nodded harder.

Mr. Wilson didn't say anything more after we got going. But his forehead was doing a lot of wrinkling and his mouth a lot of scowling, and it was making me nervous.

"Are you gonna stop for me?" I asked after he kept making all them faces.

"I told you I was your friend," he reminded me. "I've just been thinking. Here's what we're gonna do."

I leaned close so Mr. Wilson could whisper his plan to me.

When we got to my stop, Grams was waiting in the driveway. Mr. Wilson swung open the side door—but I didn't get off.

"Don't worry, I've got him," Mr. Wilson hollered to Grams. "The boy needs to make a special pit stop first. I'll have him home soon."

Grams was the one making faces after she heard that, but she didn't say no. She trusted Mr. Wilson. I poked my head up front and waved to her. She smiled and waved back when she saw me. Mr. Wilson gave her a nod and pulled the door shut, and then we kept rolling. We finished the rest of the bus run, dropping everyone off, and then we circled back and stopped in front of Missy Gerber's house.

Mr. Wilson sighed. "Well, here we are. You ready?"

I nodded.

"Good luck, then. And be careful. I'm not sure you want to tangle with Ms. Gerber if you can avoid it."

"Tell me something that I don't already know," I grumbled.

Mr. Wilson chuckled 'cause that was his sort of remark.

I shouldered my backpack and walked down the steps, careful not to bounce my baby chick too much. Then I strolled up Missy's driveway and along the sidewalk that led to her front door, and caught my first bit of luck, 'cause Missy saw me coming and met me outside before I had to knock or ring the doorbell.

"Carter? What're you doing here?"

"I brought you a present," I said. I slid my backpack off and set it on the ground. Then I unzipped it.

"What do you mean, a present? What do you have in there?" she asked.

"Look."

Missy stepped closer and gasped. "They hatched," she whispered.

"Yes, and you missed it. So I brought you this little guy to keep."

"Oh, Carter, that's so sweet."

My face and ears got real hot real fast after she said that. *Why did she have to say that?!*

"He's so cute," Missy gushed.

"I knew you'd like him."

"I do. He's adorable. But there's no way I can keep him. My mother would have a cow."

My shoulders slumped. After all that.

"I'm sorry, Carter. If you knew my mother—"

"How come you don't ride the bus?"

"My mother doesn't want me to. She says buses can be trouble, and she'd rather drive me herself."

"Mr. Wilson has me sit up front so I steer clear of any trouble. You could try that."

Missy shrugged.

"Ms. Krane is having a baby shower. There's a sign about it on the teachers' room door. That's a party where people bring the pregnant lady presents like diapers and stuff."

"I know what a baby shower is," Missy groaned, sounding like her old self.

"So Ms. Krane has lots of friends, even if your mother doesn't like her."

"Those people aren't friends, they're colleagues, and you don't know how many are actually going to the shower."

I frowned. "What's a colleague?"

"Someone you work with. You're friendly with one another because you work together, but that doesn't mean you're friends. A colleague wouldn't smuggle a baby chick out of the classroom and convince the bus driver to make a special stop for a coworker. That's something only a true friend would do."

My face and ears got hot again.

Missy smiled—but her smile didn't stay long 'cause we heard noise inside her house. Someone was coming.

"Melissa?" the Crow cawed, searching for her daughter.

"You better go," Missy urged.

I quick zipped my bag and pulled it onto my shoulder. "Are you coming back to school?"

She shrugged.

"I hope so," I said, surprising myself.

"Me too," Missy replied.

I turned then and ran to the big yellow taxi and bounded up the steps. Mr. Wilson pulled away from Missy's house just as the Crow poked her nasty beak outside.

"How'd it go?" he asked. "No trouble?"

"She couldn't keep the chick, but she was glad to see it."

"That's good."

"I think Missy is my friend."

"Yup, I think so too," Mr. Wilson agreed. "I hope she knows how lucky she is."

If you want to talk about lucky, I was lucky to have a friend like Mr. Wilson—and you better believe I knew that.

44

NO ROMANCE

Mr. Wilson dropped me off and I did my fastest speed walk up our driveway, 'cause I still needed to be careful not to bounce my little guy too much. I yanked open the front door and scooted into the kitchen. Shelby got up from her spot under the table where Grams sat cradling a cup of coffee and stuck her nose in the air, smelling something funny.

"Well, welcome home," Grams said. "Now that you and Mr. Wilson are done with your shenanigans, you mind telling me what that was all about?"

I didn't mind, but instead of telling, I showed her. I scooped the zipper-hoodie nest out of my backpack and set in on the table.

"Holy mackerel!" Grams exclaimed once she spotted Peeper snuggled in the middle. (Peeper was a good name for my baby chick.)

"*Arooo,*" Shelby howled, which was something she only ever did on the specialest occasions.

All the commotion got Brynn's and Torrie's attention and they came running from Brynn's bedroom. "Aww," they cooed when they saw Peeper.

"I can explain everything later," I said, "but right now I need help building my baby chick a proper home for the weekend. He needs to be warm and have food and water or else he'll die."

"There should be an old heat lamp leftover from Brynn's pet lizard down in the basement."

"You had a pet lizard?" I asked my sister.

"Spike. Dad got him for me on my fourth birthday. He died soon after Mom and Dad, though."

"I'm pretty sure there's a picture of you and your father with that lizard in one of our albums," Grams said.

"I think I've seen it before," Torrie said, glancing up from her phone.

"We'll look later," Grams said. "We better go and see what we can find in the cellar first. Peeper's waiting."

I was only a baby when the car accident happened, so that made some things easier for me—but I still missed my parents. Grams had pictures of them throughout the house so me and Brynn wouldn't forget them, and she liked to tell us when we reminded her of our mom or dad, which I always liked hearing—Brynn did too. Grams had more stories about Mom 'cause that was her daughter, but she'd known my dad since he was a boy, so she had lots to say about him too.

Anyway, down to the basement we went—except for

Torrie. She was busy texting and suddenly had somewhere else she needed to be, which made Brynn give her a look, but I didn't ask questions. I was too concerned with Peeper to worry about Torrie. Besides, if I'd said anything, Brynn woulda just told me it was none of my beeswax.

This was definitely a time when I was grateful for Grams being a pack rat, 'cause I found everything I needed: heat lamp, a couple small saucers for food and drink, a small tote to use as the yard, and stuff for bedding. With my sister and Grams pitching in, it didn't take long to have a new temporary home set up for Peeper. And once the little guy was settled, Brynn and Grams turned to me. They wanted the story now.

First, I had Brynn help me get a slice of her yummy banana bread and a glass of milk 'cause me and Shelby were starving, and then I sat down at the table. And in between my bites and Shelby's nibbles, I told them everything. Brynn complained a few times 'cause I wasn't chewing my food before talking, but if she wanted the story, then I had to talk. It would take too long if I did all my chewing before opening my mouth. She could close her eyes.

"You went through all that trouble for Missy Gerber?" Grams said after I'd finished my story. "The same Missy Gerber who was the most annoying girl on the planet during swim lessons and at the start of school?"

"Yeah," I mumbled.

"I think what you did was romantic," Brynn said.

"Romantic!" I screeched. "You're crazy!"

"We'll see about that in a few years."

I stuck my tongue, which was covered in banana bread, all the way out at her.

"Eww. You're disgusting," she whined.

Grams chuckled. "Just so we're clear, Peeper goes back to school on Monday. We're not raising a chicken."

"Okay," I agreed, even though I thought he'd make a great pet.

I changed my mind about that real quick after trying to sleep with him in my room. Peeper's peeping kept me up all night. I made him stay in the living room for the rest of the weekend. Come Monday morning, I was happy to take him back to his friends and family—until I got to wondering what was gonna happen when I did that.

"There's no sense in even trying to hide the truth from Ms. Krane," Grams told me after I explained my dilemma. "She knows by now anyway, trust me."

Grams was right. The Owl didn't miss anything. I wasn't worrying so much about how I was going to get Peeper back to his flock as I was about what the Owl was gonna say—or do.

Grams tried telling me I didn't need to worry about that either, but she wasn't the one who had to return Peeper. No matter, there wasn't much else I could do, so when I got to our classroom, I put my head down and hurried over to the baby chicks as fast as I could without running, 'cause that was a rule. Then, real quick, I transferred Peeper from his zipper-hoodie nest inside my bag back to his family home.

The Owl made silent flight and landed by my side before I finished. I peeked up at her, looking into her triangle eyes.

"I think *Little Chick's Big Trip* needs to be the next story you tell the Dragon. The baby and I can't wait to hear it," she said, patting me on the shoulder.

I grinned. "Yeah," I agreed. "It's an adventure story—but there's no romance," I stressed, making that clear. I was still mad at Brynn for saying that.

Ms. Krane laughed.

And Peeper peeped.

45

LITTLE CHICK'S BIG TRIP

Principal Ryan was thrilled to hear my newest saga after I got done telling the Dragon. She even went down the hall and got Ms. Garcia so she could listen too.

"That's a remarkable story, Carter," Principal Ryan gushed after I finished reading. "You really went to Missy's house?"

I nodded.

"That was very sweet of you," Ms. Garcia said.

I scowled.

"Or not," she corrected when she saw my face.

"Did you happen to see Missy's mother?" Principal Ryan asked.

I shook my head. "I got out of there before I had to."

Principal Ryan and Ms. Garcia glanced at each other.

"I heard Ms. Gerber when she was in your office last time," I blurted. I quick covered my mouth, but it was too late.

"You did?" Principal Ryan asked.

I pulled my hand away. "Yes. Can't you make her send Missy back to school?"

"No. I'm sorry, Carter, but that's not something I can do," Principal Ryan said. "It's Ms. Gerber's right as a parent to do what she feels is best for her daughter."

"But Missy wants to come back. She told me so."

"Unfortunately, that is out of our control," Ms. Garcia replied. "It's hard, I know, but try focusing your energy on what you can control. Your relationship with friends, Ms. Krane, and your grams and sister—especially with Thanksgiving coming. Let's be thankful for what we do have."

I nodded. Control what you can control, just like Grams had said. How did grown-ups do that? How did they come up with some of the same stuff to say without even talking to each other?

Principal Ryan complimented me again on my writing and said she was proud of me, and then said I'd better get back to class.

"Okay. Thanks," I replied. "Bye, Ms. Garcia."

I gathered my papers and hurried out of the office. I took the stairs two at a time 'cause I had a sudden jolt of extra energy. Ms. Garcia had just given me a great idea. I was gonna control what I could control—but I had to act fast 'cause there wasn't much time.

46

INVITATIONS

It would be more work, but Grams wouldn't mind, and I'd help. It'd give Brynn a reason to do extra baking, which she liked. It was a good plan.

First on my list were Mason and Susie, 'cause they were coming for another visit that afternoon, which was perfect timing. But before I got to ask Mason what I wanted, I had to wait 'cause he had something in store for our class.

"After talking about the ocean when I was here last, I was reminded of one of my favorite poems," he told us. "If you don't mind, I'd like to share it with all of you."

"Please," Ms. Krane said, giving permission.

Mason cleared his throat and began. I didn't hear all of the beginning words 'cause that was the first time I'd ever seen a blind person read with their fingers and I got distracted by that. But once I started listening, it was really good. Ms. Krane thought so too.

"Thank you, Mason. That was beautiful," she said.

Then she turned to us. "The special bumps and dots that Mason was touching and reading with his fingers is called Braille," Ms. Krane explained. "You may have also noticed Mason didn't use different voices like I often do when reading aloud because that isn't what his poem called for. Poetry is about rhythm and pacing, pauses and emphasis, and subtle changes. Could you hear that?"

I nodded 'cause I heard it.

"Thank you again, Mason," Ms. Krane said. "That happens to be a favorite poem of mine as well, so that was extra special for me."

Mason tipped his head all gentleman-like. "My pleasure."

Ms. Krane smiled, then picked up *Summer of the Gypsy Moths*. We brought Mason up to speed on what he'd missed, and then Ms. Krane started our next chapter. We took turns petting Susie as she scooted around our circle, making the rounds, and we all listened real close to the story, 'cause that pickle the two girls were in kept getting trickier and trickier.

When it was time for Mason and Susie to leave, I asked Ms. Krane if I could walk them out 'cause I had something to ask them. My old teachers would've been nosy and wanted to know what was so important, but not Ms. Krane. She gave me permission without needing to know anything more, which was a good thing, 'cause I couldn't tell her—not yet.

I held it in until we got outside, but then my plan jumped

out of my mouth in one big breathless burst. "Mason, I'd like to invite you and Susie to my house for Thanksgiving with me and Grams and Brynn."

"Gee, Carter, that's very generous of you, but I don't want to intrude. Thanksgiving is important family time."

"It's a time for family *and* friends," I said. "Ms. Krane is coming."

That wasn't true—yet. I planned on inviting her next, so that didn't count as a lie. It was a soon-to-be truth. I was keeping it positive 'cause that was our rule.

"Really?"

"Yes."

"Well, if you're having other guests, then Susie and I would be delighted to attend."

"Super!" I cheered.

"I'll get in touch with your grams to find out details and also what I can bring."

"You don't need to bring anything," I said. "Just yourselves."

"Carter, my dear boy, a gentleman never arrives empty-handed. Remember that when you're older."

I nodded. "I will."

Mason and Susie got in their ride then, and I sprinted back upstairs. It was a good thing school was almost over, 'cause I had an extra hard time listening and following directions after that. I couldn't wait to ask Ms. Krane next, and I knew just when I'd have the perfect chance.

The Owl glided over and landed by my side at the window after everyone else had left for the day and I was watching for Mr. Wilson. I twisted and faced my teacher. "Ms. Krane, I'd like to invite you to my house for Thanksgiving with me and Grams and Brynn."

"Carter, that's very kind and thoughtful of you, but I'm not sure a teacher should be spending time with a student's family outside of school. Thank you, though."

"Mason and Susie are coming," I said, "'cause they're my friends. So maybe you can come as a friend and not my teacher."

Ms. Krane did one of the biggest smiles then, making her purple stain crinkle and fold—and her eyes got wet. "Oh, Carter," she said, wiping her face. "My parents were hoping I'd come home, but my doctor said I shouldn't fly, so I had to tell them no. I thought I'd be spending the day alone."

"Not anymore."

"You're a sweetheart."

Mr. Wilson rolled in with the big yellow taxi, and I spun away from the window and hurried toward the door. That was enough of the mushy talk.

"I'll have my grams get in touch with details," I said, which was something I hadn't thought of until Mason mentioned it.

"Carter," Ms. Krane called. "Your grams knows about this, right?"

"Yup!" I called back, ducking around the corner and running down the hall. That was another one of my soon-to-be truths.

I skipped up the bus steps and hopped into my seat behind Mr. Wilson and didn't even wait until we were on our way. Mr. Wilson tried saying that he didn't want to impose, and that he could never leave his wife at home to spend the day all by herself. So I told him that his wife was invited too. It took some extra arm twisting, but by the time we reached my house, I had him convinced to come. I thought I was the trickiest and smartest boy alive—until Mr. Wilson saw Grams standing in the driveway and had to say something to her.

"See you later," I told Mr. Wilson, trying to get off the bus as fast as I could.

But instead of thanking me for the warning like he was supposed to, he tipped his hat to Grams. "My wife and I thank you for the invite, Mrs. Sims. I'll bring my famous sweet potato pie."

Grams's face twisted 'cause she didn't know what in tarnation Mr. Wilson was talking about, but she didn't let on. "Sounds wonderful. Looking forward to it," she replied, waving to him.

"I'm guessing you've got some explaining to do," Grams said after Mr. Wilson honked and drove away.

"Yup. I sure do!" I admitted, and ran ahead. I wanted Brynn with us when I did my explaining. This was gonna be a whopper!

47

THANKSGIVING

"You sure cooked up an idea that means we've got a lot of work ahead of us," Grams exclaimed after I got done filling her and Brynn in on what I'd done. "Cooking for me, baking for Brynn, and cleaning for you. I hope you didn't think you were getting off easy. This is an all-hands-on-deck operation."

Me and Brynn laughed. Grams might've been doing a lot of huffing and puffing, but she wasn't for-real upset. This was her getting excited.

"First thing we oughta do is get the table leaves from the basement," she directed. "We're gonna need them."

So that was it. Our getting-ready operation kicked off that night and didn't finish until late on Thursday morning. It was way more work than I expected, but it was fun too—except that traitor, Shelby, decided to keep my sister and Grams company in the kitchen instead of me. But I couldn't blame her.

Mason was our first guest to arrive on Thanksgiving. I was excited to see him, but Shelby and Susie got more excited when they saw each other. Those two made friends real fast after a couple rounds of butt sniffing.

Once everyone else turned up and we got introductions out of the way, the adults poured drinks and made chitchat, and then we found our seats at the table. Grams and Brynn had whipped together a feast that left our whole house smelling delicious, and I couldn't wait to dig in. Mr. Wilson added his sweet potato pie. Mason and Susie brought cider and yummy cookies, and Ms. Krane came with a big pasta salad. There was enough food for an army.

"Thank you for having us," Mrs. Wilson said to Grams after passing the potatoes. "This is truly nice. Our children are all grown up and moved away now, so it's been a while since Henry and I have had a big gathering for Thanksgiving."

"We're glad you could join us," Grams said.

"I agree. This is lovely, Mrs. Sims. Thank you," Ms. Krane said next.

"Indeed," Mason replied. "Not only is the food wonderful, but your invitation made declining my brother's offer to join his family in Philadelphia much easier. I'll be seeing them at Christmas anyway, and while I love them dearly, one visit a year with his wife is plenty. Don't tell him I said that."

We all laughed.

"So thanks for having me," Mason added, scooping more stuffing onto his plate.

"Oh, you're welcome," Grams said. "We're delighted to have all of you with us, so enough with the thank-yous."

"It is THANKSgiving, Grams," I reminded her, which made everyone laugh again.

"My siblings and their families are with my parents today back in Ohio," Ms. Krane said in between bites. "My doctor thought getting away would be beneficial but she advised me against flying in my current condition." She pointed at her belly, which led to more laughing.

I fake laughed 'cause I was stuck wondering if Ms. Krane had heard about the petition. Was that why getting away would be good for her? Was the petition stressing her out like Grams had said would be bad?

"What brought you out this way in the first place?" Mr. Wilson asked her.

"College. I came out here for college. And I stayed after getting my first job. There weren't many openings back home, and while my résumé and application landed me several interviews, sometimes putting a face to a name doesn't help."

"That's awful," Brynn whispered.

"It's okay," Ms. Krane said. "With this birthmark, I've had to endure comments and looks all my life—ever since I was a young kid. But most people aren't outright mean about it; my mark just makes them uncomfortable. So I kept trying and eventually got hired at a wonderful school. People there were supportive and compassionate—until it came to my pregnancy. That was something they couldn't stand behind, but I knew that going in. Maybe someday I'll find Mr. Right. But I can't keep waiting. I'm running out of time. So I decided to have this baby on my own. And I'm overjoyed about it."

"It must be hard for your parents being far away," Mrs. Wilson said.

"Yes, but they'll be making the trip this way for Christmas so they can meet their new grandchild. *Oof.* There's a kick now," Ms. Krane said, rubbing her belly.

Susie sprang from the floor and walked over and put her head in Ms. Krane's lap. "Well, hello, Susie," Ms. Krane said, petting her behind the ears where she liked it. Susie sniffed and kissed Ms. Krane's belly. We were all smiles after seeing that.

"Well, I'm sure your parents are looking forward to coming out here," Grams said, getting back to their conversation.

"Very much so," Ms. Krane replied, giving Susie more pets.

The turkey made a second trip around the table—and so did the potatoes and deviled eggs. Our friends weren't kidding when they said it was good 'cause they ate a lot. And they were enjoying themselves for real 'cause there was lots of conversation and laughing throughout dinner.

"Can we have dessert now?" I blurted. I didn't mind the grown-up talk, but a boy can only wait so long for all the goodies on Thanksgiving.

"Yes, please," Mr. Wilson agreed. "It's time to be amazed by my famous sweet potato pie."

"Honest to goodness, Henry," Mrs. Wilson huffed. "The way you talk about that pie you should marry it."

"Maybe I will," Mr. Wilson replied.

"Brynn made fancy red velvet cupcakes too!" I added, bouncing in my seat.

"My daughter-in-law was an excellent baker," Grams told our guests, "and that talent didn't miss Brynn. My granddaughter is even better," she bragged.

Brynn blushed.

"Is that something you might want to do later on, be a baker?" Ms. Krane asked my sister.

"I'd like to go to college and study business and marketing first, and after that maybe I'll open my own bakery," Brynn said, ruffling my hair.

She and Grams got up then and finally went to get the pie and cupcakes—and my day only got better from there, 'cause both were super yummy. I snuck a little to Shelby, but Susie never left Ms. Krane's side.

When all was said and done, and our company was gone and it was just me and Brynn and Grams resting in the living room, Grams turned to me. "You should be proud of what you made happen today," she said.

"Real proud," Brynn said.

I was. I was as proud and happy as I'd ever been—but life isn't always fair, and special feelings and special days don't last forever.

48

GOOD GOES TO BAD

I got to school on Monday morning, still riding my high from Thanksgiving, but that didn't last long. I skipped into our classroom and saw Missy still wasn't back. And she wasn't the only one missing. We had a sub. Where was Ms. Krane?

This was the beginning of good going to bad. All the way to bad.

Part IV

WINTER : SHAPE UP OR SHIP OUT

Lieutenant Boss

49

LIEUTENANT BOSS

Instead of Ms. Krane, a strange man sat behind her desk reading a big fat book.

"Who's that?" Kyle asked, stopping beside me and peering into our classroom.

"I don't know. Where's Ms. Krane?"

Kyle shrugged. "Beats me. But it looks like we're stuck with this dude for the day."

"I don't like subs," I groaned. "I always get in trouble."

"Don't sweat it. The only thing this guy cares about is reading his book. He hasn't even picked his head up yet. This should be an easy day."

Kyle couldn't have been any more wrong about that.

I glided over to my counter space and said hi to Camo, but not to Peeper and his friends 'cause they had moved to Farmer Don's, and I didn't say anything to the stranger in Ms. Krane's chair. He still had his nose in his book and I didn't want to get off on the wrong foot by interrupting him. But where was Ms. Krane?

Mrs. Rosa came over the loudspeaker and greeted us all good morning 'cause Principal Ryan and Ms. Garcia were away at some big conference. We did the pledge and listened to a few announcements and then Mrs. Rosa reminded us to choose kindness and that was the end of it.

As soon as she finished, our substitute rose from Ms. Krane's chair and marched to the front of our room. He marched like a soldier, spun on his heel like one, and stood real straight and tall like one, too, so I guessed he was an army guy right away. I was close.

"My name is Lieutenant Gene Boss. United States Navy. Retired. You can address me as Sir, Lieutenant, Lieutenant Boss, or any combination of the three. I'll be running this ship."

"Where's Ms. Krane?" I blurted. No way I could hold that in any longer.

"Please raise your hand to speak," the lieutenant man said. "And why aren't you sitting at your desk where you belong?"

"But where is she?" I persisted. My mouth was getting on a roll now.

"Once again, please raise your hand to speak," he emphasized. "And I asked you a question. Why aren't you sitting at your desk?"

"But where is she?"

"Wise guy, huh? In the hall. Now," Lieutenant Boss barked, jabbing his finger at me.

Kyle slid lower in his seat when I walked by.

I stepped into the hall and stood with my back pressed against the wall. I gave Ms. Krane's owl a quick glance and then the lieutenant man took his position in front of me. Everything about Lieutenant Boss was serious. His shoes were shiny black and serious. His pants had a sharp line down the front that was serious. If he'd had hair, his haircut woulda been serious.

"It's gonna be me for a while around here, and I run a tight ship," he began, getting down to business. "You understand?"

"Whaddya mean *for a while?*"

"For a while," he repeated. "Did you hear me, sailor? I run a tight ship. That means I expect you to follow the rules. There's no yelling out. You will raise your hand to speak. And you will sit at your desk, nowhere else. It shouldn't be that difficult."

Easy for him to say, I thought.

"It's my way or the seaway. You can choose to shape up or ship out. Got it?"

Was he trying to be funny like Mr. Wilson, 'cause I wasn't laughing. Where was Ms. Krane?

"No response?" he said. "Then a dose of solitary confinement oughta give you the chance to think things over. You can take a seat and stay out here until I come and get you."

My shoulders sagged. "I've done lots of time in the hall before," I said.

Lieutenant Boss grunted. Then he turned on his heel and marched back into the classroom.

So much for not getting off on the wrong foot. I got off on two wrong feet. Lieutenant Boss was a lieutenant and a boss. That was like a bad version of Missy Gerber times a hundred. And the worst was Lieutenant Boss was terrible at answering questions, 'cause I still didn't know where Ms. Krane was or when she was coming back. What was *for a while*?

50

NOBODY KNOWS NOTHING

I spent the rest of the morning in the hall 'cause Lieutenant Boss forgot about me, but I didn't care. At least he couldn't yell at me for spinning. And I got to make shapes out of the dots on the ceiling. And I got to do some thinking too—but not about me and my behavior like the lieutenant wanted. I couldn't stop thinking about Ms. Krane. And I started wondering if that dumb petition was the reason my teacher was absent.

When my brain gets going real fast like that, my mouth can race ahead of it, and my body might even do stuff it shouldn't 'cause my brain is too busy to tell it not to. That was what happened at lunch. I didn't go and sit in my spot like I was supposed to. My legs walked me over to Kyle's table.

"Did Lieutenant Boss say anything about Ms. Krane?" I asked him. I had to know.

"No, nothing," Kyle said. "Maybe she's sick, Carter. She'll be back. Stop worrying."

Easy for him to say. Must be he didn't know about the peti-tion. I wanted to mention it, but I promised Grams I wouldn't tell anyone 'cause that could be bad for Ms. Krane.

I turned away and sulked over to my spot. It was time for me to do more solitary confinement at my lunch table. I wasn't even hungry.

"Sorry, Carter," voices said.

I looked up from my sandwich to find Vanessa and Mary standing there.

"Maybe if you don't say anything and sit at your desk, you won't get in trouble and Lieutenant Boss will let you stay in the classroom this afternoon?" Vanessa suggested.

"I can't do those things and everyone knows it," I mur-mured. "I need Ms. Krane. I can only do good with her."

"She'll probably be back tomorrow," Mary said, also trying to sound positive—but I wasn't feeling very hopeful. Must be they didn't know about the petition, either.

"If there's something you really need to say or ask, whisper it to me," Vanessa said. "Or Camo. I've seen you do that, but if you're at your desk, he'll be too far away, so you better just tell me. That way you get it off your chest without getting the lieutenant upset."

I was used to kids trying to make me feel bad, but these two were trying to make me feel better. Was that something colleagues did or only friends? I wished Missy were here.

"Girls, back to your table! No loitering!" the lunch aide barked.

I glanced at Vanessa and Mary. "Thanks," I said. And then I quick passed them two of my animal cookies. They smiled and hurried back to their chairs before they got in more trouble.

I looked down at my lunch. Grams had included my horoscope today. *Your coming days will be filled with challenging moments as well as uplifting surprises. With the right attitude, you will come out better in the end.* Grams musta really liked this one 'cause she was always reminding me and Brynn that attitude was a little thing that makes a big difference—which was something some famous person said once, I think.

I was gonna try to be positive, 'cause that's what Grams would want—and Ms. Krane too. I just hoped that whoever came up with this stuff knew what they were talking about.

Turns out, none of that mattered. Things were much better with Lieutenant Boss that afternoon, but that wasn't 'cause of my attitude. It was 'cause we got to watch a movie. When subs don't know what to do, a movie is always a good idea. It helped me and the lieutenant get through the rest of the day without more problems—but that didn't mean everything was suddenly all hunky-dory.

"How was your day?" Grams asked when I got home. She was in the living room putting our fall decorations inside their tote so that we could start getting the Christmas stuff out next.

I dropped onto the couch. "Awful," I moaned.

Grams stopped what she was doing. "Why?"

I told her everything. Told her all about Lieutenant Boss

and what he'd said. "Mr. Wilson hasn't heard anything. But do you know why Ms. Krane's gonna be gone for a while, Grams? Do you think it's 'cause of that petition?"

Grams's face turned serious. "Anything I say would only be a guess. We'll ask your sister and Torrie if they've heard anything when they get home from practice. Maybe Torrie's mother has seen something on that awful Village Moms site again."

There were two problems with that. First, it meant I had to wait. Second, Brynn came home alone.

"Where's Torrie?" I asked as soon as my sister walked into the house.

"I don't know," Brynn huffed. "She didn't show up at practice."

"Well, maybe you can tell me. Has her mom seen anything more about Ms. Krane on Village Moms?"

"No idea," Brynn huffed louder. Then she stormed past me, charging toward her room.

"Brynn!" Grams snapped.

Brynn stopped, but she didn't turn to look at us. "What?"

"Ms. Krane wasn't in school today and your brother is worried. His substitute told the students he's going to be in charge for a while."

"I haven't heard anything. Can I please go now?" my sister groaned.

"Fine," Grams said, but she didn't sound too happy. I

wonder now if that was when Grams started worrying about Brynn? Not me. I was still too worried about Ms. Krane.

"How come nobody knows nothing?!" I exploded.

"Because it probably is nothing," Grams shot back, "so don't go getting your underwear in a bunch. There's a nasty stomach bug going around, so the poor woman is probably just dealing with that. She'll be back soon."

I wanted to believe her, but sometimes a bad feeling is a bad feeling.

51

NAIL IN THE COFFIN

The next morning, I took the stairs two at a time, racing to get to my classroom to see if Ms. Krane was back. I jumped past my locker and landed in the doorway. The moment my feet hit the ground, all that positive attitude Ms. Krane woulda liked rushed out of me in one big woosh. I stood frozen, staring at the man sitting in her chair, feeling worse than when I found one of our chicks not breathing.

I turned around and slunk to my locker. Even though going fast was my specialty, I moved slow as a turtle putting my things away 'cause I wasn't thrilled to be stuck sitting behind my desk.

After morning announcements, the lieutenant had us take out our math books. Math wasn't terrible 'cause Lieutenant Boss was good at explaining the rules for equivalent fractions. Lieutenant Boss was real good at rules, and he was even good at showing how we might have to do this stuff if we were trying to double a recipe or cut it in half, but he didn't like us trying different ways to do a problem. Ms. Krane encouraged that 'cause she wanted thinkers and not Simon Saysers. But with the lieutenant, it was his way or the seaway.

"Ms. Krane wants us to share if we have different ways to get the answer," I tried explaining.

"Ms. Krane isn't here," Lieutenant Boss replied.

"Where is she?" I whined.

Lieutenant Boss sighed. "Class, please work on problems one through ten on page ninety-eight. Officer Avery, follow me. I'd like to have a word with you."

Out in the hall we went. The lieutenant closed the door behind us and I slid over to my spot against the wall.

"Officer Avery, I'd hoped we could do better today."

"Will Ms. Krane be back tomorrow?" I begged.

Another sigh. "I wish I had more information for you, but I haven't been told anything about when she'll be back," he confessed—and somehow I knew that was the truth.

My shoulders sagged.

"I can see that has you upset. I'm sorry. But I can't have you yelling out in the classroom and I won't tolerate you telling me how to do my job. That is disrespectful. I'm the lieutenant here."

"You're the substitute," I said, correcting him.

Lieutenant Boss's face hardened. I shouldn't have let those words jump out.

"Take whatever time you need to get yourself under control," he said after releasing a deep breath. "When you're ready to cooperate and follow the rules, you can come back into the classroom."

And that was it. Lieutenant Boss turned on his heel and marched back inside.

Lieutenant Boss had just put me in charge of my own time-out. This wasn't a punishment. It was just quiet time to get myself under control. If I needed to get the wiggles out, I could.

I stayed in the hall a while longer and my mind got busy thinking again. Thinking that Ms. Gerber had been right all along. Ms. Krane did leave—and this was a disruption. Nothing was going the way it was supposed to—including lunch.

As I walked across the cafeteria toward my spot, I suddenly heard my name being called. I stopped and glanced around.

"Carter. Over here."

I turned and spotted Vanessa and Mary waving me over. They probly wanted an animal cookie, so I scurried to their table. They always sat with Samantha Yelber and Missy, but Missy wasn't here.

"Sit with us," Vanessa said, pointing to Missy's empty seat.

It was a toss-up who looked more confused, me or Samantha Yelber. My brain had gone foggy, so I pulled out the chair and sat down, and as soon as I did, Samantha Yelber got up.

"Not happening," she said—and with plenty of attitude, but not the kind Grams liked. She grabbed her tray and found someplace else to sit. Even though I was feeling like a zombie, I still smiled at that.

"Did Lieutenant Boss yell at you in the hall?" Mary asked.

"No. He wasn't mean."

"You were out there for a while," Vanessa said, "so we were worried he got real mad at you."

"He told me I could come back when I was ready, but I got busy thinking."

"About what?" they asked.

I shrugged. "Ms. Krane."

"She's probably just dealing with the flu or a bad cold. If it was anything worse, we'd know. That's what my mother says," Mary said.

"Same," Vanessa replied, twisting her hand back and forth with her thumb and pinky sticking out.

I tried copying her gesture 'cause Grams had told me the same thing.

They looked at me and giggled—and I laughed with them.

"At least we know that petition has nothing to do with it," Vanessa said.

My eyes popped. "You know about that?!"

"The petition?" Vanessa repeated. "Yeah, we know about it. Samantha's mom was one of the parents pushing it. And Mrs. Stinger and Ms. Hornet signed it."

"Samantha's not even in our class," I said.

"I know, right?" Mary exclaimed. "We don't know why Missy is friends with her."

"But how do you know the petition isn't the reason Ms. Krane is out?" I asked.

"Because Samantha told us it was a flop," Mary explained. "My mom says they only rounded up a handful of signatures."

Vanessa nodded. "Rumor is once Principal Ryan caught wind of it, she yanked Stinger and Hornet into her office and told them to back off or she'd be forced to take more serious action. That was the nail in the coffin."

Way to go Principal Ryan, I thought. "But you never said anything about it," I complained.

"We haven't always been friends," Mary replied—and boy, that was the truth. "Besides, my mother told me not to bring it up with anyone else in school. We only whispered about it at lunch when we sat with Samantha. Another reason we're not sorry she left in a huff. We really like Ms. Krane and don't want to make things hard for her."

"My grams said pretty much the same thing!" I said, giving that twisty thing with my hand another try.

Vanessa and Mary lost it this time. They started cracking up—but not in a mean way. I gave them a big grin.

Grams had packed me my same peanut butter and jelly and it got squished, but it was still the best lunch I'd ever had. Not only did I get good news about the petition, but I also wasn't stuck sitting alone.

52

THE SHIP GOES DOWN

I told Grams about the petition being a big flop as soon as I got home from school. And that Mary's mother had said Ms. Krane probly just had the flu too. Grams wanted to know who Mary was, so I had to tell her about Mary and Vanessa and how I didn't eat lunch alone and how they told me Principal Ryan had kicked Stinger's and Hornet's butts. And after I got done telling her everything, Grams was choking back tears.

"It's okay, Grams. Ms. Krane isn't in trouble," I said, rubbing her back.

Grams nodded. "I know," she croaked. Then she gave me a good hard hug.

Brynn was at work, but I told her my good news as soon as she got home.

"That's a relief," she said—but she didn't sound like she cared. And she walked straight to her bedroom. I didn't get a chance to ask about Torrie. And neither did Grams. We chalked it up to Brynn being a grouchy teenager—we just didn't know the whole story.

No matter, I wasn't gonna let Brynn's grumpiness spoil my night. I went to bed happier than I'd been all week.

When I got to school the next day, Ms. Krane still wasn't there, but Grams had told me it can take a while to get over the flu, so me and Lieutenant Boss got through Wednesday and Thursday and almost all of Friday before our ship started to go down.

Our first close call came when Lieutenant Boss attempted our read-aloud. He took *Summer of the Gypsy Moths* and gave it to Kyle to pick up where we'd last left off. Kyle tried his hardest, but he couldn't make the story sound like Ms. Krane did with all her special voices. None of us could!

"Lieutenant Boss, stop!" I exploded after Mary finished her turn reading. "We're ruining the book. Can't you choose something else and save *Gypsy Moths* for Ms. Krane? Please. She reads it in a special way."

I was maybe getting better at not yelling out, and I wasn't trying to tell the lieutenant how to do his job again, but those words sprang from my mouth before my brain had time to proofread them. And, boy, the classroom fell dead silent after they came flying out.

The lieutenant sucked in a big breath and his face reddened. He was mad. Real mad.

"Carter's right," Kyle suddenly blurted. "We can't read it like Ms. Krane does. And she loves reading it to us."

Lieutenant Boss seemed stunned by Kyle speaking up and taking my side. So was I. But then Vanessa and Mary jumped in and did the same, and after that, Lieutenant Boss let his big breath out.

"Okay," he agreed. "We'll save *Gypsy Moths* for Ms. Krane, if that's what you want. Why don't we stick with silent reading for this afternoon. We'll revisit doing a read-aloud after I've had a chance to find something else."

"That's a great plan!" I exclaimed.

Lieutenant Boss narrowed his eyes on me and gave a slight nod. "I'm glad you approve of my decision this time, Officer Avery."

And that was maybe the funniest thing the lieutenant had said all week. But what happened next wasn't funny at all. What happened next sank our ship.

53

SOMETHING WAS WRONG

We were on our way back from specials at the end of the day on Friday when we walked past the teachers' room door . . . and Ms. Krane's baby shower poster was gone!

I froze. My class left me in the dust, but I couldn't move. Seeing that blank door took the wind out of my sails, which meant things on Lieutenant Boss's tight ship got real rocky, real fast. Sailors were expected to file into the classroom and take their seats. Lieutenant Boss had a specific routine he wanted us to follow when it came to packing up. But I couldn't focus on that right now. This was an emergency. I ran to catch up and burst into our classroom.

"Lieutenant Boss, what happened to Ms. Krane's poster?" I hollered.

"Officer Avery, I thought we were done playing this game. It's time for dismissal and we have a checklist to follow."

"But do you know where she is?" I cried. That missing sign had me real scared, so there was no stopping my mouth.

Lieutenant Boss marched across the room to where I was standing. "Officer Avery, I haven't a clue what you're yelling about, but it's obvious you need to take a minute to get yourself under control," he said real quiet and calm. Then he steered me into the hallway and gently closed the door.

But now wasn't the time to get myself under control. I didn't need him or anyone else to give me answers. I already knew the truth. Something was wrong.

54

STRIKING A DEAL

I grabbed my backpack from my locker and took off before anyone else came out. I sprinted onto the bus as soon as Mr. Wilson stopped in the pickup circle. I flung my bag in my seat and told him about Ms. Krane's poster gone missing.

"Maybe it fell down and no one's had the chance to put it back up yet," he suggested. "Stuff like that happens all the time."

I hadn't thought of that, but I guessed that was possible.

"You'll probably see it hanging up again when you get back to school after the weekend."

"But what if I get there and it's still missing?"

"Well, then you and me can do some investigating, 'cause I'll be ready to start worrying right along with you. But we'll do it together, and not before Monday. Deal?"

"Okay."

"So no worrying over the weekend. That's part of the deal," Mr. Wilson emphasized.

"Okay," I agreed. "No worrying."

It was a good deal, but that didn't stop me from telling Grams about the missing poster and asking her if she'd heard anything when I got home. That wasn't me worrying. It was me wondering.

"No" was still her answer.

"Do you think Ms. Krane will be back on Monday?" I begged.

"CJ, I don't have a crystal ball, so I don't know."

"You always say everyone around here is in everyone else's business, but nobody still knows nothing about Ms. Krane," I griped.

"People around here love to gossip," Grams said, "but they don't always know the truth or the whole story. And good for Ms. Krane if she can keep people from spreading her business."

"I don't want to spread her business. I just want to know it. That's different."

"All's I can say is you'll know when she wants you to know. Now get yourself ready, we're heading to Brynn's swim scrimmage."

"Now?" I groaned. "But I'm hungry. I want a snack."

"We don't have time. I'll stop at McDonald's on the way."

"Now you're talking," I cheered.

A cheeseburger and fries and I forgot all about being upset—at least for a little while.

55

SWIM SCRIMMAGE

I'd forgotten today was the annual Red versus Black Swim Scrimmage for the girls' and boys' teams. It wasn't a boys versus girls thing, though. Each team was a mix of both. The girls' season had just ended, so this was their final splash, and the boys' season was getting underway, so it was their big kickoff event. The scrimmage was an important fundraiser for both teams 'cause a lot of people went to watch and it was also a great way to get kids—like me—interested about swimming in school.

The swim meets always got crazy loud 'cause all the shouting and cheering bounced off the walls inside the pool gym, but this one took the prize for loudest. I liked the excitement but Grams thought it was wasted energy 'cause the swimmers never stopped screaming for their teammates.

"Can you even hear anything with all that racket?" she'd asked Brynn once.

"The only voice I ever hear is CJ's."

"Guess your brother better become a swim coach, then," Grams joked.

I laughed. But you know what, ever since Brynn told us that, I made sure to scream my loudest when she raced. That was easy.

It was during the diving portion of the meets that I had a really hard time, 'cause Brynn was the team's top 1M diver, except you had to be silent during the diving or the referees would throw you out. So just when I wanted to do my wildest and loudest cheering, I had to zip it. I kept both hands clamped over my mouth or else I was sure to break that rule. But as soon as Brynn did her dive and came up to the surface, I let loose and screamed my head off for her.

The thing that was neat about the Red versus Black Scrimmage was I also got to cheer for Torrie and Justin. Torrie was good. She did this medley race where you had to do four different swim strokes down and back. She was usually real fast, but not today. Grams said she seemed off. If "off" meant slow, then I agreed. And she wasn't the only one. Brynn had an "off" day too.

Justin brought his A game, though. They saved his race for last and he didn't disappoint. He flew through the water. He almost broke the school record for butterfly, which Grams said was a real hard stroke. I was gonna ask him to teach it to me if I had lessons with him again.

The only part of the swim scrimmage I didn't like was when we had to wait for Brynn and Torrie after it was all over. They always took forever getting changed. I tried getting Grams to leave but she wanted to find out my sister's plans before taking off, so we were stuck standing outside the school. Brynn finally came walking out with Justin after most of the team had already left.

"Hi, Mrs. Sims. Hi, Carter," Justin said.

"Way to kick butt," I told him. "You're gonna smash that record soon."

He laughed. "Thanks."

"Where's Torrie?" Grams asked my sister. It'd been the same question all week. And we got the same answer.

"She's doing her own thing," Brynn huffed, a bit snippy.

Where's Torrie? reminded me of *Where's Ms. Krane?* "Have you heard anything about Ms. Krane?" I asked next. "She wasn't in school again and her baby shower poster wasn't hanging up."

"CJ, I'm not your personal detective," Brynn snapped. "I haven't been trying to track down your teacher. I have no clue where she is."

That stung. "What's your problem?!" I yelled.

"Enough," Grams scolded. "I don't need you two having one of your spats in public."

I glared at my sister. I was glad she stunk at diving today.

"Do you need a ride home or not?" Grams asked her.

"No," Brynn spat, snapping at Grams now.

"Fine. Home by eleven. C'mon, CJ. We're leaving," Grams said.

"Bye, Mrs. Sims. Have a good night. Bye, Carter," Justin said, giving me a thumbs-up.

I waved—but I was still mad at Brynn. Then me and Grams walked across the parking lot and climbed inside Leopold—and just in time, 'cause a rusty brown truck came roaring past, peeling rubber and spitting fumes on its way out of the school.

That just added fuel to the fire, 'cause Grams was already hot over Brynn's attitude. "Don't you ever drive like that!" she barked. "You hear me?"

I was too busy craning my neck, staring at the back of the truck to answer. I wanted to ask Grams if she'd spotted the driver or anyone in the passenger's seat, but I didn't want to make her more upset.

"You know something, that Justin is a nice boy," Grams said, breaking the silence after we'd driven a ways and she'd had a chance to cool down. "I hope your sister sees that. He'd make a fine boyfriend."

"Grams, that's gross. I don't want to talk about that."

She laughed. "'Course, maybe that's why Brynn wasn't herself on that diving board today. She's distracted with the boy."

"That's enough, Grams," I scolded, shaking my head.

She laughed more.

Turns out Grams was right about a couple of things. Justin was a good guy, and Brynn was distracted, but not by *that* boy.

56

KRITZ'S TREE FARM

I rolled out of bed and made my way to the kitchen the next morning. Grams had to be cooking a big breakfast 'cause something smelled real good.

My nose was right. Pancakes and sausage were on the griddle, but Grams was sitting at the table.

"Good morning, CJ," my sister said. "I'm sorry about the way I treated you yesterday. I was upset about something and took it out on you. I'm sorry."

I went to bed mad at her, but just like that, I wasn't angry anymore. I was hungry. "It's okay."

"Good." She gave me a quick hug, then turned back to the griddle.

I sat down across from Grams, and Brynn slid a stack of banana foster pancakes in front of me. My eyes got real big. I leaned forward and took a big whiff, licking my chops.

"Eat up," Grams said. "We've got a big day ahead."

"Doing what?" I asked, stuffing a forkful in my mouth.

"Going to Kritz's to get our Christmas tree."

"Today?!" I exclaimed, spitting pancake bits on the table.

"Chew your food before you try talking!" Grams scolded.

"Sorry," I mumbled.

"Yes, today," Grams answered. "We're leaving after breakfast so we can get there before it's a madhouse. Now, eat up."

I ate a lot 'cause it was good and I ate fast 'cause I was excited. Then I let Shelby lick my plate clean 'cause she'd been waiting patiently, and after that I thanked my sister for the special breakfast and told her to hurry and get ready. I shoved my plate in the dishwasher and rushed off to get my outside clothes on.

Kritz's Tree Farm was the best. The workers dressed like people from the movie *A Christmas Carol*, with top hats and scarves and all that stuff, so it felt like you were walking through an old village. They even had a group that sang Christmas carols. It was real festive. (That's what Brynn said.) But getting our tree was still my favorite part.

First thing you did when you got to the farm was pick any saw off the barn wall where they had them hanging and then you walked out into the field and hunted high and low until you found the perfect tree. After you found it, you had to lie on the ground on your side and saw it down. Last year was the first time Grams let me use the saw. I got halfway through the trunk, but Torrie had to finish the job for me 'cause my arms got tired. This year I was gonna do it all by myself!

It was always a great day. There was a lot to it—and I was ready to go! I had my old pants on so Grams wouldn't care when I got them dirty, and my play-outside hoodie over the top of a long-sleeve shirt and a pair of gloves and a winter hat. And my boots. I was dressed and waiting for my sister—like always. It was another round of Hurry Up and Wait. I hated that game.

"C'mon, Brynn, you don't have to get all fancy. Let's go!" I hollered.

"Give her a second," Grams whispered. "She's on the phone."

"Who with? I don't hear her talking."

"With Torrie. They're doing that texting thing. None of you kids know how to call anymore."

"I'm gonna call when I get a phone," I promised. "I can't stand typing, unless the Dragon does it for me."

Grams smirked, then quick pulled my hat down over my eyes. "You're one of a kind, Carter Avery," she said.

I fixed my hat and then Brynn finally came walking out of her room.

"Well?" Grams asked.

"Torrie isn't coming."

"But she always comes with us," I protested. "She needs to see me cut the tree down all by myself."

"Maybe next year," Brynn grumbled. She grabbed her coat from the closet and then her phone rang. More waiting.

"Hello? . . . Hi . . . We're going to Kritz's Tree Farm. Want to tag along? . . . We'll pick you up on the way."

Brynn slid her phone into her pocket. "That was Justin. He's coming with us."

"Oh, okay," Grams said, smirking.

"I'll drive," Brynn said, snatching the car keys and heading outside.

"Justin called," I whispered to Grams.

"Told you I liked that boy," she replied, giving me a wink.

57

NEAR COLLISION

It was busy when we got to Kritz's. Justin helped me pick a saw and then we headed out to the field. Grams didn't venture far 'cause she didn't want to wander all over tarnation if there was a good one calling our name near the front. That never happened, so I told her it was a waste of time, but she was gonna make sure.

So me and Brynn and Justin split up and began searching farther out. Those two stayed kinda close together, but I took off. The best trees were the ones in the way back where no one else wanted to walk—not near the front.

I put my head down and marched forward, stride after stride, determined to find the perfect tree—until somebody who wasn't watching where they were going came huffing and puffing from the next row over and stepped right in front of me. We almost collided—and I was carrying a saw!

"Carter!" a girl shrieked. "Watch where you're going!"

"Me? You watch it!" I shot back.

We'd both yelled and shouted after scaring the bejeebers out of each other, and then we just stood there, staring at one another. I hadn't seen Missy Gerber since before Thanksgiving.

"What're you doing here?" I asked after calming down.

She giggled. "What do you think? I'm getting my tree."

"Oh."

"How's school?" she wanted to know.

I frowned. "Terrible. Ms. Krane was out all week and we got stuck with Lieutenant Boss. He's as bad as they come."

"I bet he's not as bad as my mother."

My eyes popped. "Really? Why?"

"She expects me to know everything without teaching it and gets mad at me when I don't."

"Your mom is your teacher?" That sounded awful—even worse than I thought the Owl was gonna be before I knew the truth about her.

"For now," Missy said, "but we're not a very good fit for homeschooling. Most days I have to go into work with her because she can't stay home. Her business needs her. It never takes me long to get through my assignments, and then I'm left with nothing to do. It's boring. And my mother gets frustrated about that too."

"Well, if it makes you feel better, Lieutenant Boss says he's gonna be running our ship for a while," I complained.

"Of course he is," Missy replied. She quick slapped her hand over her mouth.

My forehead scrunched. "What's wrong?"

"My mother made me promise not to tell."

"Tell what?"

Missy bit her lip.

"Tell what?" I pressed.

"Carter, Ms. Krane had her baby."

My scowl deepened. "What?!"

"My mother got a call from Ms. Krane's mom yesterday. She ordered balloons and a gift basket to be delivered to the hospital."

"Why did she call your mom for that?"

"My mother's business is Gerber's Gourmet Gifts. Ms. Krane had her baby the day after Thanksgiving."

"But her baby wasn't supposed to be born yet."

"True," Missy said, "but sometimes babies come early. They're called preemies."

"Melissa!" the Crow cawed. "Where are you?"

"I better go."

"Wait. Is Ms. Krane's baby okay?"

Missy shook her head. "I don't know."

"Melissa!"

"Carter, I'm sorry. Hope you find a good tree."

Missy hurried off but I stayed frozen in place. All this time I'd been wondering and worrying about Ms. Krane—but never her baby. Until now!

I dropped my saw and turned and ran, racing back through the trees. I had to find Grams.

58

TIMBER!

"Grams, it's all my fault!" I cried, running up to her.

"What're you talking about? What's wrong?" she asked, sounding frightened.

"I used to think Ms. Krane's baby would be better off not being born than being stuck with the Owl for a mother, and now her baby is a preemie and might die. It's all my fault!"

"CJ, what just happened?"

I unloaded everything that Missy Gerber had just told me. I was all snot, blubbering and sniffling when I got done.

"Carter Avery, this isn't your fault," Grams said, taking me by the shoulders. "Just because you thought something once doesn't make it happen. You'd need special powers for that. Besides, you don't think that anymore, do you?"

I shook my head and dragged my sleeve under my nose. "No. That was before I knew Ms. Krane," I croaked.

"Okay, then. Stop this nonsense and get ahold of yourself."

"But what're we gonna do?" I asked, still worrying.

"We're gonna get our tree like we planned," Grams said. "There's no reason to panic. Lots of babies are born early, and Ms. Krane was close enough to her due date that hers should be in good shape. It'll need to spend extra time in the hospital, I'm sure, but her baby should be fine in the long run."

I sniffed and wiped my nose again. "You promise?"

"I promise I'm telling the truth. I don't think you need to worry."

I sucked in my breath and nodded. "Okay."

"CJ, where've you been?!" Brynn exclaimed. "We've been calling your name. We found our tree."

"Let's have a look," Grams said, wrapping her arm around me and pulling me close.

Brynn was no dummy. She saw I was upset, but she didn't pester me with questions. "Justin stayed with the tree so no one else takes it," she said. "C'mon."

We followed her, zigzagging our way through the rows.

"That's a mighty fine tree," Grams said when we got there. "Good pick."

"Okay, Carter. You're up," Justin said. "The moment you've been waiting for."

I looked at him with wide eyes.

"Where's your saw?" Brynn asked.

I shrugged.

"Unless you're a beaver, I don't think you can cut this down without one," Justin joked.

I cracked a small grin.

"Don't sweat it," he said. "I'll run to the barn and grab us another one. You guys stay here."

As soon as he disappeared, Brynn wanted to know what was wrong. There was no keeping my sister in the dark. Grams filled her in and then Brynn gave me a hug, which made my eyes water again.

I wiped my nose on my sleeve and looked up at her. "Is Justin your boyfriend?"

Brynn yanked my hat down over my eyes and Grams laughed.

"Okay, Muscles. You ready?" Justin asked, returning with a new saw.

I fixed my hat and smirked at Brynn. Then I took the saw and got down on the ground. And I didn't need any help. I sawed through the trunk all by myself.

"Timber!" Justin yelled.

I stood up and raised my arms in victory, a big smile spread across my face.

That was how the rest of the weekend went for me. When I got to thinking about Ms. Krane *and* her baby, I'd start worrying. (Now that I had some real information about my teacher, my deal with Mr. Wilson was off.) But if I kept busy, then I was okay—so it was a good thing Grams had lots for us to do, starting with getting our tree home.

59

KEEPING BUSY

Justin got Grams's vote and mine for being Brynn's boyfriend after he came back to our house to help us carry our tree inside and get it standing straight in our stand—which was a job that wasn't getting any easier for Grams and was still more than me and Brynn could manage on our own.

Grams insisted on feeding Justin lunch after that, and then our real work began. We had tree-trimming to do and putting out all the holiday decorations around the house. I knew Brynn more than liked Justin when she let him stay, 'cause tree-trimming was a special time for us.

We had some First Christmas ornaments from when Mom and Dad were alive and just married. And there were Baby's First Christmas ones from when Brynn came along. My favorites were the decorations we'd made in preschool 'cause they were funny. There was one with my handprint and a different one with Brynn's foot, but the silliest was the real messy-looking snowman blob that I'd glued together and Brynn's cyclops gingerbread woman.

"Whoa, I didn't know you were so talented at arts and crafts," Justin teased my sister.

"Shut up," she said, socking him on the shoulder.

I laughed. Tree-trimming was one of those happy-sad times, but mostly happy now.

Justin's mom picked him up after we finished the tree and Grams ended up on the phone, so me and Brynn put out the rest of the house decorations by ourselves. We tried playing a Christmas movie in the background at the same time, but the blasted TV was throwing a fit again, and besides that, Grams had us keeping the volume so low now that we could barely hear it anyways, so we used Brynn's computer instead.

By the time *The Grinch* ended, I was ready for bed. It had been a long and busy day, and I had baking and frosting and decorating and eating Christmas cookies to look forward to tomorrow. Justin was coming over to help—but not Torrie. I didn't ask.

As beat as I was, the second my head hit the pillow and everything got quiet, my brain took off racing with worry again. And it was double worry now 'cause I had Ms. Krane *and* her baby to think about. Luckily, Grams came in with a surprise—or I should say half-a-surprise, 'cause she didn't tell me everything. Not yet.

She walked into my bedroom and took a seat on the edge of my bed. "That was Mason I was on the phone with earlier."

I sat up. "Mason? He called you?"

"Yes, Mason. After Susie's peculiar behavior around Ms. Krane on Thanksgiving, he checked in on her. He was able to visit her yesterday. He said she's doing well—and her baby too. He says not to worry."

"Susie knew," I muttered.

"Susie knew," Grams repeated. "That dog is pretty special."

"Why didn't he call us sooner?"

"He's sorry about that. But Ms. Krane didn't want visitors or questions. She had too much going on, which I can understand. I'm not certain when she told Principal Ryan the news, but she asked that it not be shared. If it weren't for Susie, Mason wouldn't have known."

I frowned.

"CJ, the important thing is that Ms. Krane and her baby are doing well."

I nodded. "I'm glad Mason got to see her. Well, sort of."

Grams smiled. "Me too," she agreed, patting my leg. "Now settle down and try to get some sleep."

After Grams left, my mind still raced for a little while, but it was happy thoughts, 'cause her half-a-surprise did put all my worrying to rest—for now.

60

HEAVENLY DINER

I rolled out of bed on Monday morning and used the bathroom, then made my way into the kitchen to see about breakfast. I didn't smell bacon or anything yummy cooking, so that meant the usual—boring toast or a bowl of cereal.

"Never mind fixing yourself anything to eat. We'll be going out for breakfast this morning," Grams said.

"Really?! But what about school?"

"Never mind school," she scoffed, which made my eyes pop real wide. "An extra day away won't hurt you none."

Now, that did sound good!

"Go brush your teeth. And maybe fix your hair and change your shirt."

I had a gazillion questions, but I hurried off and got myself ready and then we climbed in Leopold. I tried asking Grams where we were going but she wasn't telling. This was an all-the-way surprise, my favorite kind. So I sat back and sang some of Mr. Wilson's driving songs, 'cause it felt like that kind of morning. When Grams whipped Leopold into the Heavenly Diner parking lot, I almost smacked my head on the ceiling I jumped so high off my seat.

"I love this place!" I cheered.

"Thank goodness we're here," Grams groaned. "I couldn't take much more of that singing."

I stuck my tongue out at her.

Grams got us parked and then we hopped out and walked into the diner—even though I wanted to run. I stepped through the door and breathed in the smells and looked around—and that was when I got hit with the big whopper. Ms. Krane was there. This was better than when I got my salt gun. It was better than two salt guns, 'cause Mason and Susie were sitting at the table with her!

Then something weird happened. Instead of running over to my teacher, I stepped back. Ms. Krane didn't look the same. She looked pale and tired, like a sleepy snowy owl.

"It's okay, CJ," Grams whispered, putting her hand on my shoulder and bending closer. "We invited Ms. Krane to break-fast this morning so you could see her."

"You did?" I croaked.

"Yes. Mason and I did. So whaddya say? You ready?"

I swallowed. I wanted to be ready, but my legs still wouldn't move—not until Susie came and got me. She left Mason's side and walked across the diner all by herself. She rubbed against my legs and nuzzled her nose under my hand. And then she guided me and Grams to her table.

Ms. Krane's purple stain got all crinkly when she saw us coming 'cause she smiled real big—and that made my eyes get wet and my insides hurt. But it was a good hurt. She got out of her chair and greeted me with a fierce owl hug, wrapping both her wings around me. "I've missed you," she said.

"I've missed you too," I said back—and boy, was that the truth.

Ms. Krane said hi to Grams next while Mason shook my hand and then we sat down. The waitress came and took our orders, which was a round of coffees and some other stuff for the grown-ups. I didn't hear what they got 'cause I was too focused on ordering my Belgian waffle with whipped cream and strawberries on top.

I heard what Ms. Krane asked after our waitress left, though. "So how's school going, Carter?"

I looked at Grams, then down at the table and sighed. "Not great," I confessed.

"I'm sorry to hear that," Ms. Krane replied. "What's not going well?"

"Ms. Krane, I can't do school without you. You're the best. When're you coming back?"

She grinned, but she didn't laugh 'cause there was nothing funny about how I was feeling. "Carter, the truth is I don't know. A lot will go into that decision, but if I do come back, it won't be until after Christmas."

"*If?*" I repeated. "You mean, you might not come back . . . ever? Ms. Krane, didn't you hear me? I can't do school without you."

My voice cracked but I didn't let myself cry. I kept going 'cause she needed to hear the truth. "Me and substitutes go together like me and Mrs. Stinger—and you know how bad that was. And this new guy, Lieutenant Boss, is ruining everything."

I was real upset, so my mouth was getting ahead of my brain and words were jumping out. "He yells at me if I forget to raise my hand. He won't let me spin on the counter. And he doesn't know how to read with voices. We can't finish *Summer of the Gypsy Moths* without you."

Then I sighed, and my chin dropped and my shoulders slumped. "And I don't get to be a dragon slayer anymore," I said, my voice almost a whisper.

Our waitress arrived with our food then. She passed out our plates and asked if we needed anything else. I stared at my Belgian waffle. I wasn't hungry anymore.

Ms. Krane reached across the table and took my hand in hers. "Carter, if I truly am the best, as you claim, then that means you'll prove it because I will have prepared you to continue being your best—even without me."

"You mean, I have to keep being your pudding?"

Ms. Krane frowned.

Grams chuckled. "It's the proof in her pudding," she corrected. "And yes, that's exactly what it means."

Ms. Krane giggled. "Yes," she agreed. "I guess that is what it means. But I tell you what. I will be seeing Principal Ryan this afternoon when she swings by to drop off my shower gifts that people so kindly purchased, and I'll encourage her to have a chat with Lieutenant Boss to straighten a few things out. That was something I'd planned to do myself before going on leave, but everything happened faster than I expected."

I nodded. I was glad Ms. Krane was still getting her presents, even though the shower got canceled. I just hoped she convinced Principal Ryan to have that chat with Lieutenant Boss, 'cause like he'd promised, it was gonna be me and him for a while.

"Missy still isn't back," I blurted, suddenly thinking of her. "She's being homeschooled."

"Unfortunately, I'm not sure I can help with that one," Ms. Krane said.

"I know," I grumbled.

"Chin up, Carter," Mason said. "A positive attitude is the rule. Now, let's eat."

61

WE'LL SEE

After one bite of my waffle, I was suddenly starving again. I wolfed the whole thing down—with Susie's help. She deserved a few nibbles for being such a good dog. We agreed, it was super yummy.

Grams shouldn't have told me to change my shirt 'cause I had syrup and a couple strawberry stains on it by the end, but that was nothing new. All's I can say is that the big breakfast must've woken up another part of my brain, or maybe the break in our talking gave me time to do more of that thinking that Ms. Krane liked, 'cause all of a sudden I realized something.

"Ms. Krane, where's your baby?"

Grams smirked. "I was wondering if you were gonna notice something was missing."

I made a face.

Ms. Krane took a sip of her orange juice. "Oliver needs to stay in the hospital for a little longer," she explained.

"His name is Oliver? Your baby's a boy?"

Ms. Krane smiled. "Yes. I have a son."

I smiled back. "How long does he have to stay in the hospital for?"

"Since he came early, Oliver needs special care and attention to help him grow bigger and stronger before he can leave. The doctors are hoping I can bring him home in time for Christmas—my parents are too. They're anxious to meet their new grandson but I told them to hold off. I'm fine and there's no sense rushing out here when he's still in the hospital."

"That's a long time to wait," I whispered.

"It's a few more weeks, but Oliver has his own incubator to keep him safe and warm, so he's happy."

"An incubator like Peeper had? Do you have to turn him and keep a close eye on the temperature and humidity?"

Ms. Krane chuckled. "Sort of like that. The nurses definitely keep careful watch over him when I'm not there. But it's hard for me to leave him. I spend all day and night with him, which is why I can't be in school right now."

"But when he gets bigger and stronger, you'll be able to come back?" I asked, fingers crossed.

Ms. Krane sighed. "We'll see."

All the hope I was holding rushed out of me in one big exhale. "We'll see" was the worst answer in the world. "We'll see" was just a tricky way for grown-ups to get out of telling you the bad news until later.

When the check came, Mason snatched the bill from the table. "My treat," he told Ms. Krane and Grams.

"Mason, you don't have to do that. Inviting me to breakfast was treat enough," Ms. Krane protested.

"That wasn't a treat," Grams said. "That was necessary. You've been spending sunup till sundown in that hospital. You need to eat and take care of yourself so you're able to keep caring for that sweet baby boy."

"Thank you," Ms. Krane said.

Suddenly, I found a little bit of hope in my next breath. "Well, if Oliver is gonna be in the hospital for a while, that means Ms. Krane will need to eat again before he comes home, right?"

Grams pursed her lips and stared at me.

"So maybe we can do breakfast again," I suggested.

"That depends," Mason said. "Are you paying?"

"I don't have any money!"

Everyone laughed 'cause Mason was teasing. Then Ms. Krane leaned closer. "I'll make a deal with you, Carter. If you can keep being my pudding while I'm away, we'll do another breakfast."

"Deal," I said.

"I know you can do it," Ms. Krane whispered.

Saying and doing were two different things, especially with Lieutenant Boss running our ship, but when your teacher believes in you, anything is possible.

62

DETOUR

Grams said I could take the whole day off since I'd already missed the morning, but I went to school that afternoon, ready to be my best even without Ms. Krane there. Ms. Krane gave me permission to tell the class her good news. Besides, I couldn't be her proof in the pudding from home.

I walked into the classroom when everyone was getting settled from recess. My math book, different papers, and my cow journal were waiting for me on my desk.

"That's the work you missed this morning," Lieutenant Boss explained.

"Can I take it into the hall and get started?" I asked.

"Um. Sure," Lieutenant Boss said, thrown off by my question. "We're just going to be silent reading, so go ahead and I'll come and get you when we move on to something new."

"Thanks, but could I make a class announcement first?"

"Um. Go ahead," Lieutenant Boss said, thrown off again.

I marched to the front of the room. "Attention, everyone!" I yelled. "I have breaking news." I waited for it to be quiet, even though it was quiet already, and then I spilled the beans. "Ms. Krane had her baby!" I gushed. "He came early—that's why she's been out. No flu," I said, glancing at Mary and shrugging.

"She had a boy?!" Kyle hollered.

"Yup. His name is Oliver," I answered.

"That's a good name," Kyle replied. "Oliver Krane sounds like a quarterback."

"Or a vet," Vanessa countered.

"Or a pilot traveling the world," Mary suggested.

"Or a lieutenant," Lieutenant Boss added, joining the fun. And for the first time, Lieutenant Boss made us laugh. That was when I knew we were going to be okay.

"How are Olivia—I mean, Ms. Krane—and Oliver doing?" Lieutenant Boss asked, turning serious again.

"They're doing great," I said. "Oliver has to stay in the hospital until he gets bigger and stronger, but Ms. Krane is there with him every day."

"How come you know all this?" Kyle asked. "Did you get to talk to her or something? That's not fair."

"Life isn't always fair, Officer Pattie," Lieutenant Boss said. "And sometimes people are lucky."

I wasn't sure if Kyle or some of my other classmates liked that answer, but it seemed to work. I *was* lucky.

"So when is Ms. Krane coming back?" Vanessa asked.

"She isn't sure. So just like the lieutenant told us. He's going to be running this ship for a while," I explained.

"And I'll do all I can to keep us on course and sailing smoothly," Lieutenant Boss promised.

"And we'll do our part too," I said, "'cause Ms. Krane is counting on us."

Lieutenant Boss gave me a curious look and I smiled. I'd show him.

I scooped up the things on my desk and marched out of the classroom. Lieutenant Boss watched me but didn't say anything more. Kyle gave me a fist bump when I passed his chair and Mary and Vanessa smiled.

I closed the door behind me when I stepped into the hall—and then I took a detour and kept walking. My brain didn't have time to think up this idea. It was my feet doing the talking—and they carried me all the way down to the office, past Mrs. Rosa, and straight to my Dragon's lair.

I didn't know if there was any writing in my stack of work that I was supposed to do, but I needed the Dragon's help. There were some things I needed to tell the lieutenant, and even though we'd had our conversations in the hall, it would be better if I put this stuff in writing so he didn't forget.

I plopped in my spinning chair and whirled around in a few circles to get energized, and then I slipped on my headphones and woke up the Dragon. And here's what I wrote:

To Lieutenant Boss, Sir:

I had breakfast with Ms. Krane. Her and my friends Mason and Susie too. That's why I missed school this morning. I found out you and me are gonna be spending more time together, so maybe we can start over.

Here are some things about me:

1. I live with my grams and my sister, Brynn.

2. My parents died in a car crash when I was a baby.

3. I have a real hard time sitting still and a harder time not blurting things out—but I'm getting better.

4. Ms. Krane lets me sit on the counter and spin in the classroom as long as it doesn't bother anyone.

5. For writing I go to my Dragon's lair. The Dragon helped me with this letter.

6. Mason is blind and his dog is Susie and sometimes they come visit our class and everyone loves them.

From,
Officer Avery

When I finished my letter, I hit print and took off my headphones. I'd done a good job of keeping my voice low when talking to the Dragon 'cause I didn't want Principal Ryan or Ms. Garcia to come check on me. I wasn't ready to answer all their questions. But once my ears were free, I heard a different voice that wasn't trying to keep quiet.

"I would like to speak to Principal Ryan."

At the sound of her cawing, my throat went dry. The Crow was back.

"Of course, I'll let her know you're here, Ms. Gerber," Mrs. Rosa replied. "You can have a seat. It should only be a minute."

"I only have a minute, so you can tell her this will be quick."

I tiptoed to the door and peeked down the hall. Ms. Gerber was sitting in my red chair. Her beady eyes narrowed when she spotted my head poking around the corner.

I jumped back. What was she doing here?

"Good afternoon, Ms. Gerber," I heard Principal Ryan say, greeting the Crow. "You can come right in."

Their footsteps grew closer. Closer and louder. Then they turned and disappeared into Principal Ryan's office. The door closed behind them.

I scurried to the wall between me and Principal Ryan's office and tried to listen—but there was no yelling or shouting this time. I only heard mumbling—and it didn't last long.

Next thing I knew, Principal Ryan's door opened and the Crow landed inside my space.

"Young man, you can expect to see Melissa in school

tomorrow. She's insisted on returning, claiming she has some-thing in Ms. Krane's classroom that she's never had before. I hope you can prove to me this was worth it."

I gulped and gave a slight nod. Then the Crow turned and flew off, and I started breathing again.

Was there a job for grown-ups where all you did was prove stuff? 'Cause that was a job for me. All of a sudden, I had to be Missy's proof in the pudding, too, but I was happy about that—until I wasn't.

63

MAIL DELIVERY

I waited until the end of the day, when it was just me and the lieutenant left in the classroom, to give him my letter. I wanted him to read it when no one else was around to interrupt him. And on top of that it was a special delivery 'cause I'd sealed my letter in an envelope that I found in my Dragon's lair and wrote *Lieutenant Boss* across it—which wasn't easy to spell and looked sloppy even though I'd tried to make it the legerble way.

I also added a number seven to my list, which took me a long time to write.

7. FYI: Missy Gerber might be coming back. She can be bossy because she knows a lot, but she's my friend.

"Lieutenant Boss, this is for you," I said, handing him my letter after I saw the big yellow taxi pull into the parking lot.

Lieutenant Boss took the envelope and stared at me; then I turned and high-tailed it out of there.

64

TOLD YOU SO

I got to school the next morning and Missy was already there, putting stuff in her locker.

"You're back!" I cheered.

"Hi, Carter," she said, and smiled.

I smiled bigger.

"Officer Avery, I'd like to have a word with you after everyone's gone inside," Lieutenant Boss announced, stepping into the hall.

I swallowed and nodded. Was he mad about my letter?

"Officer Gerber, welcome aboard. It's nice to have you joining us."

"Thank you, sir. I'm glad to be back," Missy replied, standing up. "And if you don't mind, I'd like to have a word with you after you're done with Officer Avery."

Lieutenant Boss shot me a wide-eyed look like, *Is she serious?* I wanted to say, *Told you so,* but I quick covered my mouth before those words jumped out.

Missy closed her locker and strolled past me and the lieutenant into the classroom. Lieutenant Boss followed her and that was a good thing 'cause I was about to burst. I couldn't keep *told you so* in much longer.

The rest of my classmates finished up at their lockers and went inside, and then Lieutenant Boss returned to have his word with me. I stood at attention with my back against the wall the way he liked.

"Officer Avery, I wanted to thank you for your letter. I found it informative—and helpful."

I grinned.

"My job as lieutenant is to get the most out of my crew. In my steadfast determination to establish rule, I seemed to have forgotten that means understanding how to get the most out of each officer. Your letter was a good reminder of that."

"I'm glad, sir."

"You mentioned that you had breakfast with Olivia. Ms. Krane. So rather than just hearing about what happened, you got to see her. I bet that was nice."

"Yes, it was. Lieutenant Boss, do you know Ms. Krane? You keep calling her Olivia."

"That's affirmative. She and I met while volunteering at a food pantry."

"*Last Stop on Market Street,*" I remembered out loud. "Ms. Krane read us that book and told us a little bit about the food pantry."

"There are several veterans who show up from time to time,

which is why I like to go," Lieutenant Boss said. "I'm able to talk to them and provide comfort and help when possible. But Olivia—Ms. Krane—is able to connect with them in a unique way. The birthmark on her face has made life challenging—"

"It's a part-jelly stain," I interrupted.

Lieutenant Boss's face twisted. "What?"

"It's a part-jelly stain," I repeated. "Her birthmark," I explained.

"Whatever it is, Ms. Krane exemplifies resilience because she's had to endure and persevere many times along the way because of it. She's a special bird."

"Owl," I corrected.

Lieutenant Boss gave me a curious look.

"She's the Owl," I said, pointing to our bulletin board.

He glanced at the board and nodded. "Indeed." Then he put his gaze back on me and handed me an envelope with my name written across the front. "Officer Avery, why don't you head inside and man your battle station. I need to have that word with Officer Gerber now."

"I warned you about her, sir."

Lieutenant Boss did something then that he hadn't ever done. He laughed. He laughed hard. "Yes, you did," he coughed.

I laughed with him. Then I marched into the classroom and took a seat on my counter space and said hi to Camo. I'd missed him. And then I opened my mail.

Officer Avery,

I appreciate your honesty. And I agree, getting to know one another sounds like a good way for us to start over.

1. I earned my teaching degree as a young man but never used it because I joined the navy.

2. I was a Culinary Specialist in the navy, which is a fancy way of saying I was the cook in charge of the kitchen. I did that for a while before changing paths and going on to become a lieutenant.

3. After retiring, I had to find something to do. Like you, I have a hard time sitting still. I tried substituting in the older grades and had a bad experience. I took the nice-guy approach and paid for it. The students took advantage of me and were downright disrespectful. I vowed never to let that happen again, which is why I showed up here meaning business.

4. Being in charge of a fourth-grade classroom is scarier than serving on a battleship. Don't tell anyone I said that.

5. I will let you continue to visit your dragon.

6. I like the idea of having Mason and Susie visit.
   I will contact them.

From,

Lieutenant Boss

I folded up the lieutenant's paper and slid it back inside my envelope. It was a good letter—and a good new start.

65

SCHOOL GETS BETTER

After a rocky beginning, we hit smoother sailing and school got better. Maybe it was my letter or the lieutenant's. Maybe it was the word Missy had with Lieutenant Boss or the fact that I'd finally seen Ms. Krane. Maybe Principal Ryan talked to the lieutenant. Don't ask me, but it was better—and that was what was important.

For starters, Lieutenant Boss saw that me and Missy were a good team, and pretty good at math too. He had us do some examples on the board. Missy did the writing and we both did the explaining. Lieutenant Boss said we did a better job at explaining than he did, and a bunch of the class agreed. Kyle and Mary got turns at the board after that, and Vanessa shared a way of doing one problem that none of us had thought of. Ms. Krane would've liked that. Lieutenant Boss was being smart and getting the most out of his crew by getting the most out of each officer.

Another smart thing Lieutenant Boss did was get the audio book for *Summer of the Gypsy Moths* from the library so we could listen to the rest of the story that way. We voted and everyone agreed we were too close to the end to keep waiting for Ms. Krane's return. It wasn't our teacher doing the reading, but I liked knowing things turned out happy for those girls in the story. I was rooting for them the whole time, especially when they didn't like each other. I wondered if Ms. Krane was rooting for me and Missy Gerber in the same way.

But hands down, the greatest thing Lieutenant Boss did was arrange for Mason and Susie to visit. I knew from his letter that he was gonna get in touch with them, but I didn't know they were coming until they showed up. I love surprises, but I wasn't the only one cheering about that one.

Lots of Lieutenant Boss's rules and routines were broken that afternoon, but he didn't get all bothered 'cause he was a dog person. He and Susie hit it off right away. That was when I knew the lieutenant wasn't really a bad guy.

"Seems like you and Lieutenant Boss have figured each other out," Mason said to me before leaving that afternoon.

"Sometimes all a person needs is a chance," I answered— and those words startled me 'cause I definitely didn't have time to think them up. I didn't know where they came from.

"Are you talking about the lieutenant . . . or someone else?" Mason asked.

My mouth opened but I didn't have any words jump out

that time. I'd thought I was talking about the lieutenant, but suddenly I didn't know.

Mason grinned. "Keep up your great work, Carter. Ms. Krane is sure to be proud."

"I will," I promised.

"C'mon, Susie. It's time for us to mosey."

"Bye," I said, giving Susie one last pat.

Mason was right, me and the lieutenant were figuring each other out, but so were me and the rest of school. Lunchtime was way better now. I didn't eat by myself anymore. Now that Missy Gerber was back, we were four at the table: me, Vanessa, Mary, and Missy. Samantha Yelber stayed with her new group of friends. Her mother's petition didn't ruin Ms. Krane's job, but it did ruin Missy and Samantha's friendship. I told Missy I was sorry about that but she said not to worry about it. So I didn't. I sat in my new spot and looked forward to it every day. And I told Grams to make sure she kept packing me a yummy snack that I could share with my friends.

"I didn't think you were supposed to share food," Grams said.

"You're not, but that's one of those rules everyone breaks."

Grams shook her head. "Just try not to get caught."

I didn't. I was fast and sneaky, so the lunch aide never

spotted me passing animal cookies, but she did come over to shoosh us one day when we got too loud. That was Grams's fault 'cause instead of my horoscope or a word on my napkin, she stuck a joke in my lunchbox.

"What's invisible and smells like bananas?" I read out loud.

None of us knew, so I flipped over the paper to find the answer. "Monkey farts!" I screeched.

We burst out laughing. That was when the lunch aide marched over, but as soon as she walked away, we started cracking up again. Kyle swung by our table 'cause he wanted to know what was so funny and the lunch aide hollered at him.

"No loitering!"

"Tell you later," I said.

Later turned out to be at indoor recess. Kyle liked my joke but he was more interested in what I was holding. The other thing Grams had slipped inside my lunch box that day was Parachute Man. Parachute Man was a blue action figure with a parachute folded up on his back. All you had to do was drop him from high up and when he fell, his parachute would open and you got to watch him float to the ground.

"Cool," Kyle said when he saw it.

"Wanna try it with me?" I asked.

"Sure! But where?"

"Follow me," I said. I had the perfect place in mind. We ducked out of the classroom and raced down the hall to the stairwell. I gave Parachute Man to Kyle and ran to the bottom of the stairs.

"Okay. Drop him," I yelled up.

Kyle leaned over the railing and let him go.

"Awesome!" we exclaimed when his parachute sprang open, slowing his fall.

We took turns until Lieutenant Boss stepped into the stairwell and caught us in the act. He was on his way back from lunch to relieve the aides from their recess duty in our classroom. Me and Kyle glanced at each other and gulped. Were we in trouble?

"Brings back memories," Lieutenant Boss said.

My forehead wrinkled. "Memories of playing with your own Parachute Man?" I asked.

"No. Memories of *being* Parachute Man," he said.

"You mean you jumped out of an airplane before?" Kyle exclaimed, taking the words right out of my mouth.

"Sure did. Me and some of the boys in the navy. Let me tell you, that gets the ole ticker going."

Our eyes shot big. "Wow," we murmured, both of us impressed.

Lieutenant Boss scanned the stairwell from top to bottom. "You've got five more minutes, then back to class. And be careful," he instructed.

Turns out we'd just given the lieutenant an awesome idea— and we found out what the next day.

66

EGG-STRONAUTS

Lieutenant Boss marched to the front of the room as soon as Principal Ryan finished her morning announcements. "I spoke to Ms. Krane yesterday after school," he began, which got everyone's attention real fast. "She and Oliver continue to do well," he said, "but she actually called to ask how things were going for us, which was perfect timing because I got to tell her about the project Carter and Kyle inspired, and get her input and permission to pursue it."

"What project?" I bawked, forgetting to raise my hand, but Lieutenant Boss let that slide.

"Yeah, how did me and Carter inspire a project? We didn't do anything," Kyle blurted right after me.

Lieutenant Boss held up his hands. "First, I have something for all of you to watch; then I will explain more." He walked to his computer and punched a few buttons and a movie popped up on the front smart board. Grams woulda needed Brynn's help to pull that off, so I was impressed.

"This is a clip from *Apollo 13,* which happens to be based on a true story," Lieutenant Boss said. He hit play.

The first thing I noticed was this wasn't a cartoon movie like all the other ones we always got stuck watching. This was a grown-up movie. The scene started with a bunch of guys wearing shirts and ties dumping boxes of stuff all over a table. Then the guy in charge said to listen up. He held up a big square block and told all the other guys in the room that they had to find a way to make that square block fit into the hole on a smaller circle object that he held up in his other hand, and they had to do it using only the junk they'd just dumped on the table. What he asked for sounded impossible, but he was serious.

Lieutenant Boss stopped the movie.

"Hey!" a bunch of us yelled.

"We don't have time to watch the whole thing," he said.

"But do they do it?" Mary asked. "Do they make the square peg fit inside the hole?"

"Yes, they accomplish the task and help save the lives of the astronauts in space who are depending on them."

"But how?" Kyle asked. "That looked impossible."

"Teamwork and problem-solving," Lieutenant Boss replied. "And now you'll be trying to do the same thing to save your egg-stronauts."

"Our what?" we squawked.

Lieutenant Boss walked to the closet and pulled out a huge black trash bag. Then he carried the bag to our front table and flipped it over, dumping stuff everywhere, just like in the movie. Some of it even spilled onto the floor. "Your challenge," he said, "is to build a structure that will hold your egg-stronaut and keep it from certain death when we drop it from the top of the school."

"What?!" we yelled.

"Parachute Man," I blurted. That was what gave him the idea.

Lieutenant Boss grinned. Then he slowed down and explained everything again. He didn't say anything much different, but we did better at listening. The challenge was to build a spaceship that would hold a raw egg—our egg-stronaut—and keep it from breaking when it got dropped from the top of the school. And we had to accomplish that by using only the stuff Lieutenant Boss had dumped all over our front table. The last thing he told us was that there were many minds working together to solve the challenge in the movie, so he encouraged us to work in teams as well.

I glanced at Missy and saw her looking at me. When it was the play yards, we got stuck working together 'cause we were the only ones not picked, but this time we chose each other 'cause we were a good team—and we proved it, until we weren't.

67

SOMETIMES SIMPLER IS BETTER

The first thing Lieutenant Boss had us do was survey all the stuff he'd dumped on the table. There were straws, rubber bands, sponges, thick and thin cardboard, duct tape, newspaper, cotton balls, a variety of plastic bags, twist ties, string, Styrofoam cups, plastic forks and spoons, napkins, and more.

Missy opened her cow journal and began listing everything.

"Looks like Officer Gerber has decided to make an inventory list. Not a bad idea," Lieutenant Boss pointed out. "The men in the movie also began by getting organized."

Everyone started a list after that—except me, 'cause Missy was my partner and writing all that stuff woulda took me till next Christmas, so I let her do it. After taking inventory, Lieutenant Boss told us we weren't allowed to touch any materials until we came up with a detailed plan that included a design sketch in our cow journals. Once our plan got his approval, we could begin building.

This was a great project. It made the slow weeks leading up to Christmas go real fast—and I thought that was more impossible than fitting a square peg in a round hole.

Everybody was anxious to get their hands on the materials, but we found out the building part was hard. There was a lot of starting over and trying again and asking for additional stuff from the lieutenant.

"Do not be discouraged. That's science. That's problem-solving," Lieutenant Boss exclaimed time and time again. He was enjoying this. So were we.

Me and Missy worked in the hall where we had plenty of space. We needed it 'cause we used straws to build an octahedron for our spaceship. That's a shape with eight equilateral triangles. Lieutenant Boss liked that 'cause geometry was good math. We used duct tape to connect the straws and hold all the vertices (that's more good math talk) together. The tricky part was figuring out how to keep our egg-stronaut safely suspended in the middle so that he didn't get hurt.

"We need a cockpit," I said.

"That's exactly what we need," Missy agreed.

So we put our brains together and came up with good ideas, but nothing was working and we were running out of time. Lieutenant Boss had scheduled our drop for the last day before Christmas break, which was only two days away.

"Don't get discouraged," Lieutenant Boss reminded us. *Blah blah blah.* But then he added, "Sometimes simpler is better."

"What's that supposed to mean?" I asked.

"You'll figure it out," he said, walking away.

I turned to Missy. "I've got to use the bathroom," she blurted, jumping to her feet. She musta been holding it for a while 'cause she ran like me when I'm ready to burst. She didn't even care that her foot kicked her cow journal and sent it flying. Her journal bounced off the wall and flipped open. The title *Annoying Boy* was written across the top in dark block letters. Our cow journals were supposed to be private, but my eyes started reading.

> Once upon a time there was a boy and a girl, and the girl hated the boy because he was the most annoying creature in the whole wide world. The girl was pretty and had many friends. The boy was gross and disgusting and had no friends. The boy didn't know how to close his yap. He was always shouting out of turn and he couldn't even manage to sit in a chair like a regular person. His mouth and his body never stopped. The only time he was ever quiet was at lunch because he had no one to talk to. He sat alone and ate by himself every day. That was his punishment for being so annoying.

I heard Missy coming and quick closed her journal and shoved it away from me. I'd read enough anyways. Her story wasn't funny. It was mean. Really mean. Missy Gerber was no different than Stinger or Hornet.

"I was thinking—" Missy started to say when she sat back down.

"Me too," I said, cutting her off. "Simpler means you can work by yourself." I ripped our octahedron apart and got up and stomped into the classroom.

"Carter!" Missy shrieked. "Carter!"

But I never stopped.

Lieutenant Boss asked if everything was all right when he saw me back in the classroom and I told him we'd decided to work alone 'cause that would be simpler.

"That's not exactly what I meant, but okay, if that's what you want," he said. "Tomorrow is your last chance to work on the project, remember."

"I know." I didn't care. I wasn't changing my mind.

Missy tried tracking me down and asking me what was wrong when we were packing up at the end of the day, but I'd had lots of practice ignoring mean people in the past.

"What is your problem?" she demanded, getting upset. She didn't give up easily.

So I whipped around and told her. "You! You're the problem, so leave me alone!" I shouted. "I never want to talk to you again!"

That shut her up. It even made her eyes get wet, too, but I didn't care about that either. I grabbed my bag and brushed past her.

68

EGG DROPS

Lieutenant Boss had been keeping a close eye on the forecast all week 'cause bad weather can halt a space launch or an egg drop, but luckily, Mother Nature decided to cooperate and delivered perfect conditions for our big event. The sky was clear with minimal wind. And it wasn't even that cold.

Lieutenant Boss got the custodians to help him get on the roof of our building while the rest of us stood on the ground, surrounding the crash site. Principal Ryan and Ms. Garcia also came out to watch.

There were seven different spaceships making the drop. All were creative, Lieutenant Boss said so himself, but you could tell both mine and Missy's had been thrown together last minute. They weren't pretty, but none of them were much to look at—Lieutenant Boss said that too. But he also told us looks shouldn't matter.

"It's what's on the inside that counts," he stressed. "You should all know that by now."

I think he was talking about more than our spaceships when he said that.

One by one, the lieutenant announced who was up. He was good at announcing, just like you'd expect a navy man to be, and he didn't even need a megaphone. Those of us on the ground cheered and held our breaths before every drop.

Kyle and Austin were first to go. They named their creation Air Jordan, but it didn't fly. Their box with wings crashed to the ground and busted open—but somehow, their egg-stronaut survived. When they saw that, they broke into a crazy dance celebration that made everyone laugh.

Vanessa and Mary went next and their egg-stronaut also survived—and so did their spaceship, which had cotton balls layered between two pieces of cardboard on all sides for shock absorption. It was a good design.

The third, fourth, and fifth egg-stronauts also survived.

"We might be looking at a class of future NASA employees!" Lieutenant Boss yelled from the roof.

Then it was my turn. I tried re-creating the octahedron me and Missy had built and used string to tie a plastic baggie to the top of my ship so that it had a parachute. The parachute worked a little, but I never got the cockpit right. When my octahedron hit the pavement, it tipped over and my egg-stronaut ejected. His guts splattered all over the sidewalk.

"Oooh!" everyone groaned.

"Splat!" Austin yelled.

Missy also stuck with our first idea except she made one smart change. Instead of eight triangles, she built a tetrahedron, which was only four. The center part of her ship became a perfect cockpit for her egg-stronaut. That musta been what the lieutenant meant by simpler.

Missy also sprinkled her egg with gold and silver glitter and drew a face on it to make it pretty, but she still had the same problem as me. Without someone to help you hold the triangles in place, it was super hard to tape them together. Her ship was weak, and not stable. When it hit the pavement, it crumpled and her egg-stronaut died.

"Oooh!" everyone groaned again.

"Splat!" Austin yelled. At least he wasn't playing favorites.

Principal Ryan and Ms. Garcia congratulated us on our projects and said they thought we'd all done an excellent job—even though that part wasn't true.

Lieutenant Boss climbed down from the roof and met us at the crash site. The custodians were nice and took care of cleaning up our egg guts while the lieutenant rounded up our crew and led us back to the classroom.

"We need to debrief and I also have a surprise for you," he said.

Normally, surprises always got me excited, but I dragged at the end of the line, in no hurry. I just wanted school to end so I could go home and get away from Missy Gerber. She'd ruined everything.

Lieutenant Boss stood at the classroom door as we filed past, but he stopped me. "Friendships can be as fragile as eggs, Officer Avery. But unlike a broken egg, they can be put back together."

"Not this time," I replied. And then I walked into the classroom and plopped in my seat.

Lieutenant Boss took his position at the front and began asking his questions. He wondered what we thought worked and didn't work with our designs, and what we'd do different in the future. What we liked and didn't like about the project. This was the debriefing part he mentioned. I didn't raise my hand or yell out any answers.

When he'd heard enough, the lieutenant told us it was time for our surprise. He walked to his computer and did more of that button pushing and this time a different movie clip popped up on our smart board.

"Hi, Class!" Ms. Krane greeted us. "I'm here with Oliver. He's home now!" She held the little guy up for us to see and the whole room filled with *Ohhs!* He was cute. And super tiny. And perfect. Ms. Krane did a great job making him. I had to remember to tell her that.

"We wanted to wish all of you a wonderful holiday season with your families."

"Hi!" two old people sang, suddenly jumping in front of the camera and waving. "We're your teacher's parents."

They quick disappeared offscreen again and the whole

class started cracking up—even me. Lieutenant Boss had to pause the video until we settled down 'cause we wouldn't have been able to hear.

"That was my mom and dad," Ms. Krane explained after the lieutenant hit play again. She shook her head. "Please excuse their behavior. They're just over the moon to be here for the holidays. They couldn't wait to meet Oliver.

"And I can't wait to hear how the egg drop went!" she continued. "Lieutenant Boss has been keeping me up to speed on everything. He says you're all doing an amazing job. Thank you for that. I knew I could count on you. Now, go have a great break and Oliver and I will see you again soon."

She waved and then the screen went black.

See us when? Did Ms. Krane know when she was coming back yet? She didn't mention a word about that.

Her video had me feeling real good and real bad all at the same time. I was happy for Ms. Krane and Oliver, happy that her baby was home and her parents got to come and see them so she wouldn't be spending the holidays alone, but seeing Ms. Krane made me miss her even more. And seeing her reminded me that I wasn't being her pudding anymore, and I felt terrible about that. I was disappointed in myself—and it was all Missy Gerber's fault.

69

LETTING OFF STEAM

I half bounded up the steps onto the big yellow taxi and slid into my seat behind Mr. Wilson.

"Everything all right?" he asked. "I'd expect a boy just before Christmas to be full of spunk, especially you."

If he'd spent the last two days eating his lunch alone again, and then watched his egg-stronaut splat all over the sidewalk, he might understand. But that was too much to tell, and I didn't want to get into it. So instead I said, "Everything's fine."

"Fine, huh? Well, I've never known you to walk up these steps and sit down all quiet, so I don't believe that for one second. But if you don't feel like talking about it, you don't feel like talking about it."

Mr. Wilson threw the bus in gear and we drove away from the school. And I didn't feel like talking about it—for most of the ride. But I'm not real good at keeping quiet. And when you try and hold the upset inside, it just builds and builds, so I finally cracked.

"Me and Missy got in a big fight."

Mr. Wilson nodded. "That happens. It's normal. Me and the Mrs. get upset with each other every now and again, too. You wanna know what helps?"

"What?" I said, eager for his advice.

"Time."

I slunk back against my seat. That wasn't a good answer.

"Trust me," he said. "Have I ever steered you wrong? A little time apart always helps. After break, you and Missy will be ready to make things right."

Mr. Wilson eased to a stop at my house and pulled the side door open. I got up from my seat and stepped forward.

"Well, see you later," he said.

"Thanks for the warning," I replied, and smirked.

Mr. Wilson laughed and I turned and jumped down the steps. Then he honked and continued on his way.

That Mr. Wilson was something else. Don't ask me how he did it, but he already had me feeling a little better.

70

CHRISTMAS

On Christmas Eve, me, Brynn, and Grams made our yearly homemade pizza and watched *Miracle on 34th Street*. The pizza was yummy, but the blasted TV kept glitching and sizzling so watching anything was near impossible. We had to rely on Brynn's computer again.

After finishing the movie, we read some of the Christmas picture books that me and Brynn had collected over the years. This was another tradition. We took turns doing the reading. Brynn loved *The Grinch*. My favorite was *The Polar Express*. And Grams always saved "'Twas the Night Before Christmas" for last.

When we got done with the stories, it was time for the impossible sleep. Grams had done a good job of keeping me busy with chores, though, so I was pretty tired and zonked out.

Come morning, the day of all days was finally here. We

had doughnuts for breakfast 'cause that way I didn't have to wait for any cooking. It was grab and go! Go straight to the presents!

I opened two smaller packages, both books, one about owls, but then Grams handed me a much bigger box. I shook it and heard things sliding and moving around. My eyes jumped wide 'cause I already had a good guess what was inside.

"Just open it," Brynn said.

I tore the wrapping paper away and it was just what I'd thought—a Lego kit. And not just any kit, but my first-ever modular. The box said *Expert* on it and it also said it was for ages sixteen and older. There were over two thousand pieces! Must be Grams knew I could handle it after building play yards and spaceships.

I looked at Grams. This kit cost a lot of money. A lot.

"Your sister insisted," Grams said. "It was either that or a new TV for the family. It was an easy choice."

I hugged Brynn super tight. She really was the best sister.

"You deserve it," she whispered.

Brynn was happy after opening her gifts too. Grams did a good job getting her the stuff that she wanted, including one of those Alexa things that you can tell to play music or make sounds or other stuff. (I didn't ask, but I got one too 'cause they came as a two-pack.) I got my sister new cookie sheets 'cause the old ones were getting rusty and I wanted her to keep baking. I thought it was a good gift. She liked them, but her favorite present was the necklace she got from Boyfriend Justin.

"'Cause you *luuu-ve* him," I teased.

Brynn didn't make a wisecrack about Missy Gerber 'cause she knew that was a sore spot, just like I knew not to mention Torrie 'cause that was a real touchy subject, but she did threaten me. "Keep it up and I'll feed you a knuckle sandwich instead of fresh baked cookies," she warned, making a fist.

"Brynn!" Grams scolded.

We laughed. Then Grams pulled out a present that she got for herself. She peeled away the wrapping paper and showed us her new . . . cell phone.

"No way!" Brynn shrieked. "You finally got one!"

"I did," Grams replied, "which is another reason the TV will have to wait. You'll have to show me how to use the darn thing."

"Absolutely," Brynn agreed, happy to help.

"You're gonna be a texter now, Grams," I teased.

"I hardly think so. I'm going to be connected is all."

Me and Brynn scoffed; then we gave Grams our present. It wasn't ever much but we could still be thoughtful. Brynn had a great picture of me and her on her phone from summer that looked a lot like a picture of my mom and dad posing together long ago. Grams loved both of those photos so me and Brynn got them enlarged and we found a nice frame that held them side by side.

You know it's a good present when the person starts crying as soon as they open it. Grams was all choked up. Me and Brynn gave her a big hug.

Wanna know something? That was my favorite part of Christmas. Seeing how happy that made Grams went straight to my heart. But I still grabbed my Lego box and dashed away as soon as we let go. I had expert building to do.

Part V

A NEW YEAR, A NEW PROJECT

71

AN UNEXPECTED NOTE

It was back to school in January. Everybody was busy wishing everybody a happy new year and talking about what they got for Christmas, but it was hard for me to feel happy when it was just more days without Ms. Krane—and more days *with* Missy Gerber.

I dumped my bag in my locker and walked into the classroom. I made a beeline for Camo. He'd been on his own for a while, so I wanted to say hi and make sure he was okay. I found him perched on a leaf catching a few rays. He looked happy.

A tree frog was a smart class pet 'cause nobody had to take him home during vacations like if we'd had a bunny or a gerbil. Camo was easy. He had a heat lamp hooked to a timer so it turned on and off daily. All we had to do was give his tank a heavy spray with a water bottle and drop some crickets inside for when he got hungry and he was all set for a week or two.

"Welcome back, Officer Avery," Lieutenant Boss said, joining me beside Camo's tank and bending to peer inside. "How's everything look?"

"Good, sir. Camo had a good break."

"Excellent. This is for you," he said, straightening and handing me a small piece of paper with my name on it.

I took the paper and turned it over. It was a note from Ms. Garcia. *Please come to my office after morning announcements.*

"Lieutenant Boss, do you know why I got this?" I asked.

He shook his head.

I shrugged. "Maybe she wants to invite me to a lunch bunch. Guess I'll find out."

Lieutenant Boss nodded and continued making the rounds, saying good morning and welcoming officers back to his ship.

I glanced around the room, and that was when I noticed Missy wasn't at her desk. Everyone was back but her. I started hoping the Crow had changed her mind and was keeping her home again—this time for good.

The PA speaker crackled and Principal Ryan's voice came across, greeting everyone at Bates Elementary good morning. She gave us her welcome back *blah blah blah* speech and let's have a great second half of the year *blah blah bah* hoorah, and then she wrapped things up by reminding us to choose kindness.

As soon as Principal Ryan finished, Lieutenant Boss gave me a nod and I got up and walked out of the classroom—but then I ran the rest of the way to the office. I waved to Mrs. Rosa on my way past her desk and made a quick pit stop to say hi to the Dragon and told him I'd see him soon, and then I skipped down the hall to Ms. Garcia's office—and you're not going to believe what happened next. Missy Gerber was sitting at the round table, waiting for me.

72

THE REST OF THE STORY

"What is she doing here?" I groaned.

"Missy asked for this meeting because she'd like to clear the air and set things straight," Ms. Garcia replied.

"What if I don't want to listen?" I objected.

"Too bad. That's not how this works," Ms. Garcia snapped, which made my eyes pop 'cause I'd never heard her lay down the law like Grams before. "I'll be in the workroom just down the hall so the two of you can talk in private. Come and get me whenever you're finished, but take all the time you need."

"Thank you," Missy said.

Ms. Garcia gave us a nod and left. I pulled out the chair farthest away from Missy and sat down at the table—but I didn't look at her.

"I've been racking my brain all vacation, trying to figure out why you're mad at me and I still don't know," she said, "but there's something inside my journal that I want to read to you. I hope it'll help patch things up between us."

Missy opened her cow journal and began. "Once upon a time there was—"

"I already read your stupid story," I blurted, shooting her a nasty glare. "I don't wanna hear it again."

"What do you mean you already read it? How?"

"When we were in the hall working on our spaceship, after Lieutenant Boss told us simpler was better, you jumped up to run to the bathroom and accidentally kicked your journal open. I wasn't gonna read it, but once my eyes got started they couldn't stop . . . I thought you were my friend."

"I am!"

"*Pfft.* Yeah, right. A friend wouldn't write all those terrible things about me."

"Did you read the whole story, Carter?" Missy asked.

"What?"

"Did you read the whole story?"

I wanted to say yes—but I couldn't. The truth was she came back before I could finish. But so what.

"You didn't," she spat after I refused to answer. "How much *did* you read?"

I shrugged. "Enough."

"How much?!" she shouted.

"The first paragraph!" I yelled.

Missy sat back. "I can't believe it. That's what this is all about. You read the first part of my story and stopped."

"It was mean stuff. I didn't want to read the rest. Anyway, what does it matter?"

"It matters a lot, Carter!" Missy said. "Listen, and you'll understand." She started reading again and this time I didn't interrupt. She got past the horrible part I already knew and kept going.

The girl had known the boy for a long time—but she didn't really know him until this year. Thanks to an owl, the girl got stuck with the boy, and the boy with the girl, for a school project. It was an important project. A matter of life versus death, so they had no choice but to work together.

That was the start of the girl seeing the boy differently. He was still fidgety, and his hair wasn't always neat, and his shirt still had food stains on it most days, but the boy was also smart, funny, and sensitive. The girl grew to like the boy.

Unfortunately, the girl was taken away by her mother, the queen, sometime later. The queen meant no harm; she was only trying to protect her daughter from an unsettled kingdom and the painful disruption caused by losing someone important. That had happened once before when she was little and her father left, leaving the queen alone to raise the girl while also fighting to keep her business going when it was just getting started. The queen did both through sheer determination and hard work. The girl tried to meet the queen's expectations with the same hard work and determination, but she continued to grow sadder and sadder.

The girl had had many friends, the kind that come and go and can sometimes be mean to each other— but the boy was different. He was brave and loyal and sincere. He proved that when he set out on a daring mission to deliver a special gift to the girl. The girl explained the difference between friend and colleague to the boy that day, but only after the boy showed her the difference first. The Annoying Boy had become the girl's first true friend.

Upon learning the truth of her young daughter's heart, the queen herself had to be courageous. And so she let the girl go.

The end.

Missy closed her cow journal and slowly lifted her eyes to meet mine.

"Is that true?" I croaked.

Missy nodded.

"Your dad left when you were little?"

"When I was two, so I don't remember him much, but Mom says I had a hard time after that happened. It was hard for her too. But we made it because we stuck together. It's always been the two of us."

"My parents died in a car crash when I was a baby, so I

never really knew them, either. But me and Brynn and Grams made it 'cause we stuck together too. It's always been the three of us."

We stopped talking and the room stayed quiet for a minute before I asked my next question. "I thought Samantha Yelber was your true friend?"

"You want to know why Samantha isn't my friend anymore? It's not only because of what happened with the petition. She wanted me to choose between you and her," Missy said. "And I chose you."

"For real?"

"Yes, for real," Missy promised.

"I'm sorry," I said. "About our fight, not about Samantha."

Missy giggled. "Me too," she said.

We might've hugged after that, but I'm not telling 'cause one Brynn is enough. Speaking of Brynn, since me and Missy were done fighting and friends again—true friends—I wished the same would happen for my sister and Torrie.

73

THE NEW PROJECT

Ms. Garcia didn't ask us a hundred questions when we went and got her.

"We're done now, Ms. Garcia," Missy said. "Thank you for letting us use your office."

Ms. Garcia looked at me, then at Missy, then back at me. She smiled. "Anytime," she replied. "Have a good day now."

"You too," we said.

Then we skipped out of the office and back upstairs to our classroom. Lieutenant Boss gave me the same kinda look that Ms. Garcia had when she saw me and Missy together, but he didn't ask any questions either. Instead, he gave me one of his nods, and I gave him a nod back. Then I took my seat on the counter space and Lieutenant Boss began marching around the room, passing out Jolly Ranchers, which made all our eyes get big.

"Now that we've got the entire crew assembled again,

you can go ahead and put your math workbooks away," he announced.

"What's this for?" I blurted. There was no way I could keep that in when he was giving us candy.

"You may consider the candy part welcome-back treat and part congratulatory treat for your impressive efforts with our egg-stronauts before break," Lieutenant Boss explained.

"That project was fun!" Kyle exclaimed.

"Yeah," everyone agreed.

Me and Missy looked at each other and did tiny shrugs and tiny smiles.

"It was fun for me too," Lieutenant Boss replied. "But more than that, it was inspiring. To see the whole ship working toward the common goal of helping someone else—your egg-stronaut—was truly special. So . . . what do you say we do it again?"

I didn't sit up straight. I jumped off my counter space.

"Yeah!" everyone cheered.

Except for Missy Gerber. "Lieutenant Boss," she said, raising her hand.

"Yes, Officer Gerber."

"That sounds exciting, but we can't do the same project all over again. There won't be any problem solving or learning."

I scowled and sat back down. Missy was my friend, but why did she have to ruin it?

"Officer Gerber, you're absolutely right. I'm not suggesting we repeat the egg drop. We need to come up with a new project."

"What?" Kyle asked.

"Exactly. What?" Lieutenant Boss wondered. "Who's got an idea?"

His Jolly Ranchers had me thinking about welcome backs, and thinking was something Ms. Krane loved. I put those two things together—and bam. "A welcome back party for Ms. Krane!" I blurted.

"Yeah!" everyone cheered again.

Lieutenant Boss pointed at me and clicked his tongue. "That could be the trick. You might have something there, Officer Avery."

And just like that, school got exciting—but not for long, 'cause Missy had to ruin it again.

"But, sir, do we know when Ms. Krane is coming back?" she asked. "Or *if*?"

That did it. All my excitement was sucked out of me 'cause *if* was the thought that scared me.

"No, we do not," Lieutenant Boss answered. "But that shouldn't matter. We can still plan a party. It will either be a welcome back party or a congratulations party. We can sort that out later."

Yeah, I thought, sitting up straight again. *We can sort that out later.*

"Here's my concern," Lieutenant Boss explained. "In order

for this endeavor to qualify as a project, there must be tasks for us to complete, similar to what we did with your egg-stronauts. So to come up with tasks, we need to think about what goes into a party, and to do that, we're going to try something called Pass the Brainstorm."

74

PASS THE BRAINSTORM

"Pass the what?" I fussed.

"The brainstorm," Missy answered. "And stop yelling out before you get in trouble."

I stuck my tongue out at her, but not in a mean way, 'cause she was right. I didn't want to push it with Lieutenant Boss. Even if he was being nice, he had his limits.

"Officers, take out a piece of paper and your pencil," Lieutenant Boss instructed.

I followed his commands, but I still didn't know what we were doing.

"When I say go, I want you to start writing down whatever you think we should have for the party—whether congratulatory or welcome back," Lieutenant Boss explained. "When I say time, you'll pass your paper to the person sitting on your left and then you'll begin adding ideas to your new list until I say time again, at which point you'll pass your paper to the left and repeat. We'll follow this routine until your original paper gets back to you."

"I don't get it," I groaned.

"Me neither," Kyle complained.

"Ugh," Missy Gerber huffed.

I stuck my tongue out at her—and this time I meant it. She was my friend, but she could still be a know-it-all.

"After we get going, you'll understand," Lieutenant Boss assured us. "Now grab your pencils. Ready. Set. Go."

There was no Dragon to help me, so I had to do this the old-fashioned way. I got *FOOD* jotted down, and then we had to pass our papers.

My new list already had *food* and *decorations* on it. I got *B* and *A* scribbled for *balloons*, but that was it and then we had to pass our papers again.

This next one mentioned *games,* which I thought was a great suggestion—and also *invitations,* which was smart too. I got *P* and *O* printed for *posters,* but then we had to pass the brainstorming again.

About halfway through the activity, when our brains and pencils were beginning to slow down, Lieutenant Boss told us we needed to start getting more specific. "For example, if food is on your list, I want to know what food," he said.

So just when we thought we were running out of ideas, we suddenly had a bunch more. Even though I didn't get anything spelled all the way out 'cause we were going too fast, I still had a blast passing our brainstorming. Round and round we went, until my paper with *FOOD* printed at the top finally landed on my desk again.

"That was cool," Kyle said.

"Yeah," everyone agreed.

"Well, we're done with cool," Lieutenant Boss replied. "Now we need to talk details. Let's start with food. I know that was on most of your lists. Can't have a party without food, I agree. So what food are we talking about?"

"Cookies!" I cried. "Chocolate chip." Then I quick raised my hand, 'cause I'd forgotten that part.

Lieutenant Boss chuckled. Then he wrote *chocolate chip cookies* on our Class Party List. And after that he went around the room calling on people to hear other suggestions.

"Now for the million-dollar question," he said when we got done with that part. "How're we going to accomplish making all of this?"

Missy Gerber raised her hand.

"Officer Gerber," Lieutenant Boss said, calling on her. "What do you propose?"

"My mom should be able to help. She runs Gerber's Gourmet Gifts. They cater for parties all the time, and even make cute gift baskets for special occasions."

"That sounds terrific," the lieutenant said, "except for one thing. This isn't your mother's project. It's ours."

I didn't know if my idea was gonna work, so instead of blurting it out, I remembered to raise my hand this time.

"Yes, Officer Avery," Lieutenant Boss said, calling on me next.

"Well, since you were chief cook on your ship once, maybe you could lead us in making all the food. If you're in charge, maybe we could even make some fancier stuff that isn't on our list?"

"Like hors d'oeuvres!" Kyle exclaimed. "My mom loves those small-bite things. Especially the ones that are warm."

"A splendid idea, Officer Avery, but making all the different foods requires a kitchen space big enough for all of us to do the work, which unfortunately, we don't have."

"We could use my mom's, at her business," Missy blurted. She was so excited she even skipped over raising her hand. "There's a workroom and kitchen at Gerber's Gourmet Gifts," she explained. "We could make it a field trip."

This was the Missy I liked. She was sharing great ideas now!

Lieutenant Boss made a thinker face. We waited while he thought more. Then he said, "It's an idea worth exploring. I'll speak to your mother."

"I'll tell her to expect your call, sir," Missy said, smiling along with everyone else.

"Excellent. Now let's move on to the rest of the list," Lieutenant Boss said.

We talked details about decorations next. And after lunch we talked details about the remaining items we'd brainstormed. Before I knew it, our first day back had ended and we had a major project with a bunch of tasks ahead of us. I couldn't wait!

75

JANUARY LESSONS : DOS AND DON'TS IN THE KITCHEN

Lieutenant Boss talked to Principal Ryan and Ms. Krane, and together they decided we'd have our party on the last day before February vacation. It wasn't gonna be a surprise 'cause we didn't want to plan it for a day when Ms. Krane couldn't come. The only stinky part was we still didn't know if it was gonna be a congratulatory party or welcome back party 'cause Ms. Krane still didn't know her plans.

Not knowing didn't slow the lieutenant down. As soon as we had our date, he called the Crow. And just like that, we had a field trip to Gerber's Gourmet Gifts scheduled for the day before our party so we could make the food. Missy said her mom was going to be there 'cause it was her place, but also 'cause she wanted to help.

All those details seemed to happen real fast, but our actual field trip was still a long ways away, especially for someone who didn't like waiting. For once, the waiting wasn't so bad, though, 'cause it turned out we had a whole bunch of stuff to do before we could go anyway. Lieutenant Boss had big plans for us now that we had a real-deal kitchen to use.

"Listen up, sailors. Now that we'll be visiting Ms. Gerber's place of business, we have a lot to do to get ready. You have much to learn about food and kitchen safety before I let you do anything close to cooking."

"What's food safety, sir?" I blurted.

"The number one rule is you must wash your hands before you even think about touching any of the food you'll be preparing."

I should've guessed. It was always hand washing.

"Don't lick your finger, then touch the food," Lieutenant Boss said. "Don't wipe your nose, then touch the food."

"Eww," a bunch of kids whined.

"If you do any licking or wiping or picking—"

More ewws.

"Then you must, absolutely must, wash your hands before continuing to cook," Lieutenant Boss stressed.

That didn't seem hard, just a pain in the neck. But that was before I found out there were even rules about hand washing. You had to use warm water and plenty of soap and you had to scrub the fronts and backs of your hands and in between your fingers for at least twenty seconds. How long was that? Lieutenant Boss told us to sing "Happy Birthday" twice and that would be good. This wasn't just a pain in the neck. It was a pain in the butt.

Next up was coughing. Just like there were rules about hand washing, there was a proper way to cough too.

"You never cough on the food!" Lieutenant Boss emphasized.

More ewws.

"If you cough in your hands, then—"

"Wash them!" we yelled. We were learning.

"That's right," Lieutenant Boss replied. "If you need to cough, then you should use your elbow," he explained, demonstrating.

We practiced. I'm a good cougher now.

Hair was next on the list. If you had long hair, then you needed to pull it back in a ponytail or wear a hair net. If you had a chef's hat, then you could tuck it inside the top. The important thing was to get your hair out of the way 'cause no one wanted to find it in their food.

"I don't want to floss with your goldie locks when I'm eating," Lieutenant Boss said.

More ewws.

After hair, it was jewelry. There were rules about that too. No dangling necklaces or bracelets or chains allowed. Those things could get caught on stuff and lead to injury. We also discussed other safety measures like making sure pot handles didn't stick out past the stove, but were turned in. And we went over pot holders and hot plates too.

My favorite was when we got to knives. Lieutenant Boss

showed us the proper way to hold a knife and how to curl in the fingers on your other hand when any chopping was needed. "You want to chop the ingredient, not your fingers," he said. He demonstrated with a plastic knife and banana on a cutting board. Then we got to practice with our own plastic knife and banana.

But some of the most fun came after we did all that learning and had to prove to the lieutenant that we were ready. He had us form small groups and then he passed out different kitchen scenarios to each team that we had to act out as a skit. The people watching had to pay close attention and try to name the safety violations. Everyone got mine when I sneezed in the bowl that I was mixing. And they yelled "yuck" real loud when I took my hand and wiped my nose and went right back to touching everything. Vanessa did a good job of grossing us out when she let her hair dangle in the food that she was making.

The skits were great, but even better was a few days later, after we'd finished acting, and Lieutenant Boss gave us a test, 'cause it wasn't a bad test with lots of writing. It was this fancy thing he called a performance task. We were each given a recipe and all the tools and ingredients for making jelly rolls. This was our chance to demonstrate how much we'd learned.

Lieutenant Boss marched around the room, keeping a close eye on us, watching to make sure we followed all the safety rules. I used warm water and soap and sang "Happy Birthday" twice while I washed my hands. Then I followed the recipe and made perfect jelly rolls—and we got to eat them too!

"That was the funnest and yummiest test I ever took!" I told Lieutenant Boss after school when he joined me by the window where I was waiting for Mr. Wilson and the big yellow taxi.

"I'm glad you enjoyed it, Officer Avery. You can thank Ms. Krane."

My forehead wrinkled. "Sir?"

"Ms. Krane has been helping me all along," the lieutenant said. "She's the one who gave me the idea for our skits and the performance task. She helped me plan it all. Even though she isn't here, she hasn't stopped thinking and caring about any of you."

I smiled. "Do we know what kind of party it will be yet, sir?" I asked.

"No, but we should soon."

"Okay," I said, turning back to the window, a bit disappointed.

"Officer Avery, you've done an admirable job of proving Ms. Krane is the best," Lieutenant Boss said next.

My eyes jumped wide. How did he know about me being her pudding?

"You all have. The class is ready for our field trip, and I, for one, can't wait."

"Me either!" I exclaimed.

And that was the truth. I never stopped talking about it on the way home. I told Mr. Wilson everything. And when I got in the house, I was still so energized about our trip and getting to work in a professional kitchen like a professional cook that I wanted to practice and show off my new skills.

Valentine's Day was right around the corner, so I decided to make heart cookies for my sister as a special surprise. Grams agreed to be my assistant—just in case.

I ended up giving Brynn a huge surprise, all right, just not the one I was planning.

76

ME AND GRAMS GET TRICKY

Me and Grams were just getting home from Farmer Don's. I needed eggs if I was gonna make cookies and we were out, so we had to go collecting. Farmer Don's hens didn't stop laying eggs just 'cause it was winter. They were tough birds. And soon Farmer Don was gonna have more eggs than he knew what to do with 'cause Peeper and friends were getting ready to start contributing, so he loaded me and Grams up with extras.

"Looks like I'll be having an omelet in the morning," I said. "Thanks, Farmer Don."

"You betcha."

Grams said her thanks, too, and then we climbed inside trusty old Leopold. Everything was real good that afternoon until we got back home. Torrie's car was in our driveway and an ugly brown pickup was parked behind it, half in our driveway and half on the grass. My heart started pounding. I knew the driver of that truck. And now I was sure it was Torrie I had glimpsed in the passenger seat. This had trouble written all over it.

I jumped out of the car before Grams even had us stopped and raced toward the house.

"CJ!" Grams yelled.

I wasn't slowing down. That was my sister and her bestie. And the driver of that truck was bad news. He didn't belong here. I burst through the front door and darted into the living room.

"Hey, little man. What's up?" Just as I'd thought. Jay was the same guy *I'd* met at the North Pole. The same bully who'd peeled rubber out of the school parking lot after the swim scrimmage. I didn't like him. And one look at my sister and Torrie squeezed together on the couch with Shelby sandwiched between them told me they didn't like him, either.

"What're you doing here?" I asked.

"Having a friendly chat with the ladies," he growled. "And they better listen. So scram, twerp."

I did what he said—but that was his mistake. He never should've let me out of his sight. I vanished to my room. I had to do something. Fast. But what?

It came to me when I glanced at my dresser. My book on owls rested next to my new Alexa. Even if owls weren't tricky, I could be.

"Alexa, play police sirens," I whispered.

"Shuffling police siren sound effects," she replied.

The sirens began, slow at first, then building momentum. And they sounded just like the real thing. I turned the volume up all the way and hurried back out to the living room and stood behind the couch.

Jay stopped his threatening talk. "I told you to beat it, birdbrain."

"You better get out of here while you can," I warned him.

"You heard what my brother said," Brynn piped up. "The cops are coming."

"Shut up!" Jay yelled. He rushed to the window and pulled back the curtain to peek outside.

That was when I made my move. I slid over to the end table and grabbed the remote. Shelby was no dummy. She must've sensed I was up to something 'cause she jumped from the couch and ran and grabbed Jay's pants leg to keep him distracted.

"Get off me, dog!" Jay yelped, kicking to free his leg.

Shelby hung on and I hit the power button. Then I cranked the volume as high as it would go. I didn't know what to expect, but Grams had been right all along. The TV couldn't handle it. The blasted thing gave one last loud sizzle and then it . . . exploded! I'm talking a great big *KABOOM* that sounded like a gunshot and sent glass and pieces flying everywhere.

"Ahhhhhh!" Jay cried.

Shelby let go and Jay jumped back from the window and stumbled. He tripped and fell and almost brought the curtain down with him. Then he scrambled to his feet and spun around, his eyes wide and scared as he searched for a way out.

"You're not welcome here," Grams said, stepping into the living room at the absolute perfect moment. She held something under a coat that she had draped over her raised arms. Something that was pointed at Jay—and that had the same long shape as a rifle.

"That first one was a warning shot. I don't know where the second one will go," Grams snarled.

Jay put his hands in the air. "Take it easy, old woman. I'm leaving," he pleaded, shuffling backward toward the door. He never took his eyes off Grams and she never took hers off him.

Jay got to the door and reached for the knob. Slowly, he twisted it. Then he turned and bolted.

Grams lowered her arms and pulled an umbrella out from underneath the coat. We looked at each other and smirked.

"Grandmas can be tricky too," she said—and my smirk grew.

But then I heard Brynn and Torrie crying and hurried over to them. They had their arms wrapped around one another.

"CJ," Torrie sobbed, pulling me into their hug.

"You could've been hurt," Brynn sniffled and choked.

"As your knight in shining armor, it's my duty to protect you," I said.

They grinned and squeezed me too hard—but that was okay.

Grams was over at the window, peeking out to make sure trouble was leaving. "I don't think that young man will be bothering us anymore," she said.

Blue lights came into view, swirling and flashing out front. "The law is here?" I blurted. "For real? How did they know to come?"

Grams pulled her cell phone from her pocket and grinned. "This darn contraption isn't all bad once you figure out how to use it."

"You called before coming inside?" Brynn asked. "But how did you know we needed help?"

"You do a very good job of protecting your brother," Grams said, sitting beside my sister, "but looking out for you is my job."

There was more hugging and crying after that, until there was knocking on our door.

Grams and Brynn and Torrie talked to the officers. It was a long story, and "more than you need to know," Brynn said, but I got most of it.

"Jay was nice in the beginning," Torrie told the officer. "He lured me in with his sweet talk and little gifts, like this dumb bracelet." She shook her wrist. "But then he changed. He became controlling and asked me for money, promising he'd pay me back. So I gave it to him. Then he needed more. But he never did pay me back, and when I asked him about it, he got mad and threatened me."

"I knew something was wrong," Brynn said. "I should've gotten help."

"You told me to get rid of him, but I wouldn't listen," Torrie admitted. "And then we had that big fight and stopped talking. I'm sorry."

"Me too," Brynn croaked.

They were hugging again. It reminded me of me and Missy after our fight—but no way was I gonna tell Brynn that.

"So what happened today?" the officer asked.

"Today was the last straw," Torrie said. "I finally told Jay it was over. He got nasty. And then he followed me here."

Like I said, it was a long story. Bottom line, Jay wasn't gonna be trouble for us anymore. The officers assured us of that much. As Lieutenant Boss would say, it was smooth sailing after that.

So instead of surprising my sister with cookies, we baked them together after the dust settled—and Torrie stayed to help. We used the new cookie sheets that I got Brynn for Christmas. And while we baked, Grams thumbed through the sales flyers that had come in the mail, looking for TVs—since I'd finally put ours out to pasture!

'Cause this time I didn't let that guy get away with being a jerk. This time I was for-real brave.

77

GRAMS *IS* THE PERSON

Grams asked me not to mention Jay and what had happened to anyone in school.

"Why not?" I whined. "It's a great story!"

"CJ, a story like this has a tendency to grow and get twisted the more it's told, and before you know it, people are adding stuff that isn't true. I don't want folks getting the wrong idea about us."

I scowled.

"Grams is right," Brynn said. "Please don't say anything."

"Please," Torrie added.

"Okay," I agreed. "Not a word. I promise. But that doesn't mean I need to keep quiet about it at home. *That first one was a warning shot. I don't know where the second one will go,*" I snarled, mimicking Grams. That was my favorite part.

Brynn and Torrie giggled. Grams gave me a look—and then she started laughing too.

Keeping quiet wasn't my strength, but Lieutenant Boss took a page out of Ms. Krane's playbook and kept us real busy in school, so that made it easier.

"Based on your excellent performance assessments, I can now officially declare you ready for our field trip to Gerber's Gourmet Gifts," the lieutenant announced. "However, that doesn't mean we're ready for our party," he was quick to add. "We still have posters and decorations and invitations to figure out."

Like I said, he kept us busy. Giving Ms. Krane and Mason and Susie their invitations became my special job, 'cause me and Grams had plans to see them for another breakfast. And Grams had given me permission to share our story about what happened with Jay with the two of them.

When that morning finally arrived, I raced across the Heavenly Diner to my teacher's table. Ms. Krane already knew about the party, but she didn't know about all the food and decorations we had planned. I handed her the invitation before I even sat down or said hi or anything else. I couldn't stand waiting any longer.

Ms. Krane took the invitation, but before reading it she got up and gave me and Grams a hug. Mason hugged Grams next and then shook my hand. I helped Ms. Krane with her chair, and finally, she opened the invitation. Her purple stain crinkled under her big smile as she read the words.

"Everybody is real excited to see you and Oliver," I said.

Ms. Krane dabbed her eyes. "We're excited too," she said, glancing down on her other side.

I peeked to see what she was looking at. "Oliver!" I exclaimed. The little guy was sleeping in his car seat on the floor. And Susie was lying right next to him, keeping close watch. "I didn't know you had him with you."

"My parents have gone back home, so I don't have a babysitter."

Hearing that scared me. If she didn't have a babysitter, did that mean she wouldn't be returning to school?

"Ms. Krane, do you know if we'll be throwing you a congratulatory party or a welcome back party?" I asked hesitantly.

My teacher glanced at Mason and Grams, giving them each a small smile, and then she looked at me. "It's going to be a welcome back party, Carter."

"Really?!" I exclaimed. "You're coming back?"

"I'm coming back after February vacation," she replied. "Lieutenant Boss knows and will be sharing the news with the class this morning."

"And Oliver's coming with you?! Yay!" I cheered, throwing my arms in the air.

"Quiet or you'll wake the baby," Grams scolded.

I turtled. "Sorry," I whispered.

Ms. Krane laughed. "It's okay, and no, Oliver won't be coming with me," she said. "I can't bring my baby to school every day. That's not how this works. I had to find a place for him to go before I could say yes to returning to work, which is why I haven't been able to share this news until now. Finding the right place took time because I'm not about to leave him with just anybody. I had to find someone dependable and that I trust—and admire."

My eyes were wide. Ms. Krane made it clear this was serious business. Whoever she found had to be special. I swallowed. "Well, I'm sure glad you found a place," I croaked. "The rest of the class is gonna be real happy too."

"You can thank your grams," Ms. Krane said.

I looked at Grams. "You found the person?"

"I guess you could say that," she replied.

I scowled.

"She *is* the person," Mason said.

At that, my eyebrows near jumped off my forehead. "Grams, you're gonna watch Oliver?!" I exclaimed.

"Yes, I am. And keep your voice down," she reminded me. "I might be retired, but I'm not incapable. Besides, I need something to do and I want to help. So this is two birds with one stone," which was another one of her old-time sayings.

I couldn't stop smiling. "Grams will take special care of Oliver," I promised Ms. Krane. "She'll make him read lots of books and she'll make sure he washes his hands when he's supposed to."

Ms. Krane chuckled. "I know she will. I have no doubts."

I was so happy after getting all that good news that they coulda served me wet cardboard for breakfast and it still woulda tasted yummy. But our waitress was nice and brought me my order instead, a warm stack of chocolate chip pancakes topped with extra whipped cream, and my morning only got better.

I picked up my fork and dug in. The adults continued chatting, but I was too busy eating to pay much attention. The stomach must be connected to the brain somehow, 'cause once the yumminess hit my belly, I got to thinking. Thinking about something that hadn't occurred to me until then. Ms. Krane coming back meant Lieutenant Boss leaving—and that wasn't something I ever thought I'd be sad about. But I was, a little.

I wiped my mouth and cleared my throat. "Ms. Krane, thanks for helping Lieutenant Boss. He told me those great ideas were yours."

"Lieutenant Boss deserves the credit," she said. "He was the one who put the ideas into action."

Yeah, I thought, nodding. He did deserve some credit. I went back to my pancakes, still thinking.

78

GERBER'S GOURMET GIFTS

"Before we load the bus to go to Gerber's Gourmet Gifts, there's something I need to give you," Lieutenant Boss said, plopping a stack of brand-new sparkling white aprons and bag of chef hats on the front table.

"Awesome!" we cheered.

Kyle's mom and Grams helped the lieutenant pass out our special gear 'cause they were our chaperones for the trip. As soon as we were all decked out, we hit the road.

"Welcome," Ms. Gerber said, greeting us with a smile when we arrived. "You all look fantastic. Very professional."

We smiled back—and at each other after her compliment.

"I hope you're ready," she continued. "We've got a big day ahead. Follow me."

Ms. Gerber brought us into a room with six rectangular tables. They were arranged in two rows of three with a lane down the middle. There were a few stools scattered about, but no chairs. She had all kinds of stuff lining the walls and even hanging from the ceiling. It reminded me of our basement 'cause there was so much.

"We call this our workroom," Ms. Gerber said. "We do most of our preparations and finishing touches in here, which is why there's stuff everywhere—but we try to keep it organized and tidy."

Now I understood why Missy's desk was so perfect. She got it from her mother. As Grams would say, the apple didn't fall far from the tree.

"From what I understand, you've already formed teams," Ms. Gerber said, checking for confirmation.

Missy nodded at her mom.

"Okay, then each team can take a table."

That worked out perfectly, 'cause we had six groups. Once we'd claimed our stations, Ms. Gerber and Lieutenant Boss went over the ground rules and gave us an overview of how things were going to proceed. Basically, we'd be preparing all the food, but only the adults were allowed to touch the ovens in the kitchen. And there was absolutely, positively no running.

"The lieutenant and I discussed possibilities and came up with your party menu," Ms. Gerber continued explaining. "It's not extravagant, but it'll put your skills to the test and will definitely require teamwork. Each group will be making four dishes: meatballs, cookies (chocolate chip and oatmeal raisin), a fruit and veggie platter, and your specialty, jelly rolls, only a little fancier."

We were all smiles. This sounded great!

First up were the meatballs. Kyle's mom passed out the recipe cards while Ms. Gerber and the lieutenant wheeled in two different carts from the kitchen, one that held all the ingredients we'd be needing and one with bowls and spoons and any other tools we might want.

After washing our hands and singing "Happy Birthday"—twice—we went to the carts and fetched whatever we needed. We were in charge. This was our project! Forming the meatballs made some of my classmates squirm 'cause sticking your hands in raw meat and mushing everything together was slimy and gross, but it didn't bother me. I'd held lots of gross stuff before—like worms with ketchup!

Each team filled a cookie sheet with small meatballs 'cause they were meant to be hors d'oeuvres—like Kyle wanted. Then one team member carried the tray into the kitchen so Ms. Gerber could slide it in the oven.

While that was happening, the other team members took care of washing the bowls and tools so they could be reused. Kyle's mom and Grams helped with that. The lieutenant wheeled the ingredients cart away and came back with it loaded up for the next recipe—cookies! We followed the same routine, first for chocolate chip and then oatmeal raisin.

When we got all done with our menu, we had a huge bowl of meatballs, a pile of cookies, a heap of fruit and veggies all cut up—we got to do the cutting!—and a big tray of jelly rolls. We were done, but we found out that didn't mean we were finished.

Ms. Gerber gathered us around one of the tables, and then she taught us about presentation—which was her specialty. "If you're in the business of trying to sell your product, the better you can make it look, the better your chances of impressing customers. Watch how you can take something as simple as jelly rolls and make them look exquisite."

Ms. Gerber placed a white plate on the table and began organizing jelly rolls on it. She made a circle pattern, but not all the way around it. She left a small slice open.

"Why aren't you putting any there?" Vanessa asked, pointing at the empty space.

"You'll see."

So we kept watching. Ms. Gerber organized the jelly rolls in a way that reminded me of a pizza with one piece gone. Then she took some squeezy-tube thing and drizzled a few lines of red jelly across the tops and drew a squiggly design in the empty space.

"For a splash of color, we add three green mint leaves," she said, sticking the leaves to the squiggly line. "And now for the finishing touch." She took confectioners' sugar and sprinkled it along the top.

"Wow! Ms. Gerber, you're really good at this!" I exclaimed. "You made boring jelly rolls look like something from a fancy restaurant."

The Crow smiled. "Thank you, Carter."

"As you can see, a striking presentation takes time and

patience," she told us. "But it's worth it. It makes all the difference. I'll admit, I can be demanding and not always the easiest to work with, but that's how my business became successful."

"I'm not good with patience, so I probly wouldn't be good at your job," I confessed.

"But you're very passionate about the things you care about," Ms. Gerber was quick to reply. "I've seen that. So whatever you do, if you bring that same passion, you'll be very successful."

The Crow was the last person I thought would be paying me compliments, but she just had, and I didn't know what to say—and that didn't happen very often. I glanced at Missy and she smiled.

"Okay, crew," Lieutenant Boss said, "it's time to make your jelly rolls look fancy like Ms. Gerber just demonstrated. Snap to it."

We returned to our battle stations and followed the lieutenant's orders. And after we'd finished with our jelly rolls, Ms. Gerber showed us how to jazz things up with our meatballs and fruit and veggies, and even our cookies. Her secret ingredient was definitely confectioners' sugar. Ms. Gerber sprinkled that stuff everywhere—but we didn't mind. It was yummy.

When all was said and done, we were ready for our party. Ms. Gerber stored the food in her kitchen 'cause the party wasn't until tomorrow, but she'd have it there for us.

"You deserve a reward after your hard work today," she

said, handing us a tray of cookies to take on the road. She must've made them earlier. They had white frosting and rainbow sprinkles!

"Yay!" we cheered.

It was late in the day, so after grabbing a cookie, it was time to pack up and head back to school to catch our buses home. Since Grams was a chaperone, I just left with her.

"So what did you think of today?" she asked after we were on our way.

"I thought it was super fun. Ms. Gerber is really good at her job—and she can be nice too."

"Ms. Gerber's a strong woman who cares deeply about her work and her daughter—and she doesn't mess around when it comes to those things. Nothing wrong with that."

"Do you think she was right, Grams? About me?" I asked.

"CJ, you're the most passionate person I know," Grams said. "You've got a long ways to growing up, but if you keep your head and your heart, I have no doubt you'll be very successful in the end. But just remember, you want to be happy too. I do wonder if that piece has been missing for Ms. Gerber. I hope today was a good reminder for her as well."

I didn't know about Ms. Gerber, but I was happy. My cookie was super yummy and tomorrow was the big day. I couldn't wait to welcome back Ms. Krane.

79

PARTY!

Since our celebration was the day before February vacation, we only had a half day of school, and we spent the whole time partying! It was a blast!

Everyone was real excited to see Mason and Susie when they made it. Too excited, 'cause we snuck Susie one too many meatballs and cookies and she got sick and barfed a big puddle all over the floor. As smart as she was, she was still a dog.

Mason apologized even though it was our fault. Lieutenant Boss told him not to worry and me and Kyle cleaned up the mess. The lieutenant didn't even have to ask us to do that. I'd cleaned up Shelby puke lots of times before, so I knew how to do it.

Susie wasn't the only one who liked our food, though. All our guests kept complimenting us. First Principal Ryan, then Ms. Garcia, and then Mrs. Rosa. Over and over we heard the meatballs were delicious, the cookies excellent, and the jelly rolls amazing. Thanks to our presentation, a lot of people thought the jelly rolls were a specialty item ordered from a bakery.

But the highlight of the party was definitely when Ms. Krane arrived. Everyone rushed to see her and get their first in-person look at baby Oliver. Don't worry, we'd learned our lesson and didn't trying sneaking the little guy any goodies.

Ms. Krane sat at the front of the room with Oliver on the floor next to her, napping in his car seat. Susie found her spot right next to him. The rest of us gathered around like we did when Ms. Krane read to us.

"He's so cute," Missy squealed, staring at the baby.

"Tiny," Kyle added.

"You did a great job making him, Ms. Krane," I remembered to tell her.

Ms. Krane smiled at Oliver and then at us. "I've missed all of you," she said. "I hope you didn't think some silly petition could keep me from coming back to see my favorite people."

My eyes popped. *She did know,* I thought. I exchanged glances with my classmates.

"Owls are tough," Ms. Krane said. "They don't back down."

We grinned.

"So tell me what you've been up to," she said, asking about us now. "Tell me about cooking all this wonderful food."

That was all she had to say. We had lots to tell. Missy had to shush me a few times so I would let others have a turn to talk, but that was okay 'cause I had my special talk saved for later.

After we got done filling Ms. Krane in on everything, and

after we let her enjoy some of our food, and after Oliver woke up from his nap and we got to see him awake, I stood on my chair and asked for everyone's attention. When I got it, I cleared my throat.

"We're happy to welcome back Ms. Krane," I started, "but we should also thank Lieutenant Boss for manning our ship while she was away. You've done a great job, sir. We learned a lot. So we'd like to present you with a medal."

None of my classmates knew about the medal 'cause it was my idea, but Grams said they wouldn't mind—and she was right. I got down and reached inside my desk and pulled out the #1 Teacher medal. It was homemade from stuff in my basement, but Grams told me that wouldn't matter. (Brynn and Torrie helped me with it—but don't tell.)

"Being a navy man, the lieutenant is sure to appreciate it," Grams said—and she was right about that too.

I approached Lieutenant Boss and he bent over so I could slide it over his head. When he stood back up, everyone clapped.

The lieutenant's jaw quivered. "Thank you," he said. "You've taught me plenty as well. This award is mine, but so has been the reward."

"The good news is the lieutenant won't be going very far," Principal Ryan announced, stepping forward. "Mrs. Stinger submitted her resignation this morning. Funny how things have a way of working out sometimes. And lucky for Bates Elementary, Lieutenant Boss will be taking her place."

"Yay!" we cheered—for the lieutenant, but I was also cheering 'cause Mrs. Stinger was outta here. It was good news on top of good news.

"Carter, that was really sweet what you did for Lieutenant Boss," Missy said when we were out at our lockers, getting ready to go home. "You know, I finally figured something out about you. Your brain doesn't come up with this stuff. It's your heart. That's why Ms. Krane put your mouse dead center on our bulletin board. Somehow she knew you were the heart of our class."

For someone who had a tough time not blurting out, a tough time shutting his trap, Missy Gerber had just left me speechless. If she wanted to talk about hearts, she'd just made mine feel pretty special.

"Thanks," I finally croaked.

She smiled big. "You're welcome. That's what friends are for."

Mr. Wilson had come to our party early, before he had to leave for his first bus run, and Grams was there for most of it, so they both knew it was a huge success, but I was gonna have to tell Brynn and Torrie all about it when I got home—except for that last part with Missy. Brynn wasn't on my need-to-know list for that one, or I'd never hear the end of it.

Epilogue

END OF FOURTH GRADE

God's Country

With Ms. Krane back in action, we got to hear her many voices during read-aloud again. We also got to do more cool projects, like an electricity unit and owl pellet dissections. Don't worry, Ms. Krane special-ordered those; she wasn't the Owl who barfed them up. And we did a lot of thinking with all the books we read and all the charts and graphs we made in math, 'cause Ms. Krane wanted thinkers and not Simon Saysers. Everyone liked my bar graph for my number of swallows in thirty seconds at the drinking fountain. With Kyle and Austin timing, I finally broke my record. I got fourteen!

Me and the Dragon spun some good stories too. I was gonna miss him over the summer—and that's saying something 'cause I used to hate writing.

I was leaving his lair when I bumped into Mrs. Stinger near the end of the school year. I could see from the box in her arms that she'd come back to get the last of her things.

Boy, there was suddenly so much I wanted to tell her. Like I am smart. And I'm not afraid to stand up for my friends. And I'm passionate and energetic and still have a hard time sitting still—but lucky for her I'd gotten better at controlling my outbursts so I kept all that to myself. The important thing was that *I* knew those things about me now. I walked past her with my head held high.

I hoped I got to keep visiting the Dragon next year. Ms. Krane promised she'd mention it to my next year's teacher, Mr. Keith, who she thought I'd get along with real well 'cause he was young and full of energy too. But if she forgot, I knew I could count on Missy to tell Mr. Keith, 'cause she was gonna be in my class and she still knew everything. As Grams liked to say, only time would tell. And as Mr. Wilson would say, there was no sense worrying about it now 'cause it wasn't gonna do me any good. Besides, now was the time for a special trip to celebrate a school year like no other.

Lucky for everyone, Leopold got to stay back and sit this one out. Turns out Grams wasn't the only one who bought herself a Christmas gift. Mr. Wilson did, too, only his was a brand-new used minibus—and we were taking it on an adventure.

"I've been thinking this could be the start of a side job for me," Mr. Wilson said. "How do you like the sound of Wilson's Tours?"

"It's got a ring to it," I agreed. "You like to drive and you've got the wheels, so why not?"

"Maybe you can be my tour guide?" he continued.

My eyes popped. "Really?"

"No, not really," Grams interrupted. "You've got to finish school before the two of you can become partners in crime."

"Partners in crime," I repeated.

"It's got a ring to it," Mr. Wilson teased.

"You two are insufferable," Grams huffed. "You can start being partners by loading our bags," she said, shaking her head and walking away.

Me and Mr. Wilson laughed, and then we began grabbing bags. Wilson's tour bus carried fifteen passengers. Eleven were making this trip: me, Shelby, Brynn, Torrie, Grams, Mason, Susie, Ms. Krane, Oliver, and Mr. and Mrs. Wilson. It was our Thanksgiving crew plus Torrie and Oliver, which meant there were a few empty seats available to hold our stuff.

After we had everything loaded, our tour group piled in. Mr. Wilson took his spot behind the wheel and I found my usual seat right behind him. Shelby sat with me, and Mason and Susie sat across the aisle. Grams and Ms. Krane were one row back. Oliver was buckled in his car seat next to his mom. Mrs. Wilson was one row behind them and Brynn and Torrie sprawled out in the rear, using our bags for pillows. We were officially locked and loaded, ready to hit the road.

Our destination: a set of seaside cottages on Cape Cod, like in *Summer of the Gypsy Moths*. "It's time to cross this one off your bucket list," Mason told me. "You're gonna see the ocean, feel it, smell it, hear it, experience it. Take it all in. It's a place big enough to take our sorrows away in one breath and give us new happiness and hope in the next wave."

He sure made it sound magical. And the crinkle in Ms. Krane's purple stain told me she felt the same way. I was eager to experience it, like Mason had said, and I wasn't the only one. Before even going to the cottages, Wilson's Tours made a beeline for the beach. If we hurried, we'd make it for sunset, which the grown-ups said would be beautiful—and romantic. Gross!

Eight hours later—thanks to traffic!—we parked at Race Point Beach on the National Seashore and unloaded. Then we began our trek down to the water. I wanted to wait for everyone, but I couldn't help it. I ran ahead—and Brynn and Torrie came with me. The others could join us when they made it.

We raced from the walking path onto the beach, across the sand, and down to the shoreline, finally stopping at the water's edge. We stood side by side as the breeze rolled in off the water, blowing our hair in the wind. The waves crashed against the shore with thunderous roars. And the ocean stretched as far as I could see in every direction. It was the biggest thing I'd ever seen in my whole life.

"It's beautiful," Brynn gushed.

"We call it God's country," a tan man wearing red shorts and a sun hat and sunglasses said as he came walking by. He held a water bottle in his hand and had his towel slung over his shoulder.

"A lifeguard on his way home after a day's work," Torrie whispered. "I could do that."

God's country, I thought. I liked that. I liked that a lot. I stared out over the water, then tipped my head back and closed my eyes, soaking in the sounds, and smells, and feels.

Sneaky Brynn and Torrie teamed up and splashed me when I wasn't looking and I shrieked. The water was cold. I chased after them with everyone laughing and the dogs barking in the background. We ran until we were out of breath and then we stopped and watched as the sun began dipping below the horizon. And you know what, it was beautiful. But I'm not gonna say it was romantic. Gross!

"Carter Avery, you've done a lot of proving this year," Grams said, joining us by the water, "but I hope by now you've proven to yourself that you're a special kid. The proof is in the pudding. Every person here is better off because of you. And even though Missy Gerber and Lieutenant Boss aren't here with us, the same is true for them too. All have benefited because they got to know you. I was wrong—you do have special powers, superhero powers, and those powers lie in your heart."

Brynn and Torrie leaned in and sandwiched me in hugs just as Shelby weaseled her way in between our legs. Grams slid behind and put her arms around all of us.

"It's 'cause of Ms. Krane," I said as I watched my teacher dip her baby's toes in the ocean a little ways down the beach. "I've decided, owls *are* tricky. She helped me be my best."

Grams nodded. "Yes, I'd have to say she deserves credit. She's a special person. The two of you were a match made in heaven."

Jelly Rolls

INGREDIENTS

1 slice of your favorite sandwich bread (more if you're really hungry)

1 tablespoon of your favorite jam or jelly (more if desired)

INSTRUCTIONS

1. Carefully remove the crust from your bread. You may use a knife (ask an adult for help) or your hands.

2. Place the crustless bread on a cutting board and use a rolling pin to flatten and spread it thin.

3. Slather the flattened bread with your favorite jelly.

4. Starting at one side, roll the bread into a log shape.

5. Carefully cut the log into small segments.

6. Eat and enjoy!

ACKNOWLEDGMENTS

When speaking with students, I'm sometimes asked what's the biggest challenge for an author. There can be many, but I often mention battling self-doubt. Writing a novel is a long journey, and there are days when the trek feels insurmountable. How do you get past that? My best advice is to surround yourself with the right people. People who will encourage you and pick you up when you get knocked down. People who make you feel good about being you, and help you be the best version of yourself.

Thank you to all the parents, teachers, librarians, and readers who've sent wonderful emails and letters my way. Your words keep me going strong. You're my people.

My deepest gratitude to Beverly Horowitz, Paul Fedorko, the Penguin Random House team, and my invaluable editor, Françoise Bui, for also being my people. I'm so lucky to have you with me.

And to Beth, Em, Lily, and Anya, you're not only my closest people, but my everything. Your hard work, commitment, and many achievements inspire and motivate me—and make me so proud. Trying to keep up makes me better. I love you all!

Potter—Jack would be proud of the work you put into this novel.

(P.S. My second piece of advice is to become a wrestler. The sport demands mental toughness.)

ABOUT THE AUTHOR

ROB BUYEA is a former fourth-grade student as well as a former fourth-grade teacher. He did not like writing as a kid but loved it when teaching, which ultimately put him on the path to becoming the author of many books. His grandmother was a big part of his young life, just like Carter's. His egg-stronaut survived when he was a student, but Missy Gerber would not have liked his boring spaceship.

ROBBUYEA.COM